THEY ALL LAUGHED AT MALIC

General Besta, who preferred butterfly chasing to pursuing the enemy.

Colonel Allegretti, fearless when mounting a woman, but terrified of even approaching a horse.

Major Peduto, whose talent lay in making epigrams, not making war.

Marika, the sensual Montenegrin beauty who climbed rank by rank from the arms of common soldiers to the general's bed.

You, too, may laugh at Malic.

For like the good soldier Schweik, and like Yossarian in Catch-22, *Malic is a very funny kind of hero.*

A HERO ON A DONKEY

MIODRAG BULATOVIC

A *Hero* ON A *Donkey*

A PLUME BOOK from
NEW AMERICAN LIBRARY
TIMES MIRROR
New York, Toronto and London

Library of Congress Catalog Card Number: 69-18520

German edition originally published by Carl Hanser Verlag

This is a reprint of a hardcover edition published by The New American Library, Inc., in association with The World Publishing Company.

PLUME TRADEMARK REG. U.S. PAT. OFF. AND FOREIGN COUNTRIES
REGISTERED TRADEMARK—MARCA REGISTRADA
HECHO EN CLINTON, MASS., U.S.A.

SIGNET, SIGNET CLASSICS, MENTOR AND PLUME BOOKS
are published *in the United States* by
The New American Library, Inc.,
1301 Avenue of the Americas, New York, New York 10019,
in Canada by The New American Library of Canada Limited,
295 King Street East, Toronto 2, Ontario,
in the United Kingdom by The New English Library Limited,
Barnard's Inn, Holborn, London, E.C. 1, England.

First Printing, September, 1970

PRINTED IN THE UNITED STATES OF AMERICA

A Hero on a Donkey

Part One

CHAPTER 1

"*Uno-due!*"

He stretched his arms, brought them together, and then raised them high above his head, touching the low, crooked ceiling with the tips of his fingers. He performed the exercise flawlessly as if on a parade ground and not between the desk and the couch. Exercising his legs was not nearly as simple; the muscles in his groin were sore. He was slightly irritated.

"*Uno-due!*"

He stroked his flabby, hairy chest and looked at himself in the mirror: "Spartaco, old man, all this was once as hard as steel." His hand slid toward his stomach which stood out like a lone island. "You never did have a waist, but this fat is too much." He squeezed his sides and went on angrily: "*Uno-due* . . ."

The clock struck twelve. "Not bad for your age." Colonel Spartaco Allegretti addressed the half-naked man in the mirror. "Not bad at all; you'll be fifty this fall and your teeth are all your own and sharp as a wolf's." He frowned at his low forehead and the coarse, strong hair that was beginning to turn gray. "You really are hairy; covered in bristles. If you let yourself go, you will look like a monkey." He caressed the hooked nose that gave his round face the look of a surprised bird. "Eh, Spartaco, how time flies; still . . .

"*Uno-due!*"

The window was open and he could hear the soldiers outside. He liked their jokes and dirty stories and would have liked to join them. But he was busy. He bent forward. The blood swelled into his temples and the veins in his neck. Even so, his hands would not reach either his bare feet or the mark on the floor. His knees shook. "*Giovinezza, giovinezza, primavera di bellezza,*" a company of soldiers crossed the square on its morning exercise. Their song was led by the gentle, passionate voice of Augusto Napolitano. Nobody could sing obscene songs more sweetly.

Colonel Allegretti hurled his vest and shirt across the room, his uniform with its medals, the revolver belt, and all other objects that lay within reach. He quickly removed his pants. He stood in the center of the room with his feet apart and fists clenched like a wrestler whom no one dared approach. The pendulum on the clock moved evenly. His own dangled. He grabbed a chest expander and began to puff: "*Uno, due, tre!*"

He tugged the expander so hard that even the framed Mussolini on the wall seemed to be straining. The Duce's jaw jutted out more than ever. The spring buzzed in the colonel's manly grasp and the King up there, next to the Duce, wrinkled his nose: the steel was too powerful for the little man on the white horse. At first the expander would not stretch to its limit and the Queen's lips swelled with the effort, her high forehead beaded with sweat, but her bright Montenegrin eyes expressed confidence in the ultimate victory of the colonel's appliance. "*Uno, due, tre . . . primavera di bellezza.*"

Sweat poured everywhere. Benito Mussolini emerged from his frame and tugged at the expander; the sour-faced little King joined him. Queen Elena walked right through the wall and into the colonel's springs. Long live the Duce! Long live the King! The expander panted and grew hot. Long live my beautiful, elongated Italy swimming in a sea of sweat, and wrestling with the steel to the accompaniment of obscene songs and the clatter of aluminum mess tins. The pendulum was stretched to the point of screaming. Long live fascism! Greasy, gaping heads shouted. Long live our fearless army and our immortal leaders! Italy writhed and bled, its geography collapsed. If the strain continues, the hairy skin will burst and fall apart. "We believe in the power of the jackboot! The world will be under our feet," said the Duce. "Hurrah!" the crowd shrieked and swallowed the springs. Several countries were erased from the map of the world and sank silently into the pale waters of the sea.

Having again defeated the chest expander, Colonel Allegretti heaved a sigh of relief. His helpers fled back to their dusty frames: the Duce wiped the sweat from his chin with somebody else's hand, while the flattened King merely whispered to the Queen, who was gazing in horror at the ravaged map. And under Allegretti's window, soldiers were singing and swearing. The colonel crossed the room: he bulged his lively Sicilian eyes, screwed up his face, and gesticulated at the map. The image in the glass was an expander. He took a gulp of air, swore at communism, and attempted to sing the "*Giovinezza*," so unpopular with the soldiers. But he felt himself much stronger than his double in the glass. The world suddenly seemed small, the sea came up only to his knees, and the mirror was too small to hold him.

The pendulum dangled lazily. The victor grew in his own eyes and in the mirror. The pendulum was mad. A quiet anger seized him; why was no one there to see him? The pendulum swung, its metallic beat withering in the great heat.

Major Antonio Peduto was covered with dust. His heart was pounding. He wore the look of a man emerging out of some perilous distance. Soldiers and girls had gathered around him.

Peduto was thin and of medium height. In addition to binoculars and other military toys, he wore a pair of dark glasses. He was slightly stooped, with a mischievous curl of hair over his forehead. Leaving his car he watched the gigantic figure of the Orthodox priest, Vukic, approaching him. The major really liked this bear of a Montenegrin because of his taste for plum brandy, poker, and certain other hobbies. But he pretended not to notice him. Nor Augusto Napolitano either, who was singing bawdy songs. Peduto was in no mood for serious conversation or for Augusto's jokes. He turned to the officer on duty:

"Is the colonel upstairs?"

"Yes, *signor maggiore*," the officer replied, "but the colonel has given orders not to admit anyone."

"Why?" the major asked in an offended voice.

"The colonel is working on important plans," the officer said confidentially.

The major's eyes moved from the flag in front of the building, the tank, and the sentry, to the saloons and the girls. He glanced at the officer and at the crowd around his car. He recalled his last meeting with the colonel, who had suddenly taken to concocting immense projects. He saw the priest tap Augusto on the shoulder and drew his cracked lips into a slight smile: "But this is extremely important, Sergeant Major."

"News from the front?"

"Yes," replied the major softly.

"Bad news?" the officer asked.

"News from the front is always bad," Major Peduto said irritably.

"By all means, *signor maggiore*," replied the officer, and before Peduto had climbed the stairs, the story had reached the crowd outside.

"*Porca miseria!*" roared one of the soldiers, kicking violently at an aluminum mess tin. "I've been here fourteen months and the news is still bad! They have been telling us for fourteen months now we'd be through with the Communists in no time! *Porco!* By the Madonna and all the saints!"

Major Peduto walked to the colonel's door and listened to a voice he recognized and liked:

"An assault on human flesh! *Uno, due!* An assault on unwanted fat! Down with traitors and stomachs! Forward, Spartaco! Long live manly prowess and beautiful Italy and her unconquerable army! Long live our leaders! For the good of the liberated peoples of all progressive mankind. *Uno, due, tre!* Long live fascism! Its healthy bodies, its strong muscles!"

The major bent toward the door and smiled.

"Why long live them? Why not me? Poor old me, even if I can't reach my feet. From now on it's long live me! Long live Spartaco Allegretti, hunter, hero, and devil, who has found a way to regain his military bearing!"

Spartaco was whipping himself into a frenzy of excitement.

"Long live handsome Allegretti, long live his expander! *Uno, due, tre!* Hurrah for him, a thousand times hurrah! Yes, after three or four minutes' rest, a staunch attack on the enemy, the Reds, and on my own rotten flesh. When the war is over, when we have won . . . *Uno, due, tre!* . . . Death to all lazy bastards, bureaucrats, and Communists!"

Major Peduto knocked.

"Who is it?" asked Allegretti.

"Inspection," said Peduto.

"And where have you been all this time, my dear pornographic inspector?" asked Allegretti. "I expected you this morning."

"Inspectors always come at the wrong time."

They embraced. Allegretti was still naked and sweating.

Peduto was glad to be free from Allegretti's sweaty embrace. He moved over to the window. Allegretti offered him the armchair and perched himself on the edge of the table. "You look thinner, you tiger."

"I'm lucky to be alive," Peduto said unhappily. "Montenegrins are a tough bunch."

"Primitives are always trouble,." the colonel said.

"Primitives aren't cunning," said the major. "Look, Spartaco, for centuries all they've had is this cult of bravery. No wonder I've lost weight."

"Have I got any thinner?" the colonel asked, running his hand over his chest.

"Not much," Peduto said, examining the colonel's rectangular body. "Try an expedition . . . "

"Here's my plan," Allegretti put in hastily. "If I get rid of a hundred grams a day, that's three kilograms a month. In five months I'll look like a man again."

"And you've got luck on your side, too," Peduto drawled, stretching out his legs. "I'd envy you if we weren't friends."

Getting to his feet with a dexterity more befitting a man fully dressed, Allegretti looked at him.

"What, another decoration?"

"A real decoration. My God, what luck!"

"Stop teasing," the colonel roared.

"It's too good to be told quickly," said the major.

"If you don't tell me, I'll explode."

Allegretti stretched the appliance all the way. "Look, Antonio, like this!"

Peduto got up and separated the curtains. He saw a small, lopsided house. Familiar and ugly. It was besieged by soldiers. He concentrated on the guitarist and smiled. But the others did not amuse him. The soldiers pressed toward the door, money in their hands, trousers unbuttoned. He knew some of the men. Some he didn't. They were excited. Sun beat on their heads.

He saw two female bodies, confined in the crooked window frame, flat on their backs, white against the walls, half covered with uniformed backs. He felt sorry for them. He remembered other brothels and the unhappy girls with legs apart and eyes ravaged.

The major was miserable. He caught sight of a soldier marching around the narrow room, leaning now over one couple and now another, as if it were the most normal of places, plucking his guitar and singing in a tearful voice: "*Catari, Catari, perche me dice sti parole?*"[1] Not distinguishing one soldier from another, these sad, female bodies writhed and twisted, as from habit, and they cared little for the soldier's ragged phrases: "*O core, core 'ngrato . . . tutt'è passato!*"[2]

[1] Katie, Katie, why do you say these words to me?
[2] Oh heart, ungrateful heart . . . it's all over now!

The smoke of Antonio's pipe grew dense. His eyes began to smart. Gently he turned.

"So, Antonio, what's it all about? What am I getting?"

"A son," the major replied softly.

The colonel threw the expander aside and cursed. He was in a rage. He paced up and down between the couch and the desk. The major chewed his pipe and watched him.

"That Albanian whore!" the colonel swore. "The filthy cow!"

"No, it's the Greek," the major burst into laughter. "Your beloved, exotic Aliki."

"What's so funny, Antonio, damn it!" the colonel said. "It's calamitous. Antonio, you irritate me. To hell with you."

"My dear Spartaco," Peduto said, "I'm laughing at myself. No woman ever wanted a child by me. Not even a whore. But you, damn you, you're the pride of our race."

"But Antonio," the colonel began tearfully, "it isn't funny. My fifth son! In rather poor taste, besides."

The major giggled and bent over his chair.

"The letters are downstairs, in the car. Half in Greek, half in Italian. We read them aloud at headquarters. Several generals were there too."

"Who?" the colonel stared.

"Vigorelli, Basso, Tozzi."

"Good thing Besta wasn't there," the colonel said, "he's such a cynic."

"He was," said Antonio. "I had no idea you knew each other."

"What did he say?"

"He laughed a lot and said he was coming to visit us."

"If I'd known you were going to bring such news, I wouldn't have ever let you in. I'm surrounded by animals," said Allegretti. "I'd be better off fighting the Communists and getting killed."

"If you do that, no need to slim," replied the major.

The colonel quickly put on his boots. Antonio puffed on his pipe and mused: "General Vigorelli roared when he read that your Greek mistress prayed for our victory."

"The Greek cow!" the colonel turned. "Ever since the whores started praying for us, things have gone badly!"

"I don't agree. Winning the heart of a whore is a most precious victory," the major said emphatically. "General Tozzi was delighted to hear that your bastard was named Cesare Claudio."

"For God's sake!" Spartaco yelled. "I already have one Cesare Claudio. She must be mad!"

Clutching the edge of the curtain, Peduto watched the priest push through a large crowd that had gathered outside, trampling everyone in his way.

"She's inspired by us, and all of Greece is too. Lots of girls write. They all begin with our glorious past and end with our liberation of Greece."

"I'm sick of your irony," the colonel said. "Aren't you upset that a bastard who may be yours as much as mine, should have such a name . . ."

"I have always found your exaggerated patriotism boring," snapped Peduto.

"Why didn't she name him Socrates or Aristotle?" Allegretti resumed the attack. "I protest as an Italian, as a person of rank, and as the father of a large family! But what really astonishes me is that you took this whore's word."

"Discuss it with the general when he comes. I'm going to get some sleep."

"I protest, a hundred times I protest!" The colonel jumped up. "I'll expose you all who've slept with the Greek bitch; that includes you. And the general."

"Protect your rank, Spartaco," drawled the major. "Somebody else's child may be preferable to demotion."

"Antonio, you don't get it." Allegretti gripped him by the shoulders. "Four children with one's own wife is unsophisticated enough. If I go on like this, I'll return to Italy after the war with a whole herd of bastards from all over the world!"

"I admire you," Antonio said. "You represent us honorably. In one of my future books I'll devote several chapters to you."

"And you can be sure that Spartaco Allegretti won't allow anyone to make an ass of him!" said the colonel. "I'm ready to take my case all the way to the top! Anyway, what's the news from the front?"

"They're not surrendering, that's for sure. They never have."

"How did you react in battle?"

"As usual. Montenegrins howl when they charge, and as soon as they calm down I shout back that they don't know the first thing about us cat-eaters. I turned one or two of their corpses over. And brave they are. They don't mind dying; like the Japanese."

"Good thing there aren't as many of them as there are Japanese," remarked the colonel.

"They believe one Montenegrin is worth two or three other men, though. They fight like tigers. Nor do they take us seriously. They call on us to surrender, and we do."

"You've got to admit this happens less and less," Allegretti was sour.

"More and more, you mean. But that's irrelevant because they don't know Italy, nor its fifty million lion hearts. They say they will not make peace until they have planted their banner in the heart of Italy. I can't make them understand that though our peninsula has been invaded many times, it has never been conquered. In the end our melancholia and pornography defeat them all. I tell them it's no joke dealing with a hundred and eighty-three million Italian pornographers, but they don't care. 'A hundred and ninety million,' I shout again, firing into their living flesh. They respond with cries of blood and freedom. 'Two hundred million!' I yell as I watch my bullets mowing them down. 'Two hundred and one million gonorrhea-stricken patriots. Two hundred and two million. . . .' "

"Your exaggerations don't irritate me today as much as usual," the colonel said hesitantly. "Calm down and give me a report."

"We are fighting for a sacred cause," said Antonio and

dramatically crossed the doorstep. "We are winning. I need sleep! If I don't get to bed, Spartaco, I'll fall asleep in your arms. Is there any other news locally apart from the massive pursuit of cats and whores?"

"Nothing," replied the colonel. "Soon there'll be no cats left! Or Communists."

CHAPTER 2

THE CLOCK struck half past twelve. The colonel was standing by the window, playing with the curtain. Everything was visible: the square with its rundown houses, the Orthodox church whose cross was obliterated by the heat and dust, and the slender mosque swarming with the customary crowds. The sky rested lazily upon the hills which cradled the shapeless little town. He heard the river as it escaped from the smells of the town, and from the barbed wire that intersected it at several points.

He let his gaze rest upon the shops that framed the square. They were utterly incomprehensible, resembling large trunks, filled with junk: beads, blades, belts and soaps, needles, arrows, knives and sabers, overcoats and diapers, rich Constantinople cloth.

The colonel was angered by all this life that crawled about the narrow streets and dragged itself from saloon to saloon, full of the stink of brandy and greasy food, old enemies drawing near to one another and whispering; close and distrusting in their Montenegrin caps and gay Muslim fezzes amid the tobacco smoke, faces now friendly, now dissembling.

Some ten yards from the flagpole stood a light tank. A soldier was standing next to it, half-dozing. His face was white with dust and fatigue, his helmet and long rifle weighing him down. Anyone passing by could have stolen both him and his tank. The sentry smiled in his sleep all the same.

The stunted Napolitano approached on tiptoe and began singing in a scarcely audible voice:

"*Nel mio cuor rinasce un sogno d'or . . .*"[1]

The sentry gave a start and grabbed his rifle. He gazed at Napolitano's blue lips and drawled in a voice close to tears:

"Ah, Augusto, it's you, you bastard."

"You're always asleep, Salvatore," Napolitano said in mocking reproach, banging him on the back.

"I've been dreaming about her again, Augusto," Salvatore said sadly. "You interrupted me just as I was about to enter her. You had to ruin everything!"

"Don't give up hope, Salvatore," Napolitano said briskly, rolling up his sleeves.

"It's no good, Augusto, she's mad about Pietro. And he thinks only of Marika."

Napolitano stared at his long fingers as they moved over the guitar. His mouth was full of pain, of metal teeth and strangled song:

"*Bolognesina mia* . . ."

Paolone took him by the arm. "Augusto, how can you sing so much? . . . You really love her, don't you, that girl from Bologna?

"She's better than my Dana," Salvatore said. "Better and more faithful. But why don't they send someone to relieve me? I'm exhausted."

"I don't know," answered Napolitano.

"Perhaps they've forgotten about me?" Paolone said glumly.

"It's as though you were condemned to it by fate!" Napolitano said.

"You're right, Augusto," said Paolone, "Like a punishment! Augusto, I heard the girls of Bologna are about the worst in

[1] A golden dream stirs again in my heart.

Italy. Everyone says so. Maybe the girl you're always moping about is no better. Why not find out about it, Augusto?" Salvatore called after him.

The guitarist heard him but did not look back. His face wore an expression of strain and longing, as he waited for Pietro.

Marika was standing by the fountain. Pietro was watching her with hungry eyes: she was beautiful, with slanting black eyes and breasts that showed clearly whenever she moved or laughed.

"Why go so quickly, signorina Marika?"

"*Debbo lavorare,* Pietro, *lavorare,*" the girl laughed, showing a row of white teeth. "Much *lavoro*!"

Pietro shivered and drew closer to the girl. "Come with me and you won't have to work."

"*Domani,* Pietro," the girl said, and picked up her bucket. "Tomorrow, Corporal."

"Tomorrow maybe I'm dead," the corporal said. "Tomorrow complications: Communists, gun, bang, bang! I die tomorrow, Marika. Montenegrins are no good. *Ammazzano* Pietro doesn't love guns, or war!"

The girl was about to say something, but she froze on seeing a large man in his fifties approaching the spring.

"Oh, my Marika," the corporal wailed. "I tell you the truth. I check *Sardo.*"

The girl raised her forefinger to her lips and then pointed to the man who was drinking from the spring.

"*Spia,* Pietro," Marika whispered. "Spy!"

"Pietro will not be quiet," the corporal said. "Pietro is in love."

The spy wiped his face. He measured the girl and the corporal with an experienced glance and set off toward the *comandatura.* The colonel saw him and hid behind the curtain. He loathed Mustafa Agic, postmaster and prewar police agent, and tried to avoid his company except when business demanded.

"Marika," the corporal said, opening his arms, "Marika *mia* . . ."

"*Domani*," the girl said, and sailed off.

The blood beat in Pietro's temples. He wanted to follow her but his knees gave way.

"Marika. Pietro is not a Fascist. Pietro perhaps is a Communist," the corporal shouted. Then he began to run after her.

"Yes, maybe I am a Communist. . . ."

"And you're proud of it, you poor lamb," the girl said.

"I am a big Communist, Marika mine," the corporal whispered. "A dangerous Communist."

"In that case I don't want you, Pietro."

"I am not a Communist," he tried to recover himself. "I hate Communists. Marika, I beg you . . ."

"No use, *soldato*. Marika wants love. *Amore*, Pietro, *amore*, and *cuore*. Now be off, you little bastard. What will people say?"

"I have love, my Marika," stammered the corporal. "Much love and heart . . . heart big . . . don't go. Pietro has two hearts. . . ."

"If you had three, it wouldn't help you with me," the girl said, flaunting her slender waist.

Pietro stood still in the middle of the square and watched her. She carried her bucket, swinging her hips provocatively.

Allegretti was in no mood to see his spy that day. He carefully drew back the curtain. Pietro had not moved. "That's no morsel for you, my little corporal," the colonel thought to himself. "You don't qualify. If you were a captain, say, you might stand a chance. I've watched you for months, lying in wait for her. If you don't leave her alone, I'll put you where it won't occur to you to go after Montenegrin whores! Besides, she's officially engaged to Captain Vittorio, your commanding officer. This evening, however, the captain is going to give his fat-bottomed Montenegrin angel to Colonel Allegretti. There's no hope for you today, tomorrow, or the day after tomorrow!"

The colonel saw Pietro go up to the fountain and plunge his head under the tap. Cooled and refreshed, he set off across the square. He wasted no time pondering which of the many saloons to enter: he went straight into the one that had a sign painted in red on a rough board:

WE SELL THE STRONGEST BRANDY, ETC.

Pietro collapsed at the nearest empty table. He looked at the proprietor, a small, skinny man, with narrow shoulders and a good face, who poured drinks energetically, looking down his hooked Montenegrin nose. His large, dark eyes alternated between an unpleasantly merry expression and brooding sadness.

Pietro looked at him. The proprietor knew the corporal and his tastes well. He brought him a pint of brandy, reminded him of a debt, and lost himself in the crowd.

The corporal grabbed the bottle. The crowd watched his Adam's apple bobbing up and down his throat as he drank without a pause. Having drained the plum poison to the last drop, he cast a dull, deathly glance at the proprietor. The walls of this saloon had no pictures of the King or his family. Nor was the Duce there. Only photographs of naked women, film stars and famous lovers, horsemen and adventurers. He was reminded of the movement of Marika's flesh, her breasts and hips. He hurled the bottle against the wall, and sobbed. He didn't hear the sound of broken glass, nor the cries of the drunken soldiers. His arms fell limp beside his body, his forehead slumped on the cold, wet table.

The walls were full of a sweet, shameful nakedness.

CHAPTER 3

COLONEL ALLEGRETTI frequently boasted of his acquaintance with the proprietor of this saloon. His predecessor and old friend, Colonel Fabiani, had said to him on arrival:

"Spartaco, this one is worth your while. People like him are capable of anything." Colonel Fabiani had cast a side glance at the unimpressive figure behind the bar. "I know what I'm talking about."

"You're recommending I keep in close touch with him?" Allegretti raised his brandy glass.

"Yes, unfortunately I can't do it any more," laughed Fabiani, "but I'm hoping to find plenty more of the same in Greece. Montenegrins and Greeks have much in common! A certain need to show off."

"Are you referring to their courage?" Allegretti put in.

"There's a world of difference between courage and the demonstration of courage," Colonel Fabiani laughed, regarding the proprietor warmly through his glasses. "Look how he scowls! The legend has it that he was discovered one summer morning in the middle of the square, next to the fountain, swaddled in woolen diapers. No one was willing to take him. The townspeople watched him cying, and argued as to whose he might be. They concluded that he had been abandoned by the circus that left the town before dawn. Then Vukic the priest came running up and, after a quarrel with the mullah who also wanted the foundling, snatched him away. This priest chose a rare name for the child: Gruban. All day he thought of a last name. Ivanovic, Petrovic, Jovanovic . . . all of them, including his own, were too common. That night, having won at cards and drunk himself into a stupor, the priest announced that Gruban's last name would be Malic, which means 'little man.' "

"Tragicomic," said Colonel Allegretti.

"All the tales I've heard here are the same," Colonel Fabiani added, and went on with his story.

"Less than two years after the christening, half in jest, the priest gave the foundling to the mullah. The mullah kept the baptized creature in his house only a few months. His cradle found its way into the home of the most pious of the local Montenegrins, a widower and a civil servant. Everyone thought: at last a proper father! But the widower landed in jail for stealing government money and the boy was taken over by two old maids. He didn't stay long with them either.

"He lived this way until he was seven or eight. Then he began to shun people, especially those who had looked after him. He wandered about with the other children, worked as a servant, or begged. He slept under bridges, in cellars and attics, in stables and ditches. When he was about twenty it was clear that he was going to be much shorter and thinner than other boys his age.

"At thirty, Gruban opened a saloon. No one knew where the money came from. The merchants and innkeepers whispered that he had robbed a safe. Others said that Malic was connected with a secret organization that invested its money in saloons and brothels."

"But why open that filthy little joint on the day our troops entered the town?"

"Who knows what they think, these Montenegrins," Colonel Fabiani replied.

"Are you sure the Communists aren't financing him?" Colonel Allegretti asked.

"Nonsense!" Colonel Fabiani drained his brandy. "No one ever got a penny from them."

"Experience teaches us all things are possible."

"But for Communists to help anyone is impossible," Colonel Fabiani said angrily. "They've no money, besides. They live by plunder and by contributions, which is, in fact, begging. If they had money, they would certainly not give it to an obscure trader. You can be sure he has no ties with them whatever!"

"I gather his place is the favorite hangout of our soldiers."

"Yes, he's done well," replied Fabiani. "He sells drink at half price!"

"Too many civilians go there for my liking."

"Montenegrins," Colonel Fabiani said benevolently. "They're never out of their saloons. Anyway, they are all yours. Study them to your heart's content! I'm off to Salonica."

Colonel Allegretti saw his predecessor off with all the required pomp and ceremony. Later he learned that it was this mysterious saloon proprietor who supplied his soldiers with contraceptives. What's more, he kept a heap of pornographic material under his counter.

"Honored Colonel, sir," Captain Brambilla reported shamefacedly, "our troops are purchasing enormous quantities of these goods. I don't know which is more in demand: the former articles, allow me not to mention them by name, or the photos of naked flesh, sexual acts, and other filth!"

The following morning Allegretti received the mullah.

"I most respectifully request, Commandant," the sly old man wound up his long-winded complaint, "that you prohibit Malic from selling these goods and especially the cure for conception. I'm thinking primarily of our Muslim population which I guard and defend to the best of my ability. What happens to the Montenegrins who are prone to every vice, especially immorality and politics, does not concern me!"

The priest, who had been drunk for months, demanded that the colonel "bring to an immediate halt the distribution of all these goods and especially of certain pills and powders that daily diminish the growth of the healthy and heroic Montenegrin people."

But Colonel Allegretti was deaf to all such protests. He took walks in the square past Malic's shop pretending neither to see nor hear anything. And in time the complaints ceased.

CHAPTER 4

THE SUN had passed right above the Orthodox church, almost impaling itself on the rusty lopsided cross. Above the dry, rotting roof, it revolved in torment like a sick spider choking in the dusty summer sun. Down below were narrow, stinking streets, cobbles and heaps of baked mud, soldiers with indolent bayonets, barefoot children playing with old tin cans, and women, like ghosts, in black Muslim rags.

The bells were ringing and the clamor that broke over his head made the air seem even more stifling to Colonel Allegretti. He wiped his neck and forehead with a handkerchief. Standing at the door of his office, he looked up at the steeple. The dust was thicker than the light.

Coughing nervously he wondered: "Why are they ringing so loudly and so long? I don't remember the bells ever being so loud." This riotous ringing, this banging without rhythm or sense raised the dust that had lain still upon the shapeless square.

At the sound of the mullah's wailing, the colonel turned his suspicious eye from the Orthodox steeple to the rickety, wooden minaret of the mosque. The mullah's hoarse, incomprehensible howling poured from the skies.

The wind dispersed the dust that rose and swirled like a column of smoke about the mosque. The colonel caught sight of the mullah. Doubled over the parapet, leaning dangerously low, the old man sang. The deep, throaty voice welled from the gaping jaws, recoiled from the white beard, and hovered over the Kasbah like a phantom. The mullah touched his cheeks with his palms and then spread his arms wide, as if, feeble yet all-seeing, he was summoning to him all the weak people who piously watched him from their shops and windows.

An inexplicable wave of fear drove the colonel, pale and shivering, down the steps. As the soldiers gathered around him, he watched the mullah's gaping, desperate face turn to the sky and then again to the faithful. Neither the bell, nor the dust that once more rose on high, could obscure this figure of despair.

"This is no prayer," the colonel thought. The troops had formed a squad. "Nor is it because somebody has died. Why should both places announce the same death? It's a revolution. That's it. That old man's been howling for half an hour and God knows how long the bells have been ringing! Fighting may break out any minute."

The colonel shuddered at the thought of having to fight with Montenegrins. He looked at the motionless squad, but took no notice of the two officers who saluted him and made their report. He was gazing over the rooftops, past the mosque and the steeple of the Orthodox church.

Accustomed to the colonel's absentmindedness, the officers waited. Side by side: Vittorio Brambilla, a short, round man with malicious eyes and a long, flattened nose; and Lorenzo Fioravanti, a giant with a big jaw and clumsy hands.

"I smell alcohol," the colonel said, "plum brandy. Who's been drinking?"

"It isn't hard to guess, Colonel, is it?" Brambilla said spitefully.

"You again, Captain?" the colonel asked.

"Me again," Lorenzo swayed. "I am sorry, Colonel."

"Don't you see, Captain, that this is hardly a suitable time to drink?" the colonel began. "You should be alert and sober! I've nothing against their damned brandy. I think it's good stuff. But it's the wrong time."

"Well put, Colonel, sir!" Brambilla interposed. "And to the point; the right time!"

"It's the right time if you ask me," thought Captain Fioravanti, barely able to keep on his feet, "for brandy and amnesia." The colonel suddenly had two heads, three arms, and several revolvers.

"Captain," he said to Lorenzo, "spare me such scenes in the future. I'm a broad-minded man and I don't like to pick on anyone, but . . ."

"But it's the wrong time," Brambilla put in, smiling at his commander.

Brambilla's remark annoyed the colonel.

"Don't you think the bells are ringing too long today?" the colonel began softly. "That old mullah has been at it for hours, too. I tell you I feel uneasy. Could it be a call for rebellion? What do you think, Fioravanti?"

"There's no one here to rebel, Colonel," Lorenzo said. "They are singing and chanting out of boredom. It's Sunday. Also, more people have been dying recently."

"You're obviously in a good mood today," the colonel said, and looked quickly at his other captain.

"Yes, I tend to agree with you, Colonel, sir," Captain Brambilla said seriously. "We mustn't forget that Montenegrins are capable of anything. You have no idea what cunning foxes they are."

"In other words, Captain, you are also suspicious," the colonel said importantly, clearing his throat.

"Yes! The bells may be sounding someone's death, they may be burying their heroes, but we mustn't forget, Colonel, that Communists are capable of exploiting a simple funeral for propaganda purposes. They say people are dying under the Fascist yoke, hold a political meeting, and move straight from the funeral to attack us with arms concealed in the coffin . . ."

"In the coffin," the colonel echoed.

"Yes, in the coffin," Captain Brambilla added. "They aren't choosy about their methods!"

"I see you've made a thorough study," the colonel said coldly.

"Communism is my specialty, Colonel."

"And the sin of my youth," said the colonel softly, and looked around. "My orders are general readiness. Strong patrols in town. If these idiots don't stop praying, drown out the noise with volleys from every weapon at hand."

"In what direction, Colonel?" Captain Brambilla interrupted again.

"At the enemy, of course," the colonel raised his voice, "from every weapon at hand. And not a bird is to be allowed in or out of town until tomorrow morning. Immediately arrest those on list number two. All persons found in the streets are to be searched, including the funeral procession and the deceased."

Vittorio Brambilla hiccuped and shuddered.

"This time even dead Communists are dangerous, don't you agree, Captain? As an expert on communism, you must be aware of that!"

Lorenzo Fioravanti looked at them.

Vittorio Brambilla turned pale.

The colonel removed his hand from his revolver.

"I trust you've understood."

"Yes, sir," said Captain Brambilla feebly. "What about persons on list number three?"

"I must remind you that as a captain of the valiant Venezia Division and an intelligence officer to boot, you should know better than to inquire about matters that have not been raised. Besides, list number three contains only one person of any interest, that dreadful Gruban Malic."

"What's to be done with him, Colonel?" asked Brambilla.

"Nothing," the colonel replied nervously, "take no notice of him!"

"I understand, Colonel," the captain said.

The colonel looked at Lorenzo sharply. "Have another drink and sleep it off. Until tomorrow at ten, and report for duty sober. Sleep well, Captain!"

"Fetch Horatio," ordered the colonel.

Three soldiers set off at a run. They searched the yard, the headquarters, the square. Horatio was nowhere to be seen!

"But where the hell is Horatio? He's gone again. The bastard! He was here a minute ago. I'm sick of your jokes. Is he upstairs in headquarters? Or at the saloon around the corner? He isn't anywhere. He's gone for a walk, the old bastard! Christ, the colonel will court-martial us or put us right in the front line!"

The colonel was having a private discussion with Captain Brambilla: he was whispering and gesticulating, making circles and crosses over Vittorio's head.

"I would like a word with your fiancée, Captain," the colonel said softly. "Be as obliging as you are zealous and ask her to come to my office. Or bring her yourself."

"With pleasure, Colonel," the captain said, relieved that no one could hear them.

"I would like to ask her a few questions," the colonel went on. "Do you understand?"

"Perfectly, Colonel," said the captain, turning deathly pale. "I'm prepared to carry out any order from you. But . . . couldn't I . . . ?"

"Not this time," the colonel said sharply.

The captain's eyes glazed, his chin quivered. But he remained calm.

Their confidential talk was interrupted by several soldiers, who led up two mares and Horatio, a well-kept pure white stallion. But the colonel had completely forgotten about Horatio and his afternoon ride to the airport.

He was afraid of all animals, but as commandant he was entitled to a horse and could think of no excuse not to accept the animal. Instead of patting him, the colonel went up to him, grabbed the horn of the saddle, and gave him a piece of sugar.

Two lieutenants on the mares and the soldiers awaiting final orders watched the colonel as he stood motionless by the horse. This was not the first time they had witnessed the colonel's lack of courage in mounting Horatio.

"Heh, Giovanotto, old man, you're not in good form today, are you?" the colonel said to himself. "All the same you must get on Horatio and ride to the airport. Come on, put your foot in the stirrup, lean back, and give a jump. If those peasants can do it, you can too. Are you afraid of getting dust on your pretty boots, or that you won't be able to get your fat ass off the ground, or that you'll split your trouser seams . . . ? Come on, take them by surprise!"

Brambilla pushed a chair up to the colonel. The colonel gave a nervous, embarrassed cough and cast a look of hatred at the silent men. Standing on the chair awkwardly, he mounted.

Brambilla's long, rubbery smile disgusted him. He snapped at Lorenzo:

"Captain, stop hiccuping and go to bed. Now."

"Yes, sir," Lorenzo Fioravanti said.

Horatio bucked under a clumsy spur and the colonel just barely managed to keep himself in the saddle.

The lieutenants followed the colonel, who seemed not to know where he was going or how to control the horse. Fresh and frisky, the horse longed for a gallop.

CHAPTER 5

"IL MONTENEGRINO, Signor Malic," the colonel said to himself, remembering Colonel Fabiani. "I must write dear Enzo and tell him that this engaging Montenegrin saloon owner was the first person in town to look at me with contempt! The jolly Tuscan will remove his glasses and laugh until the tears roll down his cheeks! Yes, I'll tell him that immediately after my arrival our *Montenegrino* announced that he was not afraid of anyone, least of all the Italians who put grease in their hair, sing too much, and eat cats. I'll tell Fabiani that the *carabinieri* wanted to shut down his saloon and arrest him, but I ordered them to leave him alone. As an Italian and a professional soldier, I have high regard for spontaneous protest, a form of patriotism."

Colonel Allegretti felt sympathy for small, unimpressive people like Signor Malic. But Fabiani had sought to prove to him that it was just such people who were often ringleaders of rebellions.

"Because they're small?" Colonel Allegretti had laughed, "or because they wish well for mankind?"

"Because they're small," Fabiani had said with conviction,

"because they're insignificant and insulted. Remember our march on Rome in twenty-two; all those dwarfs and idiots!"

They were descending an uneven slope that ended in a bridge. Horatio sensed his master's fear and arched his neck to stop the saddle from slipping down onto his mane.

Around them ran children, raising a dust that made the colonel shudder. He longed to be free from these ghostly beggars and their throaty voices.

The colonel thought of the gaunt Greek revolutionary, Janis Duros, who engaged in the sale of cattle and quack medicines and in petty thievery as well. The hare-lipped Signor Greca was caught sticking anti-Italian leaflets on fences. This bandy-legged patriot cried under the gallows, "Long live free Greece! Down with Italy and fascism!" The colonel spared his life and was soon afterwards transferred to Albania.

The old wooden bridge swayed. The colonel was afraid Horatio's hoofs might go through one of the many holes whose presence he noted with apprehension. The bridge was loaded with cattle. The sweating sheep bleated and huddled in ugly clusters; donkeys, overloaded with firewood, heehawed, proclaiming the hour of noon; the cows mooed and switched at flies, their tails striking the colonel on his boots, trousers, and neck.

White with dust, the shepherds moved amid the cattle with their long sticks. Some carried baskets and sacks of nettle, others were hidden under loads of hay and dry branches. They mercilessly beat the cattle to make room for the soldiers, and pressed themselves against the rotting rail of the bridge.

Lieutenant Riva's burned face bore an expression of false anxiety. The goats, donkeys, and scattered calves prevented him from wiping the traces of cow dung from the colonel's neck and trousers. He knew the colonel dared not let go of the reins for long enough to take out a handkerchief and wipe the dung from his forehead and chin. He wanted to laugh. He glanced at Arturo, looking for traces of support. But Arturo pretended not to have noticed either the colonel's predicament or Riva's amusement. His gentle face looked strained; he was trying to guide Horatio across the crowded bridge.

The chaotic ringing of the bells and the mullah's yelling were more audible than ever. The colonel felt that the mullah's groaning, belching, incomprehensible words of Oriental prayer were directed against him, that the bells were clanging for the sole purpose of warning him.

On the other side of the bridge, at a spring, the lieutenants cleaned up the colonel. He was still gripping the reins as he gazed at the many-headed crowd on the bridge. The narrow, shrunken river writhed around the bridge's wooden piles.

And just as Arturo and Nicola were polishing the colonel's boots, the firing began. The colonel's heart throbbed. He seized his binoculars: from the trenches that enclosed the town, soldiers were firing. He raised himself in the saddle: from the concrete fortifications came the crush of artillery. He watched the large, black barrels smoking, the shell cases recoiling, and the soldiers tripping around the ammunition boxes.

The blood beat harder in his temples and he seemed to be swelling in the saddle.

"Well, children," he whispered. "Now let's see who wins: their infernal ringing or our shiny weapons?"

The sky thundered. The motley mass on the bridge shook. Horatio flipped back his ears and glanced at the green river. The colonel longed to shoot, to try out his new revolver with its gold-encrusted holster. But, seeing the glum, frightened faces of his escorts, he felt sick and continued on his way to the airport.

CHAPTER 6

AS THE SHOOTING split the heavens and the banners fluttered, Captain Brambilla saw Lorenzo Fioravanti separate himself from the crowd, take a step forward, and then stagger to one side, colliding with an NCO. The man fell, but the captain didn't notice.

"For God's sake!" said Brambilla.

Lorenzo turned on the captain with clenched fists. Who knows what would have happened if the soldiers had not blocked his way?

"Men, did you see that?" hissed Brambilla. "And in public too, in front of civilians! That's what alcohol does to a man!"

The soldiers jostled one another and sneered but remained standing in front of Lorenzo, who made no move.

"You pitiful bastard," Lorenzo Fioravanti said quietly, his eyes filling with a bloody mist. And he set off across the square as if propelled by some dark force. Nobody dared stop him. The closer he got to the saloons, the more he swayed. The soldiers exchanged glances, their eyes covertly seeking Brambilla, who stood somewhere in the crowd hissing like a snake:

"I'll report him to the colonel! And to the general! Our army does not permit its officers to soak themselves in alcohol! And to cause disorder compromising our glorious forces!"

A sharp thirst baked Lorenzo's lips. His tongue was swollen, his palate dry. He trembled. He was dizzy again. He raised his head high and gasped like a fish on the hot sand. He knew he was going astray, but could not stop himself.

A wave of singing and a deafening din greeted him as he crossed the threshold of Malic's saloon. He made his way toward the counter where Malic was standing and overturned everything. He leaned on the counter, grabbed a glass of brandy from a tray, and drained it.

Malic looked at him in surprise. The captain jerked the tray from his hand and turned away. He emptied glass after glass and shivered. He returned the wooden tray to the proprietor and looked at the crowd. He recognized no one.

"*Amico,*" one of the girls said, putting her arm round his waist. "Friend!"

Dolled up and corseted, the girl mistakenly thought he was looking at her.

"*Amico,*" the girl said, stretching her wide, thick lips, "give me a drink."

The captain was silent, staring into the smoke. He heard Augusto's guitar and plaintive song, and somewhere beyond Napolitano's familiar song, the lascivious laughter of a girl.

"*Signor capitano,* you've forgotten me," the girl said, thrusting her face right into his.

For a moment he sensed the warmth of her presence, the touch of her rounded thighs and flattened stomach. She wound herself about him, blowing behind his ears, seeking with a thievish skill the buttons on his trousers.

In his eyes a darkness was gathering. He felt revulsion at the hands that caressed him and the voices that were uttering his name to the accompaniment of laughter, and he longed to be in a cleaner, quieter place.

"Console her, Captain," someone said, striking a chord on a guitar, "can't you see she's a thirsty cat, Captain!"

The girl stood on her toes and passed her moist lips over his. He felt the touch of her cold, sharp tongue and shuddered. As she repeated her performance, he sniffed a wave of cheap army perfume and grabbed her by the hair. A mist broke over his eyes and he suddenly was pulling her hair and striking her.

"You bastard!" someone yelled.

"Leave our baby alone!"

"She may be carrying your child! Shame!"

Lorenzo Fioravanti reached the door of Malic's saloon.

"You'll pay for this!" the girl shouted, smoothing her ruffled hair. "Right now!"

"You show him! He asked for it!"

"Pay her, Captain, pay her, by God!"

"Five blows, fifty lire!" the girl said breathlessly, seizing him by the collar.

He was silent.

"Do you hear, you beast; ten lire a blow!" the girl hissed. "And you owe me fifty lire, that makes it a hundred."

The strings of Augusto's guitar were ready to snap. The singing grew louder and there was a stench of brandy and male sweat. He wanted to escape.

"*Paghi, canaglia!*" the girl said. "Pay, you swine! Or I'll go straight to the colonel."

Staggering toward the door, Captain Fioravanti pulled a wad of notes from his pocket. "Let her divide it up with Malic," he thought and threw it into the din and smoke.

The roar of the guns drowned out the song. He walked down the street as if demented. The sun burned his hands, beat on his forehead.

"Are you still shooting," he whispered to himself. "Still? Why don't you stop, you idiots! Can't you see it's getting you nowhere? Just scaring yourselves. Shooting'll get you nowhere, my scared rabbits!"

Like tangled steel chains, shells whistled over the roofs. The bombs clanged as they flew from the mortars, some vanishing without echo, others exploding before they reached the blue spine of the mountain. He saw the soldiers looking down their barrels, through their sights, and frantically rattling the bolts of their rifles and machine guns, pressing triggers and shouting, yelling and swearing, blaspheming the gods.

The mountains were dark and still, huge, awkward monuments with blotches of last year's snow on their peaks and in their gulleys. Nothing could stir them, let alone ordinary gunfire. He looked up at them: proud and invulnerable, crowned in mist and fear. He looked around: the decrepit and filthy little houses, among which he wandered like a lunatic. "Oh God," he whined, "what is this, hell or just wilderness!" He started running, leaning to one side as if balancing on a beam. "Oh, dear mother, tell me why I am here!"

He fell near a crossroads and, raising his head, caught sight of a beggar, a child of five or six. The thin neck could barely support the large, shaggy head. The boy sat between a pair of crutches, his legs crossed, his hands in the dust. In front of him lay a cap with several coins in it. Enjoying the pain in his bruised elbows and knees, Lorenzo gazed into the boy's blue eyes. They were so badly inflamed that the pupils were scarcely visible. Flies settled on his oily, straw-blond hair, but the boy didn't move. "Maybe he's dead," Lorenzo thought, and shuddered. "Or did he turn to stone while begging?"

A man was approaching. Still motionless, the boy sensed this and when the mullah drew near, greeted him in a low voice:

"Alms, in the name of God . . ."

The mullah cleared his throat awkwardly and threw a coin into the boy's cap.

"God be with you," the boy whispered.

The mullah gave the boy a look of revulsion, his nervous coughing, as it were, warding off a false and alien god. He hurried on his way.

Lorenzo and the boy were now alone in the square. Lorenzo looked into the boy's wasted eyes. Feeling his stomach rising into his throat, he said to himself: "You have a boy like this too. You, and hundreds of others, who have been driven here. Your son must be dead; you've had no news of him or of Anna for ten months. If he's survived the air raids, he is sitting on some bridge, begging."

"What's your name, little boy?"

The boy was silent; Lorenzo's throat contracted.

"Come, my good boy, tell me."

The boy seemed to be asleep again.

"You are a good boy," Lorenzo Fioravanti said tearfully, "like my Gaetano. Say something."

The boy was motionless.

Tears gushed from the man's eyes. He shook all over, grabbed some earth, and sifted it through his fingers.

"Son," he began, "Son . . . little boy . . . speak to me. I

can't bear to see you sitting still like this. You look dead . . . there, tell me, do your eyes hurt a lot, can you see me?"

But the little sage with the withered legs made no movement.

Feverishly Fioravanti took a handful of coins from his pocket and threw them down in front of the boy. The boy's lips parted. Shaking with sobs, Fioravanti was uncertain whether he spoke. He watched him feel around with his dirty little hands and gather the coins and wanted to go up to him and kiss his crippled knees, his wasted legs and the ugly crutches.

It seemed as if they were the only two under the hot sun that day, they alone were condemned to burn and perish. Fioravanti's head spun, his lips dry with thirst.

He looked up and saw the empty burning sky, the rotting naked roofs, the mute windows with their wooden bars, and realized that there was no one there to hear his protests. A sharp spasm twisted his face and neck and he slumped to the ground. His teeth were biting into the hard, sun-baked clods. The sky above him grew darker. Somewhere nearby he could smell brandy. The light in the sky grew dimmer and it seemed as if the stars were falling in clusters into the dust and into the boy's cap.

CHAPTER 7

THE GUNS CONTINUED to rumble, more loudly than ever, but the colonel was no longer in a panic. Riding carefully, he gazed into the dark-blue depths of the mountains, whose sharp rocky peaks reached up to the sky. He knew that these mountains were filled with rifles. The thought of an encounter with them made him feel thoroughly uncomfortable.

He approached a field that had been hastily converted into

an airport and concluded he would have been better off if he had stayed in his rooms, if only to have enjoyed the company of Vittorio's Marika. He coughed nervously, paying no attention to the peasants who had come to watch him. Horatio was dawdling, but he didn't have the courage to spur him on. He couldn't wait to get to his plane and forget the strange terror that came from the mountains.

Dismounting was difficult without a chair. The soldiers watched with amusement as he slid from the saddle like a sack.

When he was finally on the ground, the colonel experienced a powerful sense of relief. Casting aside the bridle and his whip, he walked to the small plane which had once been the property of the local sports club. The colonel had had it overhauled and repainted. In place of *The Brave Montenegrin*, he had personally written in *Il Romano*.

In the sun and heat the guns continued unabated. Colonel Allegretti leaned against the fragile wing and asked if all was in order.

"Yes, Colonel," replied the corporal.

"Can we take off, then?"

"All is ready, Colonel."

The colonel examined the plane's wings, tail, and fuselage once more and asked for the pilot.

It took a long time to find the pilot. He was swimming in the river. Meanwhile the colonel examined his little plane with affection. He recalled that upon its capture he had recorded this great military conquest in a special communiqué to the High Command for Montenegro, Greece, and Albania. He had explained that during the struggle to capture the aeroplane, thirty-four heavily armed Montenegrins had been killed and some twenty taken prisoner.

But neither the Montenegrin, nor the Greek, nor the Albanian High Command had ever acknowledged receipt of this message. "Well, there you are, these people will sabotage you whenever they get a chance. Still, record all your successes and wait in silence until your heroism is recognized."

Although the day was hot, Turiddu Barbagallo's teeth chattered. Wet and unbuttoned, he approached the colonel, who had always loathed him. Coming to attention right by the aircraft, he tried to explain himself.

"That's all right, Turiddu," he said.

"But, Colonel . . ."

"I said it's all right," the colonel repeated. "Are we ready to take off?"

Turiddu choked on his words, a flush spreading to his eyes and ears.

"Can we take off?" the colonel shouted in his usual manner. "Can we take off, Turiddu, take off! Can we take off?"

"Certainly, Colonel!" Turiddu cried happily. "Why not?"

The colonel looked at him: the large jaws, the strong sunburned neck, the long arms and short legs.

"Then let's get going, Turiddu."

"Yes, sir!"

"Have we enough gas?"

"Enough for another ten or eleven flights, Colonel."

"Good!"

The soldiers laughed.

Horatio whinneyed.

The plane climbed with the speed of a sick bird.

Turiddu skillfully manipulated all kinds of wires and levers. The colonel wiped his cheeks and forehead; his hands were cold and clammy. Turiddu coughed and fiddled with his instruments. He said nothing, while reassuring himself that he was still in one piece.

"What the hell made me get into this monster," the colonel thought. "In these troubled times most people avoid taking the slightest risk, but I go rushing to my grave! Mad! To hell with my *Il Romano*. To hell with the whole air force! To hell with all armies! And the Italian army! And to hell with this short-legged badger Turiddu who puts me in fear of death every single day!"

They were already flying over the little town.

He knew well the sooty roofs, the deformed chimneys, and the crooked, filthy little streets that seemed to lead nowhere. They flew over the church and the mosque, but he dared not lean over to see whether the mullah still ululated or whether the hairy Montenegrin ape still moved beneath the bells of the Orthodox church.

"Can you see anything, Turiddu?"

"People, Colonel."

"What are they doing?"

"Some are moving and some are not, Colonel."

"Are they gathering in groups?"

"Yes, Colonel. They're going into the saloon."

The motor hummed.

"Any rumors of an uprising? You spend a lot of time mixing with them."

"They just moan and groan, Colonel."

"Do they curse us?"

"Well, Colonel . . . they do, no sense in saying they don't. But again it depends. There are those . . . "

"And what do you say to them when they do?"

"What can I say, Colonel? I'm nobody, just an ordinary soldier. It would be different if I were promoted. But as it is, they all say: Turiddu, he's only a soldier, Turiddu's no problem. Turiddu'll never get anywhere."

The colonel gave him a look full of unconcealed loathing.

The sly eyes and round lips with their unchanging smile angered him. "Badger," the colonel said to himself. "A real badger!"

A suspicious knocking of the engine brought the colonel up with a start. He squirmed in his seat.

"I told you to get that thing fixed," he said, feeling a certain constriction in his throat.

"But it can't be fixed, Colonel," the soldier retorted calmly.

"Well, what's the problem, Turiddu?" the colonel asked angrily, hiding his shaking hands in his pockets.

"I don't know exactly," the soldier began haltingly. "But somewhere inside, Colonel, in the motor."

"And you, being just an ordinary soldier," the colonel said, emphasizing each word, "would not be able to put it right, of course. Eh, Barbagallo?"

"I guess so, Colonel."

"If you manage to stop these sinister noises by tomorrow night, you'll get your promotion," the colonel whispered.

"I always do my best, Colonel," Turiddu said with a blush.

They were flying over the square. The colonel could see the flag on its mast and the tank with its sentry. From high up, people always looked unreal. Usually, as he looked down on the napes of their necks, he would sneer at them in amusement. Figures that moved with arms spread out in argument. But today the smile did not come to the colonel's lips. The people on the ground were alive; death was far removed from them.

He saw Turiddu's face reflected in the mirror that gleamed among the instruments.

The motor gave a suspicious cough.

"Barbagallo," the colonel began, "listen, Barbagallo!"

"Yes, Colonel," Turiddu said.

"Are you sure we can get down?"

"No, Colonel, I am not."

They were descending; they were already close to the minarets. The colonel's eyes were full of mist and he couldn't see a thing. He rubbed his cheeks and forehead. He wanted to scream. But, instead, he asked with a forced calm:

"What is your last wish, Barbagallo?"

"Promotion," Turiddu replied in a trembling voice, "And to leave Montenegro, Colonel."

"Back to the airport, Corporal," the colonel barked. "Just be careful. And get us down alive. Then we'll get drunk on that plum brandy poison of theirs. Eh, Barbagallo?"

"Right, Colonel," the pilot brightened. "Corporal Turiddu Barbagallo has a great liking for their brandy. He adores it."

Terror gripped the colonel's intestines. He closed his eyes and pictured life on the ground. He saw himself standing on the square, in his office, his room, with Vittorio's Marika. He listened to the knocking of the engine.

"If I ever get down in one piece, I'll make my life quite different," he decided. "I'll go into Malic's saloon and mix with the soldiers, those simple good people who salute indiscriminately the pictures of naked women on the walls. I'll get drunk like my Barbagallo, or like Captain Fioravanti. I was so unfair to him. Or I'll get so drunk that they'll have to carry me across the square. I shall be alive and happy, five or six times more alive than I am now in this damned plane. I'll kiss Gruban Malic on his warm human forehead and give him a ridiculously large tip and a watch because he's not a charred ugly corpse in a burnt-out plane, because he lives and breathes.

"Nor will I be a beast any more," he thought feverishly. "I'll recognize that child in Greece, regardless of whose it is, and all the other bastards they claim I've produced. I'll recognize anybody's child, if only I get down alive. I'll even recognize communism, yes, those bastards too! They've two legs and two arms and they breathe with lungs not gills. And I'll be understanding toward every other kind of trash. I'll embrace and forgive everybody. I'll release half of the prisoners jailed for spreading Communist propaganda. I'll make Brambilla a major and then have a real go at his fiancée; I'll put my head and nose between her big luscious breasts, bite her tits and navel, and lower down. I'll have her and eat her, not once, but over and over again, and I won't move from between her legs till I feel I'm no longer in this plane, that I'm alive again, that I'm on good, rough earth. No one will ever make me get into this idiotic contraption again!

"Corporal, what would you do in my place?"

The question took Turiddu Barbagallo by surprise. He was afraid to tell the truth. He caught sight of the colonel's miserable face in the mirror.

"If I were in your place," Turiddu stammered. "If I were in your place . . ."

"Stop stammering, you miserable pig!"

"If I were in your place," the corporal began again. "But, Colonel, I couldn't be in your place. One of these days you'll be a general."

"But if you were in my place," the colonel said firmly, "and if you were in this plane, what would you do?"

"Well, if I were in your place, Colonel, I'd never get into this plane again," the corporal said. "Not into this or any other."

"Why?" the colonel asked, feeling his breath growing shorter.

"The risk, Colonel. Forgive my saying so, but when a man gets into a plane he can never be sure he'll live to get drunk again. You know, I used to dream about planes when I was a young boy."

"You don't care for them much now, do you?" the colonel interrupted.

"I don't, Colonel," Turiddu whispered. "Between you and me, I'm an Italian first and a soldier second. But now that you've promoted me, I'll say I'm against driving as well. That can kill too."

"How about sailing?" the colonel inquired jocularly. "The navy?"

"That's dangerous too," the corporal replied quickly. "Suppose a ship is sinking and you swim like a rat. No sign of help anywhere. It's every man for himself. You flounder with your heart in your mouth, as they say. And then a monster of a fish comes and snap! And that's the end of all your rank and decorations."

"You approve of fighting only on dry land?" the colonel said, watching the roofs around the airport.

"I'm not for fighting, but I'm for dry land," Barbagallo said, laughing at his own joke. "When one's country is at stake, that's a different matter."

"Where do you come from, Barbagallo?" the colonel asked, once he felt the undercarriage touch earth.

"You're always asking me that, Colonel," the corporal said mischievously. "I'm from Marsala, Sicily, western Sicily."

"I should have known," the colonel said insultingly. "You're a proper *terrore*."

"But you are from there too, sir," Turiddu plucked up courage to say. "You're from Trapania. We're countrymen. My aunt married a man from Trapania. A nice place. It's got all the salt you could wish for."

"Barbagallo," the colonel shouted, "open the door and get lost! And if I have to wait for you again, I'll have your stripes. Do you understand?"

"Yes, sir," Turiddu Barbagallo said, helping the colonel get down. "I'll stay right by the plane and I won't even go swimming!"

Colonel Allegretti felt the earth under his feet. He cast a look of loathing at the plane and at the soldiers drawn up at attention. He passed them in silence.

The guns still thundered. He began to think about Vittorio's fiancée.

Part Two

CHAPTER 1

"THIS FIRING is too damn much," Major Peduto thought, crossing the square. "We're wasting ammunition. We've been firing for a whole hour. It's all quite useless. No one, except we Italians, enjoys shooting in the air so much. There isn't a soldier on earth to match an Italian when it comes to firing artillery at some poor hare. To say nothing of the fact that this damn barrage won't let me get any sleep! Oh, Spartaco, you devil, I'll get you hanged yet!"

The major paused. He glanced at the sentry in front of the tank. Salvatore's face was sad. Antonio liked his large, lively Calabrian eyes. He wanted to go up to him, pat his hunched shoulders, and tell him not to be sad, that he would find a girl for him, two, three, five girls. But he was so tired he couldn't move. He fingered his beard and whispered to himself: "My little *Calabrese,* at this very moment, as you weep and I sway on my weary unwashed feet, I've decided to write about you. In this comic book, you'll wipe your tears with your fist and long for relief and some filthy whore. But, for the sake of a good story, no one will come to relieve you, the sun will burn through your helmet and singe your eyebrows. Don't be angry, my young friend with burning eyes, that I go on observing you until this foolish, pornographic war is over. If you leave before your time, my dirty book, my symbols, and all my anger will have gone the way of the wind. So stay put and bear with my injustice."

The day was hot and ugly. The sun was strong. Nearby

someone was singing. Not Augusto, his favorite among the soldiers. Major Peduto wanted to leave the square, to forget for a moment all he had seen and heard. He looked at Paolone under his helmet swarms of flies rose from the shit scattered around the tank. In the meantime, Salvatore coughed dryly and paced up and down.

At the fountain the major pondered which way to go. "Rest and sleep out of the question," he thought. "I won't go to bed," he added, as if defending himself. "Time spent in bed is time lost. I haven't seen enough today. It's time I wet my old throat."

His eyes sought Malic's saloon. He saw the sign and his heart jumped. From the half-dark pit came noise and song. He went in, aware that his eyes had never before beheld a filthier hole, and wetting his lips in anticipation. Shouts of joy greeted him.

"Long live the major!"

"Down with the army!"

"Long live the army!"

Waving nonchalantly, the major pushed his way to the counter. He walked round a lieutenant who attempted to stand at attention and salute him but instead fell into the arms of another drunken soldier. The major squeezed Brambilla's hand and then reluctantly greeted another captain. At last he caught sight of Pietro. Pietro's childish face was swollen with tears. In front of him was a row of empty glasses. Augusto Napolitano was sitting next to him, singing. Whenever he came to the refrain: "*Lontano da te,*"[1] Pietro would burst into tears.

Major Peduto reached the counter and greeted the proprietor.

"How about a glass of the real stuff, *signor maggiore?*" Malic said, "Purer than tears and stronger than thunder."

"That sounds good," the major said, taking the glass.

[1] Far from you.

"You must have had a hard trip," Malic said maliciously, filling up his glass.

"Pretty busy," the major consented, noting that Malic's eyes were framed in long lashes.

"And as proof that all went as planned, you're here," Malic said with an insincere smile. "All in one piece."

"I got back," the major said, pushing forward his glass which Malic deftly filled. "I trust you have no objections?"

"I do, but it doesn't help," Malic said. "As you can see, I am here too!"

"I'm glad you are," the major said sincerely, and laughed. "What would I do without you?"

Failing to grasp his meaning, Malic said: "Who knows whether I shall be here much longer. There isn't much fun in keeping a saloon nowadays."

"There is always the black market," the major said spontaneously. "Or pornography. That's exciting, almost as good as being a revolutionary."

The singing grew steadily. Augusto was again in a trance. Peduto liked his voice. He gazed at the photographs on the wall: a man kneeling with his head between a woman's knees. She, all aglow, displaying herself. A middle-aged man with his tongue thrust, like a dog's, into a sliced peach. A woman taking a bite from a live banana.

"And he has the nerve to say nothing happens here," the major said cheerfully, catching sight of still another series of photographs. "Look at that!"

"You must have been away some time," Malic said.

"Wonderful!" the major responded, thinking about how he would begin his next chapter about Malic.

"The days are long and the nights still longer," Malic said. "We manage to amuse ourselves."

"And how!" the major echoed, draining his glass with sensuous enjoyment. "You must have had plenty of trouble getting these from Paris."

"From Rome," Malic said pointedly. "Some are from Milan, others from Bologna and Venice. There are some I haven't put up yet. The work of your garrisons in Albania and Greece."

"Of course!" the major exclaimed. "It's all the work of Italians. There's no more human or more corrupt nation in the world. All this is a reflection of a mad, wonderful people, the most pornographic people on earth! We will always be remembered for our brothels, our gonorrhea, our syphilis, and our own peculiar capacity for suffering. Yes, excellent! Here is a real encyclopedia of Italian poetry."

The major's hands shook. Malic said that he had a few other things of interest under the counter, but Peduto was not listening. He jumped from his chair and eyed each picture carefully: "Poor little fellow," he said, "that one on the left. Look, he is sucking and drinking it in . . . he's really going at it, poor man! And those two doing the sixty-nine! My wonderful, corrupt country, who wouldn't give his life for you! I love you and adore you, my filthy Italy!"

Peduto was ecstatic. He drew out a thick notebook and jotted something down.

Once more the saloon was shaken by the thunder of guns.

"What else do you have for me?" the major asked, stroking his beard.

"French letters, *signor maggiore.* Something out of this world! From Rome. They're the best yet. Softer than the softest silk. A completely new model!"

"What do you mean, a new model?" the major laughed good-humoredly, pouring himself a drink.

"That's what it says."

"Long live the war, if we can't have peace!" cried Peduto. "Long live the Italian war . . . the war that never lasts long but is long remembered!"

"How many packets shall I put aside for you, Major?" Malic asked. "Two or three?"

"Ten."

"You should always put some aside when you can get them," Malic said.

"Fifteen then," Peduto said, taking another drink.

"They're not so expensive either," Malic added.

"Make it twenty," the major banged on the counter.

"How about a complete set of photographs, *signor maggiore?*"

"All right," Antonio said, the brandy burning his throat and dulling his thought. "I'll take anything you have!"

"Then I'll make you a parcel of two or three packets of Abortina. The medicine's name is its best recommendation. It's another excellent little product, fully tested and approved by both the army and the civilian population."

"Might I ask where this universal miracle is produced?"

"In Albania."

"Staggering! I thought their specialites were grease and stench. Dear God, how grateful I am to you for the opportunity to tour this land you've created by accident. Tell me about Abortina."

"I supply our people and your army, and the outlying district as well. In times like these one has to think more of others than of oneself."

"How much of this miraculous stuff have you got?"

"I'd say enough to abort all your occupied territories, including Greece, Albania, and Abyssinia."

"I always thought Montenegrins a gifted, intelligent people. You make so much of honor that you get on my nerves. You're like the ancient Greeks."

"I've never been in Greece so I don't know what they are like," Malic said. "But I know what you are like."

"We'll discuss that when I am sober," Peduto said.

"I'm changing my profession," Malic said, pushing aside a number of bottles.

"We'll talk about that, too, some other time."

"We may not have a chance."

"Of course we will," said Peduto, clutching the thick notebook under his arm. "The two of us won't get away from each other as easily as that."

"I don't understand," Malic said, handing him the parcel.

"Just as well. Who does?"

The major's attention was engaged by two drunken, mustachioed Montenegrins who took turns embracing Pietro. Pietro was weeping. People stared into his face, poured brandy over him, and wiped him with dirty rags and dirty hands. Pietro spread his arms as if to ward off the sound of dirty army songs. He whispered softly: "Marika *mia* . . . where are you?"

"Marika *mia,*" Colonel Allegretti whispered in a trembling voice, gripping her breasts as he had gripped the chest expander a while ago. "Marika, my sweetheart, my darling," he added, covering her neck with kisses.

He was thrusting himself between her rounded knees, and forcing aside the arms that had tried to cover her nakedness and the sharp points of her breasts. He longed to lay her flat and take her. But the supple body resisted skillfully and the sweating colonel kept slipping down beside her. "Marika, why?" he uttered feebly.

"Later," the girl said nervously. "*Dopo,* Spartaco. Plenty of time."

He fingered her smooth body with shaking hands, swinging her from one side of the bed to the other. The girl giggled and slipped from his grasp like a fish. When he finally caught her again, he plunged his teeth into her thighs. He bit her shoulders and licked her breasts and kissed her stomach and groin. Her fingers were in the colonel's hair, as if caressing him, but in actual fact preventing him from slipping beneath her navel. His voice was hollow and sweaty:

"Don't torture me."

"*Dopo, ragazzino,*" Marika said. "Later!"

"Why later, Marika?" the colonel said, his lips pressed to her navel.

"I want you to promise me something first," Marika said. "Will you, *ragazzino*, will you?"

"I will, dearest," he shuddered. "Anything you say!"

"Will you keep your promise?"

"Of course, darling."

"Then take me up in your wonderful plane," Marika twittered. "Every day I watch you flying over the town, looking down on everybody, and my heart leaps. Spartaco, will you let me?"

Spartaco fell silent. His head slipped lower and lower. "First promise," Marika said calmly.

"I promise," the colonel said.

"Say it like this: I give you my word as an Italian and an officer that I'll take *la carissima signorina* Marika for a trip in my plane."

The colonel repeated her words. His lips were dry.

"*Si*, you can take me for a little ride," the girl purred in a sing-song voice. "I want everyone to see me with you, the commandant. I want them all to be jealous! All Montenegro will envy me!"

"But Marika *mia*," the colonel said weakly, lifting his head a moment from where it lay on her groin.

"You mean, you won't?" the girl flared. "*Bene*, then there'll be no . . ."

"But Marika, I don't know when I'll be going up again in that damned thing."

"Why don't you know?" she interrupted him. "You're the commandant and you must know everything."

"I'm holding it for the main offensive," the colonel said. "For the decisive battle."

"Then get up and get dressed," the girl said. "*Subito!*"

The colonel gripped her waist. A new strength entered him. "Very well, *carina*, I agree. We'll fly!"

"Promise me you'll summon Captain Brambilla today and tell him I've been with you and all the rest of it," the girl said.

"If you go on like this, you'll be dead drunk," Captain Brambilla told himself. "You're pretty far gone now, and you can't forget. That shaggy ape has had your Marika. No, you'll never forget that. Wait, have another drink. Some day he'll get it."

The captain thought of sticking a knife in Colonel Allegretti and throwing him into a ravine. The image frightened him and he quickly got to his feet. He swayed and staggered to the counter. Malic and Major Peduto were still talking. He looked at the pictures on the wall, the slender waists, the powerful breasts, and rounded backsides. One of the girls was Marika.

"Another drink," Brambilla said quietly.

"Here's two," Malic served him promptly.

"Give me three," the captain said, placing the money on the counter.

"Bravo, Captain," said Peduto.

The captain smiled ingratiatingly and bowed. He raised his glass and drank to the major's health. Peduto went on talking.

"All right, dear Malic. You're partly right. But try to understand my point."

"That won't be easy," said Malic. "Forgive my frankness."

"I've always appreciated frankness and honesty," Peduto said. "Especially from an enemy. But in this case I can't agree with you."

"You ask too much, *signor maggiore*," Malic said, looking him straight in the eyes.

"Any other Montenegrin would accept an offer like that with open arms," Peduto said.

"But you always forget I'm a patriot. Money means nothing to me. A true patriot, *signor maggiore*. Why should that surprise you?"

"What if I ordered you to put some other pictures among these truly excellent photographs?"

Malic put aside the bottle and glasses. He looked straight at the major.

"What would happen then?" Peduto repeated, taking his glass with an unsteady hand.

"I don't know," Malic said firmly. "We'll see."

"I order you, more or less informally, to put up portraits of the royal family and the Duce as well as scenes of our successful battles," Peduto said. "Of course the place of honor belongs to Mussolini, our unconquerable and infallible leader."

"An excellent idea!" Brambilla exclaimed.

Peduto liked sycophants. He favored the captain with a long, artificial smile and then turned again to Malic.

"I want to see our pictures on all your walls. Our glory, the glory that makes my heart contract with pain. We must mingle the photos you've already got with those of our leaders, who are guiding us toward victory and better life with a wisdom hitherto unknown. I want our glory and our pornography in one and the same place."

Peduto had never been more excited. His fine, gentle blue eyes were full of tears; he was shaking.

"Is it hard for you to do what I ask?"

"There's only one little snag," Malic said. "Your soldiers will take these pictures down. It happened before and it'll happen again. They spit on the members of your royal family, as well as on Mussolini. The Queen was the only one they spared."

"Do you recall the names of those idiots?" Captain Brambilla asked. "For a good price, of course."

"No use asking him such things," Major Peduto said. "He hates telling tales. You'll have to find someone else, Captain."

Augusto Napolitano thrust himself between Peduto and Brambilla, and sang:

> "*Amato mio, sta natte o mai,*
> *Mi bacerai, ti bacero . . .*"[2]

[2] Oh, my loved one, tonight or never,
You will kiss me, and I'll kiss you . . .

Brambilla thought of Marika, and the colonel. He had never felt such jealousy. Peduto's mirth angered him and he clenched his fists. His eyes were filled with tears.

Peduto gently pushed the guitarist away. It didn't become Augusto to sing such soft, depraved songs and he requested that he stick to his good-natured obscenities until the end of the war.

"We'll put these pictures up at once. And if anything happens to them I'll have you in front of a military court," Peduto said feebly. "Understood?"

"Understood." Malic turned pale. "Will you have another brandy?"

"Yes. Pour one for the captain as well. But I want you, Brambilla, to go to the colonel first. He has a heap of photographs. Ask him for them. We'll pick out the best and the most symbolic for the walls."

"The commandant won't receive me," Brambilla said tearfully.

"Tell him I sent you."

"Promise here and now that you'll have your picture taken with me," Marika purred.

The colonel was silent.

"If you don't promise, you get nothing."

"Hold on, Marika," Allegretti said.

"I want to be photographed with you in front of headquarters," Marika said, "and I want to have the bunkers and our beautiful flag in the background."

"What good will that do you, darling?"

"I always think of the future. Once the war is over, those photographs will mean a lot to me. A proof that we shared the good and the bad. Right, my bumblebee?"

"I'll bet you've got hundreds of such pictures."

"Not hundreds, but a few. The first one was with a soldier,

just after you had entered town. He was a good boy. We were together for three weeks. I left him the minute he proposed to marry me. Then there was a lieutenant but he was killed. Then Major Peduto; I was photographed with him several times. I tired of him soon enough. He has a lot of children everywhere, and he likes to gamble and promises to marry all his women in Rome. Also, he used to write down what I said. I didn't like that. I liked Colonel Fabiani best. We were engaged to be married, but it was ruined by the Greeks. 'My Montenegrin angel,' he said to me, 'I have to put down those Greek rascals. Perhaps I shall die.' I never heard from him so I gave up. But we had a wonderful photo taken! I was armed to the teeth, he cuddled up beside me. We looked ferocious. We had a guitar between us and I was holding a helmet in my lap, full of flowers he had picked himself. I also had my picture taken several times with that fool, Captain Brambilla. He is now my fiancé. He's married, has three children, but wants more. He hates his wife. She won't have any more. He'll take me to Italy. It's all in writing. His wife has no objections, but she wants to keep the children. Also, she wants us to buy her a small pharmacy. We have agreed. She'll mix medicines, we'll make love. And spend his father's millions. His father is dying, you know."

"Shut up, will you?" the colonel snapped.

"If I find out you are married," Marika said, "and that you have a child, you've had it! Just try to tell me lies! I'll find out the truth through the Red Cross."

"Forget the Red Cross," the colonel shouted.

She had never seen him so aroused. His lips were trembling. But she couldn't help herself.

"Say you'll do it, my hairy *calabrone*, a picture, yes? Or no love!"

With the skill of an old and experienced hunter and tenderly, as if touching precious gold, he caressed the soft, fine fur between her legs. Lowering his head, he said:

"I agree, my bunny rabbit . . . everything."

Major Peduto leaned across the counter and tapped Malic gently on the shoulder.

"You, *Montenegrino,* you probably think I'm a patriot, too?"

"I have no objection to that," Malic said. "Every man should be patriotic."

"Why would you worry about things like that?" Peduto asked, trying to draw him close. "You run a saloon, that's all. What do you care about fascism and communism? All nonsense. You make as much money as you can and keep quiet. And let us wallow in our own shit. At least they pay me well. And promote me mercilessly. I shall very likely die a general. Me a general! Impossible, isn't it? Sex and poetry is all I care for. Irony! Sheer irony!" the major concluded, and brought his fist down heavily on the counter.

"What's irony?" Malic asked.

"You and me," the major said.

"Is it the same as pornography?"

"More or less the same," Peduto retorted with growing excitement. "But the word pornography sounds better and is far more universal. There is no more exalted word than pornography. Give me another drink, but make it stronger this time!"

Peduto put the bottle to his lips and drank. "I have plenty of weaknesses, pornographic ones, of course. I like you and I don't want to quarrel with you over patriotism. I like you and I like Paolone out there by the tank. For me you are both metaphors."

"He must be out of his mind," Brambilla thought. "How can he like this mad Montenegrin, who decorates his walls with shameful pictures, and that Paolone who's surrounded by shit?"

"Friend," the major said, "let me embrace you. I wish you luck and success in life. May you survive this sexual, filthy, infected war and get rich in the process. And, if you manage to save your head, I hope you will employ me as a porter in one of your brothels."

"If only I dared, I'd order him taken out," Captain Brambilla thought. "Of course, he'll get into trouble, the swine. He doesn't deserve his rank, or his decorations. He'll pay for having wooed Marika while she was my fiancée. I know what I'll do! I'll write to the High Command for Montenegro, Greece, and Albania, and have him black-listed along with that hairy beast Allegretti. Well, Major, just you keep up your friendship with this Communist dwarf!"

"*Carissimo*," the major went on, his eyes full of tears. "I honestly want to help. You are the only one who earns his bread honestly. You alone have overcome darkness and pornography!"

Brambilla and Malic were speechless.

"Yes," Peduto stammered. "This red, shaggy, dirty ape with his major's rank is dying to help everyone. I want you, as one of my favorite metaphors, to leave this wilderness. Neither you or I are fit to live in a country whose people are so quick with a knife. The place for you is Italy, the country with feeling, with the deepest pathos known to man. Why not marry my cousin? She has some money. She's going to live in Milan. In fact, I've already written to her about you and she has asked for your photo. She'll send you hers. She'd come and get you. I'd like to help you both. I'll help you open your first brothel! She is a lamb, a good quiet girl. A lamb! She'll obey you. One of her legs is a bit short, but she's inherited a nice sum and she isn't a virgin."

Malic thought it immoral to get married while one's country was in danger. He took a drink from the major's bottle.

"She's religious," the major said. "She prays all day long and curses the one who first took her. Looking at you, I now see what you two have in common: your eyes are almost identical: large and dark, and shot through with brownish veins. And the lashes, too. If you open a brothel, this drunken officer, this debauched old gambler will be your regular guest: he will also show his medals and badges to the clientele and describe our campaigns so as to put Italian glory and Italian pornography in the right perspective."

Peduto picked up a bottle of brandy and the package Malic

had prepared for him. He turned from right to left, shouting at the soldiers crowded around the counter.

Brambilla and Malic found the major's muddled and garrulous talk incomprehensible. Love and victory on all fronts, the bombardment of Montenegro, fascism, his pious relative, and the gonorrhea he had avoided. Dust fell from him as he swayed in front of the counter, gesticulating to express himself more graphically.

Peduto reached out and accidentally embraced one of the girls. She pressed herself against his uniform and thrust her knees between his. He had no idea who she was.

"Three weeks I've been waiting for you, Antonio," the girl said, revealing a row of bad teeth.

"I once knew your name," the major said unsteadily.

"Kiki," the girl said. "*Tua cara* Kiki."

"All right, Miki, what do you want?"

"I am Kiki, aren't I?"

"Yes, you're Riki," Brambilla echoed contemptuously.

"I'm a little drunk, Miki," the major stammered. "Grab the captain."

"I'll sober you up," the girl said, putting her arm around his waist.

"I'll give you fleas," Antonio said.

"I'm full of them already. Come on, dear, come on, freckle-face."

"*Evviva signor maggiore!*" someone yelled from the crowd. "Long live the major!"

"Don't surrender, Peduto!" cried an officer.

"Long live poker!" someone else said.

"Kiki, angel, what are you waiting for?" the officer said. "Grab him! That's a good girl."

Kiki's knees were still between the major's.

"You must forgive me this time," the major said. "We'll do it tomorrow. Or the day after. I haven't got a penny. Drunk everything. Be off, there's a good girl!"

"You can pay later," the girl said. "You don't have to pay

cash. You already owe me something, anyway, don't you remember?"

"I don't," the major said. "But then I enjoy not remembering anything."

"*Andiamo,*" the girl said. "Come. I'll let you have it for nothing. My sweet, darling Peduto."

"Riki, my precious Miki, I must confess that on my trip I picked up a rather impressive dose of Montenegrin clap, in addition to fleas and bugs, and I wouldn't want to make you unhappy."

"But I already have it," Kiki said. "Mine is Italian. Lucky it isn't syphilis. *Andiamo!*"

Antonio pushed her away gently.

"I love you," she said, grabbing the holster around his waist.

"I love you, too," the major said, looking for the bottle. "But go away."

"If you love me, why won't you come with me," the girl asked, stretching her thick lips in a melancholy smile.

"Because I hear shooting."

"Who cares?"

"They'll be killing my metaphors."

"What are metaphors, darling?"

"I really have a swine for a commander," Captain Brambilla thought to himself. "How can he ignore his rank and his medals? I won't rest until he is demolished."

The major was now looking at Pietro who lay on the floor stock-still, his arms by his sides, his eyes glazed and insane, staring into the smoke as if dead.

"Riki," the major said hoarsely, "go and help Pietro."

The girl looked at him in surprise.

"Miki, can't you hear me?"

"He looks as if he's going to die," the girl whispered.

"Do it or I'll shoot you!" the major said. "Quick!"

The girl went up to Pietro and caressed his hair.

"Kiss him," Peduto roared.

Kiki looked at him sadly.

"On the lips," Peduto said.

The girl obeyed. But Pietro didn't move. He was hot, sweating, completely oblivious to what was going on around him. The girl kissed him again, but he only breathed more deeply and touched the filthy floor with the tips of his fingers.

"Unbutton him!"

The customers rose to their feet. They were silent, except for Napolitano who continued humming his song. They watched the girl unbutton the stiff military shirt. She caressed his smooth Sardinian chest.

"I can't do anything with him," she said desperately. "I couldn't wake him if I was the devil himself."

"Poor man," said Malic.

"Call the doctor," someone shouted. "Or the *padre*."

Everyone looked at the major: he was clasping a bottle to his chest. His eyes were bloodshot, his face grim.

"His trousers too," Major Peduto screamed at the top of his voice.

"But, Major," the girl whispered. "I can't go on. I can't."

"The trousers too!"

"But I love you, I really do . . . "

"And I love you!" said the major. "Quick!"

The girl obeyed. Pietro Portulo did not move.

"Now take it out and shake it!" the major said between his teeth. "That should bring him round."

She had done as she was told, but Pietro was breathing still more deeply.

"Faster," Antonio whispered. "Stop that guitar, Augusto!"

She was doing all she could with an amazing skill, but Pietro remained half-dead.

"Slowly now, up and down," the major commanded, his voice trembling. "I know our dear, good Pietro will wake up. That's the way! We must help him; we are human beings, we've drunk and sung with him. That's it, Riki, my love. That's it, again, and again! And don't cry, *carina,* don't cry! We've got to bring poor old *Sardo* around."

Pietro ground his teeth, raised his hands from the floor, and crossed them on his stomach. As he began to sob, Augusto's guitar rang out:

> *"Ma la canzone mia più bella sei tu,*
> *Sei, tu, la vita . . ."*[3]

The crowd strained to understand Pietro's words. Some said he was talking about his mother, others thought it was about his sister.

Pietro sat up. Wet through, unbelted and unbuttoned, he slowly got to his feet. He looked around, but recognized no one. He felt strange female hands upon his body; his skin itched. Softly, he whispered:

"Marika, my love!"

Even the major was astonished by this statement. He looked at Captain Brambilla and then at Pietro. The girl concealed her face with a handkerchief. Napolitano struck the strings. Waving his arms about him as if seeking something in the dark, Pietro moaned: "Marika *mia* . . . Marika, my poor darling . . . "

Captain Vittorio Brambilla took advantage of the uproar to slip away from the saloon.

"I don't give in so easily," Marika said holding the colonel's head between her legs at a reasonable distance. "If I gave in as easily as all that . . . there'd be nothing left of poor me."

"Let me, or kill me," the colonel whispered.

"I'll let you. I won't kill you," Marika said, and giggled playfully. "But first you must say yes to everything. Everything."

"Yes, I say yes," said the colonel. "To everything."

"Say you are mad about me," the girl demanded.

"I am mad about you," the colonel conceded gloomily.

"And that since you've been in Montenegro, Greece, and Albania, you've never loved any girl as you love me," Marika said.

[3] You are my loveliest song,
You are my life . . .

The colonel's breathing was heavy.

"Spartaco," the girl began, "you must understand. Your saying this is as important to me as love. Say it sincerely, *calabrone*, I don't want soldier's lies! Watch your words!"

"You're right," Allegretti said. He had reached the end of his strength. "Since we liberated Abyssinia, Greece, Albania, and Montenegro, I've never loved another . . . nor shall I . . . nor shall I, I'm sure, till the end of my life . . . "

"Perfect!" Marika cried like a child. "We'll spread it around! All Montenegro must know it: and all the liberated countries and all the garrisons, and the High Command!"

"Now let me," the colonel moaned. "Just a little, *cara*. I've promised you everything you've asked and I've said everything you wanted me to say."

"Promise," the girl continued, gradually freeing his passionate head, "that you'll recognize the child I will bear you nine months from now as your own."

"Dearest," the colonel said, now openly desperate, "I'll make a confession now. Don't curse me. I've already got five: four are mine. Of that I'm a hundred per cent sure. But the fifth . . . the fifth is no more mine than anyone else's. Five, *carina*, do you know what that means, a scandal!"

"You'll have a sixth, I'm certain, and it'll be your favorite," Marika said as tears came to her eyes. "If it's a son, we'll put him in a military school."

She was waiting for his final yes. She watched his head fall lower and lower.

"Promise," Marika said, in a halting voice. "Promise, love!"

The guns roared. A heavy explosion shook the house. The windows rattled, the doors gave. Blind with passion, he stuck out his tongue like a dog.

CHAPTER 2

CAPTAIN BRAMBILLA tottered down the street. The guns boomed. But all he could hear was Pietro's crazy words: "Marika, my life!" The further he walked, the more he was possessed by disgust for Pietro. "What does he want from my poor girl?" he wondered, "and what right has that filthy, drunken *Sardo* to speak about my fiancée? The moment he said 'Marika, *mia vita*,' I should have punched him like a man; that would have taught him to leave other people's property alone."

The shutters on the colonel's windows were closed. He felt a vague and oppressive sadness: "Who knows how he is questioning her now," he thought, and his breath grew short. "My poor darling, they are all plotting to take you from me."

He passed several officers without returning their salutes. Soldiers were running about blowing whistles. Suddenly he paused and no longer felt drunk. He was in a cold sweat. "My company is waiting!"

His soldiers were waiting for him in the shade, in front of the mosque. They were singing and drinking. Some were in shirt-sleeves, others in breeches, most of them were barefoot. One of them was sitting on the steps of the mosque playing a harmonica.

"Is everything in order, men?" Brambilla asked.

"Yes, Captain," the swarthy sergeant major reported.

"Any suspicious people around?" the captain asked, amused by his own question.

"Yes, Captain, sir," the sergeant major replied. "And he is dangerous, too!"

"Where," Brambilla asked, automatically reaching for his revolver.

The sergeant major pointed upwards. The mullah loomed white on the minaret. The gunfire obliterated his singing. He was flailing his arms, touching his cheeks, peeking out of the little windows.

"What makes you suspect him, Sergeant Major?" the captain asked. "Is he armed?"

"I pulled his beard, but still he refused to speak to us," the sergeant major said seriously. "He must be concealing something. Also, he refused to drink with us."

The soldiers nodded in agreement. The captain's head swam, brandy beating at his temples. The sergeant major went on explaining, wrinkling his low, coarse forehead.

"Shall I shoot, Captain?" a soldier whispered. "That'll shut him up!"

"Why not pinch his boots?" Brambilla suggested, and was immediately disgusted with himself.

He marched limply alongside his soldiers and thought: "My poor girl, is he still torturing you? I will not allow you to visit him again. No, a thousand times no, not even if it costs me my rank! I'll give them hell, anyone who touches you," the captain whispered to himself. "I'll kill the lot of them! I'll pour gasoline on them and burn them and then I'll run away with you to the other end of the world or straight into the Communist guns!"

The soldiers were kicking up a lot of dust. The sun was scorching hot. The captain's head seethed.

"The mullah, Captain," a soldier said suddenly.

The captain lazily ordered a left turn. The soldiers obeyed.

"The mullah!" the soldier repeated angrily. "Let me kill him. He stole my boots. That's why he won't come down."

The captain ordered them to hurry up. Once again he heard the church bells and spotted a crowd of townspeople dressed in black. He marched at the head of his unit. His thoughts were with Marika as he came face to face with the funeral procession.

In front of the coffin marched Vukic, the fat priest, his beard reaching to the middle of his chest. The men were bareheaded. The women wore black headscarves.

"Search!" Brambilla ordered. "Men, surround them!"

"*Signor capitano,*" the priest stuck his chest out. "We are bearing the dead."

"Hands up!" Brambilla snapped.

"We are in a hurry," the priest said. "The poor soul has been waiting since yesterday to be buried. He's beginning to smell."

"Was he a Communist?" the captain asked, as he searched the priest and raised his long, black robe.

"He was nothing," the priest said, blushing with shame because he had no pants underneath. "He was a pauper, a good man. An old soldier."

"You're all good people," the captain said. "And soldiers too, but you are all Communists!"

The children wept because the soldiers pulled their ears. The women screamed and swore because the soldiers did not merely search them. The most obedient were the men because they knew that silence was the quickest way to be rid of evil.

They found a knife on the sexton and bound him. He burst into tears and ran to the priest like a helpless child.

"But this is our sexton," the priest protested. "Sacristan, *signor capitano.*"

"You're all sextons," the captain replied harshly.

"But he is a man of God," the priest was angry. "A man of the Church. I answer for him."

"Put him in jail," Brambilla ordered. "Some man of God!"

"*Signor capitano,*" the priest said, and advanced toward him. "What you've found on my sexton is no weapon. It's a simple kitchen knife . . ."

"In the hands of a Communist fanatic," the captain interrupted. "But I am not going to argue with you. A kitchen knife: who needs a knife to bury people!"

The ugly sexton wept.

Brambilla went up to the coffin and kicked it with his boot.

"It's got something in it," he said, and looked at the priest.

"Of course it does," the priest said. "A corpse, *signor capitano*."

The captain surveyed the crowd. The men lowered their heads. The women began to cry again. Brambilla's dull gaze rested briefly on the rotting plank roofs, the tips of the surrounding hills, and on the misty mountain that appeared so often in his nightmares. He shuddered.

"Open it up!" he barked.

"But I beg you most humbly," the priest wailed. "I beg and beseech you not to do it. *Signor capitano, prego, prego, prego!* Let us not disturb a poor man to whom life was unkind."

Quivering with a strange, unreasonable fear, Brambilla watched the weeping women and the bare-headed men and thought they might attack him.

As the lid was raised a foul smell hit his nostrils. He almost threw up. With the movement of one accustomed to dealing with the dead, the priest removed the silk cover from the corpse and Brambilla saw a recumbent figure in gold-embroidered Montenegrin dress covered with flowers and decorations. An old Montenegrin revolver rested next to the man's shriveled head.

"Arms!" Brambilla thundered.

"*Egregio signor capitano,*" the priest was offended. "He was a soldier. A hero. The revolver was a personal gift from King Nikola of Montenegro, whose daughter is your own Queen. And ours. I tell you, a personal gift from the King!"

"But what does a dead man want with a weapon?" Brambilla fumed.

"It accompanies the poor man to his grave," the priest said. "It was his wish."

"Nonsense!" Brambilla said. "A lie!" he added, and with a handkerchief picked up the revolver that lay next to the flattened, silent Montenegrin.

"Who knows what this was meant for!"

"The black earth, *signor capitano*," the priest said.

"The red earth," Brambilla replied, screwing up his eyes meaningfully.

"Sergeant Major, search the corpse, then take them all, in twos and threes, to the cemetery. Be on your guard," he added quickly, "and listen to every word they say!"

The men knocked the coffin lid back into place with their rifle butts. Brambilla ordered the rest of the soldiers to patrol the streets and search everyone, and should the bells go on ringing, to surround the church.

Brambilla went straight to headquarters. Gripping the revolver in his handkerchief, he said to the sentry:

"I wish to see the commandant."

The soldier regarded the ugly rusty revolver with open amazement and said:

"He's busy, Captain. Will you please wait."

"May I ask what he is doing?" Vittorio asked, and regretted the question instantly.

"He's interrogating a dangerous woman spy."

"It's been going on for some time," Brambilla said. "More than two hours!"

"She seems unwilling to talk, Captain," the soldier said from beneath his helmet. "And our colonel keeps pressing."

"Can you hear anything?" Brambilla asked. "Any voices?"

"I heard a gramophone playing," the soldier said, as if revealing a great secret.

The captain looked in the direction of the square and at the flag in front of headquarters. The dust rose thick all the way up to the top of the mast. "Why is that swine questioning you so long my dear, gentle girl . . . why is he forcing you to confess, my defenseless lamb . . . ? Be wise and brave as you've always been and don't let that Sicilian thief, that southern bastard, trick you . . . he must be up to something if he has kept you this long . . . and you're so good, so gentle and childlike, I'm afraid you'll give in to him. . . . "

For a long time he stood there listening to the guns and the bells. He held onto the dead man's revolver, as if it were a strange gift to be ceremoniously presented to an important person. The revolver was hot, as if heated over a fire.

Gruban Malic and two men assisted Pietro to his feet and led him up to the counter. His face was pale, his eyes vacant. He gripped the edge of the counter and gazed about him. He had no idea where he was. His knees were weak. He wanted to collapse and shut his eyes, to sink into a long oblivion.

A sad-looking girl ran up to him and buttoned his trousers and blouse.

"He's a marvel, this *Sardo,*" she said to Malic, putting a cup of black coffee to Pietro's lips. "Why can't you love me, my poor *caporale,* instead of losing your head over that whore who has eyes only for officers . . . "

"What is this?" Pietro grunted.

"Black coffee, *caro,*" the girl said. "Drink it. It'll sober you up."

"I don't want to sober up," Pietro said wearily. "I want to die."

"That's all right with me," the girl said." Drink this coffee though and then maybe you will die."

"Good," Pietro whispered, and drank it.

Major Peduto was fast asleep. Sprawled in a deep, soft armchair, his hands on his stomach, Malic's package on his lap. Kiki stood beside him, gazing at him religiously. She unbuttoned his blouse and kissed his hairy chest. She whispered gently. "Sleep, Antonio darling. My poor tired, freckle-faced love . . . "

Pietro gazed at the bright opening of the door.

"Don't you see he wants to go out?" Malic asked the men who were supporting him.

They were on their way. All three of them swaying. Malic

made a note of what Pietro owed him and followed them to the door.

"Give us a hand," one of the men protested, as Pietro collapsed.

Malic led them out into the middle of the street.

With a feeling of genuine disgust he left them by the tank.

"Now you can take care of him yourselves," he said.

Malic saw them abandon Pietro by the tank as they set off toward another saloon.

His own counter was under assault by the girls and soldiers. Malic was bitter. "All this is shit! I never thought it would be this bad. It's high time I did something about it."

Left on his own, Pietro was seized by fear. The heavy artillery firing. The echo of distant explosions. The sky above quivered in an eternity of burning heat. Pietro breathed heavily, inhaling the dust. He wished someone would come and take him away into the shade. He caught sight of Captain Brambilla standing in front of headquarters, clutching a revolver wrapped in a handkerchief. Pietro felt sorry for him. He strained to get a clearer view of Brambilla, his eyes filled with tears. He looked up. The windows of the colonel's apartment were still closed. Again he looked at the captain.

"Why are you looking at me, you Sardinian dog," Brambilla said to himself as Pietro swayed. "I've got enough trouble as it is. Get out of my sight, you bastard, or I'll kill you with this damned revolver. Be off, or I'll go stark raving mad. The sun has been scorching my eyes and brain for a whole hour!"

Pietro shivered. The mast with four flags spun around him. He wished he were down by the riverbank, which is where he went whenever he felt depressed. But no one would take him to the river now. He rested his forehead against the tank, and didn't notice how hot the steel was.

CHAPTER 3

WITH THE SPEED of a highly skilled magician, Malic was pouring out brandy and distributing it. The guns were silent, the sky clear and burning, yet he was in no mood for small talk with the clientele draped over the counter. Captain Brambilla was full of brandy and anger. Had he been less drunk, he would have been more offended by Malic's mood, he would have shaken him out of it.

Pietro was behind Captain Brambilla, overcoming him completely. He was angry, almost in tears, and Lieutenant Nicola Riva and another man were trying to humor him. They were drawing a sketch in the air and on the dirty tabletop and making obscene motions with their fingers.

"Yes, Pietro, yes!" Riva belched.

"I don't believe you," Pietro whined.

"*Sicurissimo,* as sure as we stand here," Nicola Riva cried, swaying across the table. "I'm telling you because I like you."

Pietro shook his head in disbelief.

"Who hasn't slept with her!" the soldier said in disgust. "You can count them on your fingers. Valerio, Nino, Giangiacomo, and the one that hanged himself, and . . . "

"And me!" the lieutenant said, taking up the brandy bottle.

"It's not true," Pietro whispered.

"Nicola," the soldier said, looking at Riva. "He doesn't believe you. Prove it to him!"

"You can't prove it to me," Pietro said, taking another swig from the bottle.

"And what if I show you some of her hairs? What then?" Riva asked mischievously.

"How come you have them?" Pietro asked inaudibly.

"I took 'em by force," Riva said, "and departed owing her fifty lire."

"Nicola, you're lying," Pietro said feebly. "Nicola, I'll kill you!"

"Show him what you have, Lieutenant," the soldier said.

"Nicola, why do you have to lie?" Pietro asked.

"What's this then?" Nicola opened wide his broad mouth and thrust a handful of chicken feathers under Pietro's nose. "What do you say now, Corporal?"

A general burst of wild and drunken laughter drowned Pietro's tears.

But Gruban Malic remained undaunted. He looked at them contemptously and thought: "I will have revenge on all of you! I give you my Montenegrin word of honor, you'll have reason to remember me!"

They were now embracing Pietro, wiping his tears with sleeves and soiled handkerchiefs, and he longed to run away. Feathers floated everywhere. Bottles and glasses were raised. Toasts resounded both in Italian and Serbian: the name of the most renowned woman was uttered with feeling. Pietro wept like a child.

"I'll get you first of all," Malic said to himself, looking at Brambilla. "You come here to spy on everybody. Your nose has grown sharper, your cheeks thinner with the spite that's eating into your guts. So, Captain, relax awhile; you're at the top of my black list."

Malic again caught sight of the photographs Major Peduto had stuck on the wall: above the middle-aged man with a long dry tongue, Benito Mussolini; another important personage, right next to the girl with a banana in her mouth; a member of an illustrious Savoy family, snapped in Montenegrin dress, gazing at the navel of a large-breasted woman with legs spread wide; a general planting the Italian flag on the ruins of the Acropolis; soldiers in white helmets madly pursuing naked Abyssinian warriors, with raised arms in surrender.

He hated these faces, just as he hated his customers. He felt a quiet hatred and contempt for them since that day in April of the previous year, when they entered the town in their dirty trucks and tanks which they were quick to abandon in search of eggs, chicken, and women.

He had his first quarrel with them in the autumn: he had refused a certain *maresciallo* a strange favor. The plump sergeant major with floppy ears had tried to embrace him and kiss him. He sported his perfumed bottom around, looked at him passionately through his lashes, and waved money in front of his nose. Malic flapped him on his soft hand and cursed him loudly. But the *maresciallo* was fearless in his passion: he leaned over, opened his well-shaped mouth, and sang into Malic's ear: "*In guerra il culo é la cosa migliore.*"[1]

Wild with anger, Malic swore and spat at him and chased him out. For several months he expected to be interrogated. Nothing happened. The perfumed *maresciallo* went elsewhere.

The second encounter was with Peduto early that spring. He demanded from Malic a list of the Communists in the village.

"You've come to the wrong place, *signor maggiore*," he replied, expecting the worst.

"You would have lire to burn," Major Peduto explained drunkenly. "And not just lire either!"

"You must understand once and for all that for Montenegrins there are more important things than your lire," Malic had replied indignantly.

"Too bad, for you and for me, Montenegrino," Antonio had said, draining his tenth brandy. "You are in an excellent position, in the center of events, so to speak. But there's nothing I can do about it. You are a Communist and I am a pornographer."

For the first time since he had opened the saloon, Malic

[1] In wartime, the best thing to have is a piece of ass.

was deathly afraid. Several people had overheard the major's words. The next day they greeted him cordially and even called him *compagno* Malic. He felt more humiliated than ever.

But no one ever believed that he would get away with his treatment of Colonel Allegretti.

"The colonel requests," the courier said, "that you bring him in person a complete set of your French magazines, the photographs, two boxes of medicine, as well as anything else that might interest him. And a bottle of brandy," the soldier added.

"If he were King Emmanuel himself, I wouldn't obey his command," Malic had said, his guests staring at him in terror. "The only way I'll go will be under escort."

His words were carefully translated to the colonel's courier. The crowd spent a whole hour commiserating with Malic. They predicted that, to set a precedent, the colonel would have him hanged by the balls. Or else, he would banish him from Montenegro and ship him by boat to Africa where the natives would roast him and eat him up. Some feared that the whole town and all of Montenegro might suffer on account of Malic.

But the courier came back flushed with excitement. He personally bought the items from Malic, added a generous tip, and formally presented the colonel's card: *Auguri e complimenti.*[2]

And today, as he poured out a brandy for Captain Brambilla and for the colonel's courier, he recalled that after the strange incident, which was as comic as it was frightening, he had suffered nights of sleeplessness.

He also disliked that loud-mouthed, greasy Turiddu Barbagallo, who had not ceased drinking and singing ever since his promotion. He was now pushing between the tables, pinching the girls, banging his comrades on the back, and singing:

> "*E alle donne brutte un aeroplano,*
> *E alle belle un . . . in mano . . .*"[3]

[2] Compliments and good wishes.
[3] For ugly women an aeroplane,
For beautiful women one . . . in the hand . . .

"*Montenegrino,*" Turiddu said, "one for Lieutenant Riva, one for Augusto, and one for Pietro, and something for those two whores. It's on me."

"And who's paying for those five bottles last month?" Malic asked.

"*Compagno* Malic," Barbagallo said. "One for the captain, too, he is falling asleep."

"When are you going to pay up?"

"Why mention such unpleasant things to a man who's just been promoted?" Barbagallo interrupted. "Don't you know that a long and powerful Italy is behind the man you are addressing?"

"I'll throw you out," Malic said.

"Corporal, I'll take your drink on condition that you pay up tomorrow," Captain Brambilla said drowsily.

"A large brandy on Barbagallo," a girl said, coming up to the counter, thrusting her rounded, low-slung behind at the corporal.

"I won't have a drink unless you promise to pay up," Captain Brambilla repeated.

"I promise, Signor Captain," Turiddu stammered, and quickly turned to the soldier next to him: "How about a game of poker? I've got a fourth."

"No," the soldier replied.

"I will," said the girl.

"Out!" said Turiddu.

"How is our plane, Corporal?" Captain Brambilla said.

"The peasants tried to break off a wing and someone stole a tire."

"Barbagallo, what did you do before you joined the army?" the courier asked.

"I worked in a condom factory."

"What did you do there?"

"I was a model," Barbagallo answered with dignity.

The saloon resounded with laughter.

Malic watched Brambilla, who had dozed off, and felt a wave of anger.

"You sly devil," he said to himself. "You squinting bastard, get out of my saloon or I'll show you a thing or two. I'm no longer the harmless proprietor of a saloon who makes tons of money in speculating on the black market." He recalled the first time he came across the pamphlets. Nobody had even asked whether he wanted them. He was innocently opening a package of contraceptives, obscene photographs, and Abortina, which was wrapped in sheets of red paper bearing the slogans: "End the army of occupation! Down with degenerate Italy! Death to fascism! Freedom to the People!" He had studied these desperate calls late into the night; a mass of words and phrases. He could not understand them at first.

Day after day the valuable merchandise arrived, wrapped in these same red sheets.

Big, important words warmed his heart. He was so excited he couldn't sleep. But it bothered him, that he didn't know who was sending him these dangerous documents. One morning he was surprised to find that he had memorized the pages by heart. "I must be thinking the same ideas!" he said to himself.

"And then," he recalled, "I started wrapping my merchandise in these same red leaflets. They laughed at me. The Montenegrins translated the long, complicated sentences for the Italians. Not that they knew what it was all about, but they were frightened, so they tore up the leaflets or tucked them in somebody else's pocket, women stuffed them in their bosoms or under their skirts. But I stood boldy behind my counter and told my story. I began to think like the man who had written those slogans and I wanted to meet him. I began dreaming about him; each night he looked like somebody else, and that really confused me. Time passed and I kept hoping the captain would come and ask me about the wrapping paper. But no such luck. I really wanted to have a fight with him. I was ready to go tc the gallows."

Malic pulled out a sheet of paper with a large red star in the middle, put it on a tray next to a glass of brandy, and delivered it to the captain.

The captain drained the brandy and his eyes rested on the leaflet. He was familiar with it. For days he had been looking for its author. With the tip of his pen he followed the lines, to create the impression that he had never seen this document before.

"Well, *signor capitano*, it's a shock, isn't it?" Malic thought. "I hope this time I've earned jail, not just interrogation. Why don't you show everybody what I've thrust under your nose and then have me escorted to the commandant!"

Calmly, as if for amusement, the captain shaded in the red star, the hammer and sickle. He glanced again at the text: "In a superhuman effort, Montenegrin Partisans have killed fifteen Italian soldiers and captured twenty of them." He read on, comparing the translation with the original, printed on the left side of the leaflet, and grinned. He skipped the lengthy, verbose sentences and returned to the figures, which he altered: instead of fifteen he wrote fourteen and instead of twenty, thirty-five. Then he added: "A truckload of salt, macaroni, and ammunition was also captured." Once again he checked the text and returned the tray with the empty glass and the leaflets to Malic.

Malic almost collapsed with anguish. "Captain," he said to himself, "you're a swine! Stop grinning, you bastard, or I'll be at your throat. You'll never survive my fist, so keep away from it."

Augusto came up to the counter. His eyes were red, his hair greased in place. He placed the guitar by Turiddu's ear and was about to sing.

"Enough of your Neapolitan wailing!" Turiddu said unpleasantly, pushing him aside.

"But, Corporal," Augusto whined, "I don't sing for money . . ."

"I want something cheerful!" Turiddu barked.

"Turiddu, you must pay your debt," Captain Brambilla suddenly joined in.

Turiddu nearly collapsed as he tried to stand at attention.

"I hate you too, Turridu," Malic thought. "You're a coarse bastard and a gambler. I'd like to smash your drunken, gaping mouth and your metal teeth!"

Barbagallo disappeared into a dark corner. He grabbed a military blouse from a table, wrapped something in it, and hastily slipped out of the door.

"Men! On parade," a soldier shouted.

"Not again," someone complained. "*Porca miseria!*"

"Shut up, Leo!"

"The major's orders!"

"That Peduto! He's lost at cards again, I'll bet."

"Shut up, Leo!"

"Get ready, men!" Brambilla barked, leading the way.

The soldiers crowded to the door.

"I've lost my blouse!"

"I can't find my belt." Augusto was frantic. "Or my revolver! I've been robbed! What shall I do?" he asked Malic in despair.

"Don't be upset, Augusto," Malic said. "Nothing will happen to you. Ten days inside, that's all. Now get going!"

"*Montenegrino,*" Augusto burst into tears. "*Fratello mio, caro,* I've already been inside three times. Once for singing, once for drinking, and once for having been robbed, like today. This time they'll court-martial me, hang me!"

"They won't, Augusto," Malic said.

"They will. You've no idea how strict they are! The gallows or the front line, what's the difference? You don't happen to have a blouse, *Montenegrino?*" Augusto said hopefully.

"Why should I have one?"

"Where are those I sold you?"

"I gave them to the Communists." Malic wanted everyone to hear him.

"What about the telescope? And the revolver?"

"Everything," Malic said nervously. "I gave them everything."

"If you find out who's robbed me . . ."

Malic led Augusto to the door. Outside, Captain Brambilla was shouting at the soldiers, waving his arms, as if to defend himself against the dense, hot air.

A sultry command echoed out. The squad moved involuntarily. "Go now, Augusto," Malic said.

Augusto stepped across the threshold and walked down the dusty, rutted road. His face was twisted with fear and pain. His eyes were sadder looking than ever.

CHAPTER 4

THE COLONEL had one hand between Marika's legs; the other surveyed Marika's breasts, her groin, the rounded stomach, and deeply cut navel.

"I must get up," he told himself, "get dressed, and inspect the troops. Horatio's calling me, he is ready for his exercise and his sugar. Peduto is organizing the soldiers for my arrival. The townspeople want to see their liberator. I must leave this little devil here, forbid her to dress, lock her in, and get going."

"I want it like this," Marika purred, pointing to a picture from Malic's collection.

"The battalion is waiting for me," Colonel Allegretti said, his eyes resting on the photograph Marika was studying in fascination.

"I've changed my mind," Marika said, taking another picture from the night table. "Look at them, *calabrone*, look! Ah, *dio mio!* You Italians are the greatest and most cultured nation! Antonio is right. Here, *caro*, this way! Come on!"

"Later," the colonel said, pressing the oval mound of her belly. "After I've addressed the troops."

"Why can't they come here? You could talk from the window up here. You don't even have to put your pants on, and I'd be down here touching you and stroking you. Like this. There, my darling Allegretti: come, stand up, just once more . . ."

"Nonetheless, I cannot inspect the troops naked," the colonel said.

"You don't have to inspect them," Marika said, pulling him by his member. "They don't need you. Darling, why are you hiding, *galletto italiano*, my little snail."

"Yes, but I believe in discipline," the colonel said anxiously. "One must raise their morale all the time. We're in a foreign country. It's hot besides. One has to think of everything. Let your little snail rest his horns."

"Can't you feel something kicking under your hand?" Marika asked, picking up a new photograph.

"I don't think so."

"It's a small Allegretti playing," Marika said. "A future high officer in the army."

"And what about Malic's medicine?" the colonel asked, letting his hand wander downwards.

"I take no medicine from a Communist," Marika replied. "I just won't, and you can't make me!"

"Then don't talk to me about future army commanders," the colonel said. "What difference does it make who sells the stuff?"

He was interrupted by the telephone. He removed his hand from Marika's navel, and raised the receiver.

"Yes, speaking, Mr. Agic," and to humor Marika who hated the local chief informer, he grimaced in disgust. "I hear you."

"How are you, *signor colonnello*?" the voice inquired.

"Well," the colonel was sharp.

"Is the heat too much for you?" the voice asked.

"Yes," the colonel replied, furious. "And how are you?"

"Burning alive. I've just come from the river."

"Any news?" the colonel inquired nervously. "Or are you calling to tell me you're hot?"

"There's news, *signor colonnello*," Agic said. "I just thought I'd break it gently."

"Well?" the colonel asked.

"Well, in the first place that criminal, that Signor Malic."

"What's my *Montenegrino* been up to now?"

"For the last few days he's been distributing leaflets to the soldiers, you know what kind of leaflets I mean. To the townsfolk too. He threw some people out of his saloon and called them Fascists. When they called him a Communist, he loved it. 'I am a Communist,' he told them. He said he would personally skin us all alive."

"Go on," the colonel said.

"And the medicine he is selling," Mustafa Agic went on. "A widow I know had dreadful pains, awful pains. If I hadn't personally helped her, who knows what would have happened. We should find out who prepares the wretched stuff. His indecent pictures, they're flooding the whole town and corrupting the people. I've been requested by our community to let you know."

"Go on," the colonel said.

"*Signor colonnello,* Malic should be expelled from Montenegro."

"Go on," the colonel said impatiently. "Everything you've told me so far I know already."

"Your soldiers drink too much," Agic said, afraid the colonel would say he was aware of this too. "Drinking and fighting. Just a few minutes ago I separated two of them. Two sergeant majors fighting over a whore, if you'll forgive the expression. I have their names. They both come from Naples."

The colonel cleared his throat. "The mullah's wife had a baby," Mustafa Agic said. "A boy. It's not his. They say the father is your very nice pilot *signor caporale* Turiddu Barbagallo. He hung around the old man's house. As soon as the mullah went to the mosque, he'd be at his wife!"

"What do they say in town?" the colonel asked, and winked at Marika who was giggling.

"They don't know about it yet," Mustafa Agic said. "Anyway,

there are many stories around town about your young airman. But more of this later. As for the mullah and the child: the old man's weeping with joy and surprise. Everybody is congratulating him and suggesting he give his son a fine Italian name. I was at his house with signor priest and I tried to persuade him to name the boy after you. But, *signor colonnello*, he refused! I asked him if it was because he was a patriot or a Communist, or because he didn't like you for some reason. He said it was neither, and that he'd be glad to have you as the godfather. He wants the child named Muhamed. He asked me to explain our customs regarding godparents to you: the child's hair is cut and he receives a substantial gift and that is all."

"Good, I accept," the colonel said. "You may tell *signor muezzino* that, busy as I am with military and political matters, I'll shear his youngest child for him. We'll make it a real occasion!"

"*Magnifico!*" Agic yelled into the phone. "Marvelous! I'll run straight to his house and tell him. I'm afraid he may have a stroke when he hears you've agreed."

"Yes, it is wonderful," the colonel said. "But you have told me nothing about the main problem. You know very well I want a list of all Communist sympathizers. As soon as possible."

"The only man I am sure of was the baker, and he hanged himself a week ago. Had he lived, we would have uncovered the whole organization. Too bad he was so quick and escaped us."

"Was his death political?"

"No. His girl was unfaithful. Your pilot was mentioned in this case, too. To say nothing of the priest: he loved her so much he beat her every day."

"And what's the news about the most dangerous of all Communists? That really interests me," he added as Marika tickled him.

"Caught," the voice in the receiver rasped. "We've got him!"

"Why didn't you tell me at once!" the colonel yelled. "That's what matters!"

"I always like to leave the best for last," Mustafa Agic said. "If I'd told you that first, you wouldn't have listened to the rest. I know you: you get as excited, pardon the comparison, as a *giovanotto*."

"Tell me all about it!"

"I don't know all the details now. He is a big man, dark and silent. He was caught in the woods at a village some fifteen miles from here. The description fits absolutely. I used to know him well. A typical Montenegrin idler. Deadly at the card table. He used to take pictures without putting film in his camera and made fools of our people. He took their money too. He's got what's coming to him."

"Let me know the moment he is brought to town," Colonel Allegretti ordered. "I have to hang up now. I'm tired and I have to make a confidential call to Rome. *Complimenti*, Signor Agic."

"*Signor colonnello*!" Mustafa Agic cried in panic. "Your promises! You haven't forgotten?"

"You're right," the colonel said quickly. "I'm getting absent-minded. Yes, I'll send the thirty pounds of macaroni."

"But you've sent me that twice already," Mustafa Agic said.

"All right then, a package of the best spaghetti," the colonel said.

"I've plenty of that too, you've been most kind and generous."

"Then I'll send you five or six bags of wheat," the colonel said. "That's worth more than either macaroni or spaghetti and a bag of sugar," said the colonel with a sigh. "*Complimenti*, Signor Agic."

The colonel replaced the receiver, collapsed on the bed, and swore violently. Marika jumped on him like an infuriated cat.

"Now I want it like this," the girl said, and began to finger him.

"Another time. That idiot tired me out."

"I want an admiral," Marika said. "Don't forget I'm Montenegrin and titles and rank mean a lot to us."

Her fingers spread out all over him like feelers. She wriggled and squirmed, contorted herself, tried everything. She spoke warm, juicy words. She transformed herself into a snake, a spider, an octopus that no man could escape.

All the colonel had to do was hang by her neck, squeeze her around her slender waist or her smooth thighs, catch the coffee-colored tips of her firm breasts in his mouth. Her dark curls touched his eyelids and his swollen lips, and surrendering himself for the umpteenth time that week, he closed his eyes and released his already expended force. All he was aware of was that he was underneath her, that his nose and mouth were buried in the soft, scented hollow between her breasts and that she trod him and crushed him with knees and elbows, scratching and stabbing him with her sharp nails.

At last Marika impaled herself on him and saw a mass of stars. Her voyage was stormy and longer than ever. He spoke of heaven and the eternal sun and she of ships, of masts and admirals. She revolved upon him like a top and again he promised her everything, even things she didn't ask for.

"You mustn't send Brambilla and Pietro away," she said.

"We'll talk of that another time," the colonel answered sleepily, and again thrust his hand between her legs. "Do you want to have them around?"

"I want to torture them," Marika said.

"Take this letter to Peduto," the colonel commanded as Marika got up. "It's on your way."

"You're beginning to give orders," Marika said, arranging her long hair. "I like it better when you obey."

"No pussy, I'm asking you," the colonel said.

Taking the letter, her hand on the doorknob, Marika said:

"Goodbye till tomorrow, my sweet, hairy *calabrone*."

"Till the day after tomorrow, Marika *mia*," the colonel said, feeling his eyelids closing. "My dear one, my Montenegrin love!"

Going down the stairs, Marika carefully opened the envelope and read: "My dear Peduto, be a good man and take my place. I presume you know who has been caught. Inspect the troops and deliver a speech. The longer, the better. You were right: a man's got to adore her. Drop in around seven or later. Spartaco."

The sentry saluted. Marika gave him a look of contempt. A whole squad of helmeted soldiers saluted her. She noticed Paolone by the tank and felt sorry for him but went on.

Marika was not intimidated by the sharp squeal of trumpets that accompanied her to the square. Boldly and directly, as if carrying out a death sentence, she went up to Major Peduto.

CHAPTER 5

GRUBAN MALIC slammed the door of his saloon and rushed out into the street. The platoon of soldiers did not scare him. Commands echoed on all sides, ordering the troops to retire or to advance as the case may be. The sound of trumpets and drums mixed with townsfolk crowding around the bars. Guns thundered in the distance. Soldiers were singing. The mullah's sad, ecstatic voice rose from the mosque. The bells of St. Peter's Church rang out. The Lord's Day choked in the light and in the dust raised by the hastily maneuvering companies.

"This drilling won't get you anywhere," Malic thought. "You can play as much as you like, but you're finished. You don't know what you are up against. You might just as well sing."

Hands in his pockets, he moved boldly among the soldiers. He saw Marika as she approached Peduto.

The soldiers singing "*Giovinezza*" assumed a momentary, lascivious silence. Marika was searching her bosom for the colonel's letter. She took her time locating this important missive. She writhed and bent, feeling and fingering herself, her breasts popping out of the military shirt.

The sky shook with distant gunfire. Major Peduto waited. In a further attempt to produce the document, Marika twisted her skin-tight skirt. The letter dropped on the ground. Peduto stooped to retrieve the letter, but Marika beat him to it. She straddled the letter and, thrusting her tight, oval bottom toward the army, leaned over and, pausing a moment, picked it up.

She was greeted by trumpets, drums, and the yellow cymbals as she straightened herself slowly, langorously, exposing the soft skin behind her knee.

The major read the message. "You were right," he repeated the commandant's words, and then elaborated. "She's the sort men always want to mount." He measured her rounded body. "Yes, I certainly was right," he thought, casting a rapid glance over her thighs.

Peduto asked for the microphone. The military band clamored as the girl swayed before the ranks.

"Listen to them playing, extolling a behind. They've had it," Malic thought. He caught sight of Captain Brambilla. "I've got another leaflet," he said.

"I have two," Brambilla said. "Would you like to borrow them?"

"Yes," Malic said, "Yes."

"Later, in your saloon," Brambilla said.

"Men!" Major Peduto shouted into the microphone. "Gallant soldiers! I have summoned you here to give you great news."

"*Evviva*!" the square vibrated, "*Evviva*!"

"Our invincible army . . ." Major Peduto was amused by the tone of his voice, "Our invincible . . ."

"Long live our invincible army!"

" . . . army," the major went on, "with the aid of our old friends, the Montenegrins, who are bound to us by glorious memories, has succeeded in capturing our greatest enemy! Our enemy and an enemy of the majestic and glorious Montenegrin people! He was taken this morning, some fifteen miles from here; in an hour or two, we shall have the pleasure of seeing him!"

"Long live our cunning army!"

"Long live our Montenegrin friends!"

"Long live Major Peduto, the organizer of our victories!"

"Men!" Peduto tried again in a tired, hoarse voice. "The news I have given you, with tears of joy in my eyes, is of far-reaching significance! After two years of struggle we have managed to capture one of the most dangerous of Montenegrin animals, the Communist criminal who spared neither our precious blood nor that of our Montenegrin brothers! We have every right to rejoice today, to celebrate and embrace our long-suffering Montenegrin brethren! However, once more, men, I stress the need for order, discipline, and obedience! And in the name of our dear and indefatigable commander, the colonel, I congratulate you on a great victory. . . ."

Townsfolk crowded around the soldiers, bearded old men, frightened women. Half-naked children with hungry eyes slipped between the closely packed companies to get a better view of the eloquent major waving his arms, clenching his fists, bulging his eyes. The loudspeakers were hidden in the tops of trees and suspended from telegraph poles. Heads peeked out of small windows. A few students volunteered to translate the major's speech for the frightened populace. "Montenegrins!" Major Peduto went on, stretching out his arms to embrace the entire nation. "Brothers and friends! Rarely have we had reason to be so entirely happy. The destroyer of our peace has been captured due to the extraordinary efforts of our brave soldiers! The man who burned your houses, corrupted your sons and daughters and drove them to their deaths, is no more! And today, you can look with a clear conscience into the eyes of our Queen, the good Helena who sends you her greetings. Today you can tell her of a great victory and I am sure that the good heart of our Mother will leap with joy and that she will have vivid memories of her native land, of her Montenegro that is free at last!"

"Hear, hear!" someone cried.

"Long live the Queen!

"Yes! Long live the King!"

Extracting himself from the crowd, Malic caught sight of Marika; she too was applauding. Malic cleared his throat, gave her a push with his shoulder in passing, and went on. The girl followed him and asked in Italian:

"What's new with you, friend?"

"Plenty," Malic said, looking over his shoulder. "Plenty!"

"Tell me," Marika said, applauding the major.

"Later," Malic said.

"Tell me now," Marika begged, "come on, tell me now."

"Put your hand in my pocket," Malic said.

"Balls!" the girl shrieked affectedly, pulling her hand away.

"Is that all?" Malic asked between clenched teeth.

"And paper," Marika said.

"Take it out," Malic said. "Quickly!"

With two fingers, the girl carefully extracted a heap of leaflets. She flipped through them with the speed and skill of an experienced gambler.

"I've seen this one, but not that one. Brambilla had this one, and Peduto that. These with the red star, the colonel's got a whole bunch of them."

"Well, what do you say?" Malic asked proudly.

"They're nonsense," the girl retorted. "Nothing to do with me!"

Blood rushed to Malic's head. He grabbed her arm.

"You silly girl, this 'nonsense' is making the world tremble. And it's giving your friends a headache!"

"Who cares," Marika said. "I've seen them all. And, anyway, I don't really know what it's all about. These long, difficult words, all this fuss! It isn't for simple people like us."

"It's no use talking to you. You don't understand anything."

"And you are deep, aren't you? Why are you staring at me like that?"

"You'll take these leaflets to your friends," Malic said.

"Why bother? They have so many they could lend you a few."

"Go to hell!"

"*Amico,* don't be a fool," the girl said gently. "Some day this stupidity will cost you your head. Watch yourself! I may not be able to help you."

Malic was crushed. He turned the corner and walked toward the priest's house, down a street that curved and twisted in sharp bends. "First of all I must deal with the Church," he thought.

A prostitute walked toward him. "Hell, an honest man can't breathe for whores," he thought. Mustafa Agic, the local spy, slowly and carefully followed her. "Spies and whores, they make life rough," he thought. "But if they follow me today, that's just what I want."

In front of the priest's house, Malic ran into a servant girl with red cheeks and blue-veined legs. He gave her the usual pinch. "Why didn't you come? I waited for you."

"You look a bit pale today," the girl replied, putting her forefinger to her lips. "Have you been drinking too much?"

"Shove your hand in my pocket."

"No," the girl protested. "Who knows what you've got there?"

"Anything you find there, you can have," Malic said, moving closer.

"Not so loud," the girl whispered pointing to the window of the priest's room. "He's asleep."

"Drinking again, the bastard!" Malic said, and handed the girl the bundle of leaflets. "When he wakes up, give him this. Or better still, go and wake him. Go on, love! And tonight we'll have fun. I have some of the latest specialties, so you don't have to worry!"

The girl shivered. She tried to say something again but was too excited.

The priest suddenly opened the window and loomed large with his long matted beard, bleary eyes, and rotten teeth. His shirt sleeves were rolled up and he had a wet rag tied round his head.

"And what business is it of yours, you booze-selling bastard, whether I've been drinking or not," he roared from the window. "I drink and I pay for it, with my money honestly earned too . . ."

"No, it isn't," shouted Malic. "You got it by robbing poor people. That's how you earned your money!"

"Get out of my yard, you red scum!" the priest screamed. "Get out, you swine! You corrupt our people. Get out of here with your leaflets and your lies!"

The priest's voice drowned the distant thundering and the noise of the trucks on the street.

"If I come down . . . If I catch you, I'll castrate you! I'll castrate you like a goat!"

"Come down if you dare, you hog, I'll shave off your filthy beard right here in front of the people you rob and cheat! Swindler! Drunkard! Gambler!"

"Get him, you people!" the priest screamed. "Hold the red bastard!"

"We'll try you, you long-nosed drunk! We'll hang you by the balls right in front of the proletariat!"

"And who is 'we,' you long-eared swine?" the priest asked, leaning out the window.

"We, Communists!" Malic said, beating his chest.

"What in God's name have you got to do with the Communists?" The priest coughed and choked with laughter. "You scum, you bastard, you!"

"I've always been red in spirit!" Malic cried, raising his fist. "Red as blood!"

"Get out of my sight!" the priest bellowed. "Don't bring misfortune on my house, you atheist, you apostate! Seize him, good people, tie him up . . . take him straight to the commandant, to the colonel . . . Brothers, call the army, run a tank over him!"

"You can't destroy me. Behind me stand the masses of revolutionary workers," Malic roared as the sweat poured down his face. "I'm strong and indestructible, a true Communist!"

"Agic, what are you waiting for!" the priest screamed. "Call the police! Shoot this blasphemous Communist dead on the spot!"

A crowd of people had gathered around Malic, who was foaming with rage, waving his arms. He pulled out a bunch of leaflets and hurled them at the soldiers who had arrived to deal with the situation and were roaring with laughter instead.

No one moved as Malic grew more and more berserk. The mullah on top of the mosque stretched his arms in conversation with God Himself. The church bells were tolling as if marking the death of many. The dust, like an inexorable sea, choked and enveloped the crowd that had gathered around Malic.

"I gave that drunken, bearded swine hell," Malic thought, pushing his way through the crowd. "If he provokes me again, I'll shoot him and show everyone how I feel about God, the Church, and the priests! It's high time I dealt with the mullah too! He also blabbers too much."

Marika went up to him and said:

"You've had it, Malic!"

"I hope so," Malic said proudly.

"They are going to arrest you, you know. They are mad at you."

"That's too bad."

"I don't know if I can help you. A lot of people heard you. That bastard Agic was pleased."

"I'll have him hanged too," Malic said. "By the feet!"

Marika opened her pretty lips in surprise. One of the whores walked up and turned to Malic. "Malic, I think I'm pregnant."

"By whom?" Marika snapped.

"Brambilla," the girl said. "But I shall say it's the colonel's. He adores children, as real Italians do."

"I'm already in my fourth month," said another girl. "The child's Peduto's but I've accused Captain Vittorio."

"Whores, whores," Marika screamed.

"Get away from me, you traitors," Malic yelled as he walked away.

Marika followed. But he quickened his pace and vanished into the crowd. He wandered left and right, forward and backward, unable to escape the blare of the loudspeaker.

"Brother Montenegrins!" Major Peduto was still at it. "Your place is with Italy, the country that loses every battle but wins every war! Let us stand firmly together and await victory in love and unity!"

Mustafa Agic approached the major and whispered something to him. The major's face suddenly lit up. He grabbed the microphone and cried:

"Beloved Montenegrins! Brother Moslems! Soldiers! Any minute now we shall be seeing the greatest traitor in Montenegro! Lieutenant Riva's company, which captured him, is in town!"

"Hurrah!" the soldiers cried. "Hurrah! Hurrah, a hundred times hurrah!"

The townspeople were silent. The prostitutes huddled together in a group, whispering among themselves: "Poor Vuk Vukov. Our poor Vuk. They couldn't have caught our Vukovic as easily as that."

"Why not? They've got dogs."

"Someone must have betrayed him. He was brave, our Vuk."

"Who'll wreck their bridges now?"

At the sound of motorcycles the crowd panicked and made way for Riva's troops. The motorcyclists, dressed in leather jerkins, goggles, crash helmets, and boots, dashed into the square.

Out of the dust loomed the figure of Nicola Riva. In one hand he held a bottle and in the other a revolver. His tunic was unbuttoned, revealing a skinny chest.

Behind him marched his soldiers, more drunk than their drunken leader. Passing in front of the major's rostrum they shouted, "Long live the Duce, the King, our commanders, great Italy, and free Montenegro!" Their rifles were decorated with small Italian flags and contraceptives.

Surrounded by drunken trumpeters playing a march, and by the drummers beating mercilessly upon their instruments, marched the notorious traitor, a huge, bearded man who towered above the soldiers. His nose was large and hooked, his ears prominent, and his forehead at least four inches high. From beneath his hairy brows a pair of dark, deep-set, frightened eyes looked out at the excited crowd. He was barefoot and in rags that flapped as he walked out of step with his escort. On his chest was hung a cardboard sign:

THE MOST DANGEROUS TRAITOR IN MONTENEGRO.

The delighted major beat his chest, pulled his hair, stomped his feet on the rickety rostrum, poked the officers gathered around him, pointing his forefinger toward the sun-baked hills. The troops fired above the frantic crowd, pouring lead into the dusty sunlight, the human cries, and the stench of the town.

Gruban Malic knew better. Had he been closer to the rostrum, he would have said to Major Peduto: "Listen, you mad devil, you! You're wrong! That blood-stained man you've got isn't our hero Vukovic but our poor, humble, mute Rasko who meanders all over the place, lives on alms. You're wrong, Major, and you are making a fool of yourself and of your soldiers. The man you think you've caught is waiting to get you in some thicket. Let poor Rasko go, and stop fooling yourself."

Rasko was led across the square. The church bells rang terrifyingly. The mullah was a patch of white on his mosque. Women wept, for Rasko and for their own lost sons. Mustafa Agic struck himself on the forehead and hurried to headquarters. Meanwhile the colonel was dreaming that he was in an aeroplane and about to plunge down over the roofs and into an abyss and that a mischievous Marika was tickling him.

CHAPTER 6

ALONE IN HIS SALOON, his accounts for the day completed, Malic went to the window. The tired and frugal people were turning down their gas lamps, and the darkness on the square grew thicker. He felt fatigue in every muscle: "You should lie down and have a good rest, and not open your eyes for a long time," he whispered to himself. "Dream that you're a man and that no one can do anything to you."

The last of the drunken soldiers were leaving the square. He heard the sound of Augusto's guitar and of his broken singing:

"Che bella cosa è na jurnata 'e sole."[1]

Malic recognized the voice of Barbagallo's victim. He heard the sound of distant firing and beamed. "We'll beat you," he said to himself. "We'll beat you, even if you rattle your arms round my shop all day long. There's no end to our strength. Don't you see that we hate your flag, that we loathe your barracks and everything you've brought us?"

He gazed into the darkness.

He thought he saw Rasko's battered, bloody feet. He knew this huge man well, his wide jaw and his wrinkled neck. Better than most people. But no one knew why Rasko had come to this little town some ten years ago.

He always hung around the shops and mills. Montenegrins would cross themselves and Moslems would stand wide-eyed as they watched him fling hundred-pound sacks over his shoulder.

[1] What a wonderful thing is a sunny day.

When he was out of work, he would stand in front of the church or the mosque, mumbling, drawing his hard mouth into a smile, stretching out his arms imploringly. He feared nothing but soldiers and guns. During the Italian maneuvers he never left the ditches in which he lived. He witnessed a hanging one day and vanished. No one knew what had become of him.

Except for Malic. The peasants told him they had seen Rasko wandering along the roadway, gray as the earth, mumbling. They offered him bread, cheese, and salt. Impenetrable as a rock, he took what they gave him and stubbornly continued on his way. He gnawed the bread and cheese, gazing up at the sun that burned his dusty lashes. He came to a water mill and cooled his battered feet in its stream and watched its wreath of white foam.

Suddenly he spotted a few soldiers. Rasko dashed down the road, his rags and tattered trouser legs flapping behind him, clutching his sack loaded with old shoes and rags. The soldiers ordered him to stop. They would not hurt him. They only wanted to know where they could find some Communists.

He didn't hear them. He hoped to make it to the woods. They began to shoot, over his head, thinking that the whine of the bullets would stop him. They shouted to nearby peasants in the fields to bar his way, to seize him, but they pretended they didn't hear either. Lieutenant Nicola Riva ordered the motorcyclists to catch him.

But Rasko had vanished without trace.

Some students arrived. They told the lieutenant that the man they were looking for was only a bandit, that a Communist would never be as shabby.

"Then he's a priest," said Riva. "Or a mullah . . . he's got a beard."

"But why should a priest run away from us?" asked the sergeant major.

"If he's not a priest he's a beggar," Riva said. "Plenty of them about!"

"True, but no beggar ever ran away from us either," objected the sergeant major. "Why should this one?"

"He is a bandit," Riva concluded, taking a swig from his bottle. "A bandit disguising himself in rags."

"Maybe, Lieutenant," agreed the sergeant major.

"I think so too," whispered a corporal.

"And not just any old Communist."

"You bet," said Riva. "He's the leader we've been after for two years now, the worst of these red devils . . . Vuk Vukovic . . ."

The lieutenant peered at the dark mountains, full of such cold terror.

The crowd watched Riva's soldiers surround the ravines.

"We are going to catch him, if it takes all night," the lieutenant ordered.

They searched for him in the bushes and down by the hedges among the nettles.

"He's lost his sack!" the sergeant major shouted.

"Bravo, Sergeant Major!" Nicola replied. "Well done. See if there are any papers."

"It's full of bread crusts," the sergeant major shouted. "The people are feeding their leader. He's got enough bread to last him five days, and clothes. . . . Good God! Everything is here!"

"He's well camouflaged," the lieutenant said, not daring to stick his head out of the ambush. "But where is he?"

The man was not to be seen anywhere.

Suddenly one of the students spotted Rasko up a dark tree, amid the thick foliage. Every gunbarrel turned up to the tree.

The sergeant major, with a corporal and ten soldiers, surrounded the tree. The lieutenant breathed a sigh of relief and took a gulp from his bottle. The peasants wondered why the troops didn't shoot immediately.

"We want him alive!" cried Lieutenant Riva from the bushes. "Watch what you're doing!"

"He won't come down," said the sergeant major. "We'll have to take him by force."

"Poor Rasko," the peasants said. At first the soldiers pleaded with him: if he betrayed one Communist stronghold he might even be pardoned. Rasko was silent, a large black nest in the crown of the beech tree. For a whole hour they fired over his head. They offered him a lot of money and other good things. "Our poor Rasko," people said.

Finally someone suggested an ax. But the soldiers knew nothing about felling trees, and they asked the peasants to help. While the peasants wielded their axes, the troops surrounded the tree, which began to lean to one side. Holding their bayonets in front of them, and tossing their grenades around like apples, they never once took their eyes off the black, monstrous fruit in human guise.

The beech tree crashed to the ground, and Rasko found himself looking straight into the muzzle of a machine gun. He had no time to raise his hands. They bound him and led him onto the road.

Lieutenant Riva delivered a short speech, full of fear and brandy. They had captured an important Communist commander. Italy and Montenegro should celebrate together, and separately.

The celebrations began with a thunderous volley. Every available weapon was used. Grenades were thrown into the silent stream. The lieutenant was the first to interrogate this great and mysterious Communist. He offered him brandy, clapped him on the back, smiled cunningly.

Rasko trembled.

The lieutenant's words were big. He dropped names that the crowd of students and soldiers had never heard of. He dispatched his fastest motorcyclist to town with orders that he should be met by the band which he had abandoned at the Muslim graveyard when he set out.

The peasants crossed themselves. Riva said again and again: "It's no use calling on God now. You should have taken better care of your leader when you could."

The peasants went on crossing themselves, watching in silence as the drunken, happy soldiers left their village.

Gruban Malic stood by his window. The warm night thickened like clotting blood. The gas lamps had long been turned out. Stars danced over the rooftops. Dogs barked, and in the distance Augusto whispered more of "O *Bolognesina*." A knock at the door broke Malic's reverie. He expected the worst.

Two men entered: one short and fat, the other thin with red hair. They were wrapped in huge capes and wore dark glasses. The fat one went up to the counter and pushed his twin-horned Italian cap back on his head. In a half-whisper he said:

"Comrade Malic, are you sure there are no agents in your saloon? We must not be seen."

"And who are you?"

"We must not be seen," repeated the redhead. "We must be invisible, so to speak. Turn that lamp down a bit, will you?"

Malic did as he was told, and the two men grew still darker. Again he asked:

"Who are you?"

"That's unimportant," said the fat one, pulling his greasy cap down over his ears.

"You'll learn soon enough," added the redheaded man.

"Are you from the movement?"

"You've guessed," said the fat one.

"Why didn't you say so?" Malic grinned, offering them seats. "Where have you been all this time?"

"Fighting," the fat one said, removing his hat and disclosing a sweaty bald patch. "They've doubled the sentries besides."

"They are losing the war," said Malic.

"They're done for," said the redhead. "It's hard to say who's advancing quickest: the English, the Americans, or the Russians. Something to remember Nineteen forty-three by. Turn the lamp down a bit more!"

When Malic had done this, the fat one whispered:

"You were brilliant today. As if you were reading from a book. In the name of the movement, we congratulate you! Listening to you, we realized that you're one of the outstanding Marxists in this country. A real Marxist!"

The blood rushed to Malic's cheeks. He wanted to ask them what a Marxist was. But the word stuck in his throat. "Marxist," he said to himself. "So, I'm that too, am I!"

He grabbed a bottle of brandy. The redhead looked at him reproachfully.

"Thank you, comrade, but revolutionaries don't drink."

"Then what can I give you?" Malic asked uncertainly. "How can I help you?"

"That is why we are here," the redhead said, jamming his glasses more firmly on his nose.

"Make yourselves comfortable, comrades," Malic said. "And take off your sunglasses, if you like."

"There you go again!" the fat one said. "Revolutionaries never take off their dark glasses, and they have no time to be comfortable."

"You surely don't sleep in those glasses!"

"Yes," the redhead said. "That's where we differ from other people. Remember that!"

"I've waited for you for a long time," Malic said. "Months, years you might say."

"As you can see, we came at the right moment."

"Was it you that has been sending me those pamphlets?" Malic asked timidly.

"Maybe," the redhead said nervously, drawing up a broken chair. "We'll talk of 'those goods' some other time, in daylight. But we must get to the point. We really need your help. We haven't got much time. We must be at our headquarters before dawn."

"For the movement I am willing to do the impossible!" Malic said decisively.

"Why not what is possible?" the fat one said. "The movement needs money and you are the only man we can turn to. We'll give you a receipt."

"That would be an insult," Malic's voice trembled.

"What did I tell you, the man is a Marxist!" The redhead turned to the fat one. "True Marxist pride. They don't make them that way any more."

Malic was confused.

"For the movement, I'm prepared to give my life," Malic said.

"The movement needs money. No offense meant, but that's the way things are. Be on your guard and take good care of yourself."

The fat one looked at his watch. Malic pulled a wad of notes from his drawer and put it down on the table.

"Is that enough, comrades?"

The comrades nodded and walked to the door.

"How are things at the front?" Malic whispered.

"Excellent! Nineteen forty-three!"

"So I thought! Give the comrades my regards and say that I'm thinking of them," Malic said. They departed.

"I knew they'd come," Malic thought. "And they did! I'm not alone any more: the Revolution is thinking of me. Captain Brambilla, Major Peduto, the priest, Mustafa Agic, everybody must know it as soon as possible. Let them touch me if they dare! The World Communist Movement is behind me! You are a lucky man, that's all there's to it. You've never been this lucky in your whole life," he repeated, wiping the sweat on his forehead and neck. His hands shook as he went up to the counter. He poured himself a glass of brandy and emptied it. "Have another drink," he told himself, "you've earned it."

Clasping the bottle, he walked over to the armchair. "There, sit down and rest a little. You've been on your feet all day." He took one swig from the bottle and then a second and then a third. His head was beginning to spin. "Have another big one, Comrade Malic," he whispered. "Get drunk like a man, and then off to bed with you."

He drank and listened to Augusto's sobs in the darkness. He

thought of the dumb-struck Rasko. "That's enough, Communist," he told himself sternly. "No more drinking! You are no longer a simple saloonkeeper." He tried to get up and look through the window: "Perhaps they're out there somewhere, in the darkness, the men with the cloaks and dark glasses. It doesn't matter if they are not. They'll be back soon. They can't stay away from me long."

He dropped off to sleep with the bottle in his arms. He dreamed he was in fetters, but it did not stop him from marching. He was followed by Riva's company; bayonets, trumpets and drums, escorting him to the presence of Captain Brambilla, Major Peduto, and Colonel Allegretti. They had him bound but were afraid and dared not come close to him. The bells clanged. The mullah announced the midday hour and the news of his arrest. His arms were bloody from the chains, but he felt no pain. He was so huge that the major, the colonel, the whole lot of them didn't even come up to his shoulder. He marched in front of the troops and whispered: "You can't do a thing to me; I'm not alone any more. I've warned you time and again."

Meanwhile his two mysterious visitors were at the priest's house, playing cards and having a good laugh.

Part Three

CHAPTER 1

"DON'T GO YET," Marika begged. "Please don't."

Weary and hot, Colonel Allegretti crawled out of bed. "You know, they've been waiting for me now for hours."

"Let them wait."

"I told them I'd come at once. They're expecting me."

"Good thing I'm not their commandant," Marika said. "I'd let them stand at attention all night."

"Wouldn't you even have mercy on me?"

"No," the girl replied. "And, anyway, are they more important to you than I am?"

"No, but they've been waiting so long that it's embarrassing," the colonel said, slipping on his trousers and boots. "And for heaven's sake don't shout! We don't want everybody to know you're here."

"What do those idiots want anyway?" Marika said, throwing off the crumpled sheet.

"How should I know?" the colonel asked. "For two days they've been asking for me. They say it's urgent."

"They're lying."

"You never know," the colonel said, surveying himself in the mirror. "We'll see."

"They're lying," Marika said. "They're Montenegrins."

"Some of my people are with them," the colonel objected.

"Then I'm wrong."

"You think Italians don't lie?" the colonel asked, smearing brilliantine on his luxuriant hair.

"They don't lie," said the girl, curling herself on the bed and digging her teeth into her knees. "Particularly if they give their Italian word of honor."

"You might be wrong, you know," the colonel said.

"I'm never wrong," Marika retorted and stretched herself full length on the bed.

With measured strides, the colonel went up to the bed and stood at attention.

"At ease!" the girl commanded.

"Be a good girl and give me my cap."

"Come back soon," the girl said, placing the cap below her navel.

"Give me my cap, my darling, and tell me where you want to be kissed."

"Here," the girl said, pointing to the cap.

The colonel sat down on the edge of the bed and did as she commanded.

"Wait," he protested, "Wait . . . I'm in uniform."

The colonel drew his fingers through her hair, stood up, and walked over to the door. He looked at her, naked and dark-skinned, and felt panicky at the thought that he might never see her again.

His office was at the end of a narrow passage. Mustafa Agic, open-jawed and smiling, was waiting for him. The priest and the mullah were also there, along with a tall, pock-marked old man dressed in ceremonial Montenegrin dress. Agic introduced him as a Montenegrin who loved Italians as dearly as his own people, who respected the Queen as one would one's own mother, a man who marveled at the colonel's military cunning, his power of command and bravery.

The colonel listened carefully to Agic's introduction and urged his guests to sit down.

He passed cigarettes around with an expression of false pleasure and satisfaction, and then sat down among his guests.

"Gentlemen, I request your forgiveness," the colonel began,

"for having kept you waiting. What a life a soldier leads! No fixed hours! We are always at the call of higher interests."

"We understand," Agic volunteered for them all. "We understand completely. Please don't worry, not on that score at any rate."

"So," the colonel said, ignoring Agic. "There you are, inspections, more inspections, talks and consultations, plans and strategy, tactics and the boring daily routine. Believe me, I don't get much sleep. And I'm continually on the line to Rome. But what can I do for you, my dear gentlemen?" the colonel asked. "How are the people?"

That was the only sentence he could say in Serbian.

Beads of sweat broke out on the tall, pock-marked forehead of the old Montenegrin.

"We've never had it better," he stated in Italian.

The colonel looked worried.

"What language is the gentleman speaking?"

"*Signor Montenegrino* answered you in Italian," Mustafa Agic said.

"Many thanks, honored Montenegrin," the colonel replied. "Many thanks for the compliment," and glancing at the priest, he asked: "And you, my dear sir . . . ?"

The priest came alive. Blood rushed into his huge nose and temples. He brought his fist down on the table and roared so violently that the colonel almost jumped up.

"*Dunque*, that snake!"

"What snake?" the colonel asked.

"That snake," the priest screamed, showing his large sparse teeth, "that red, poisonous viper!"

"Which one are you referring to?" the colonel asked. "As you know, one fell into our hands two or three days ago and is now behind bars."

"Malic!" the priest thundered. "That bandit!"

"What's my dear *compagno* Malic been up to this time?" the colonel asked with a smile.

The priest's eyes bulged. "You call him dear and *compagno*! That swine, Colonel, did I hear you right?"

"Yes, he's marvelous," the colonel said enthusiastically. "Marvelous, marvelous!"

"That red devil is the town's problem number one!" the priest said desperately.

"You must remember my dear sir that we no longer have problems."

"*Signor colonnello*," the priest rasped, "I don't believe you."

"Let's be human," the colonel said, stretching his arms, "And not think only of triumphs and victories. Live, and let live, as the saying goes," he stated, passing cigarettes around again.

"But, *signor colonnello*, haven't you heard what the bandit said to me the other day? He said terrible things and everyone laughed at me . . . a man of God! He said things for which he should have been arrested immediately. Signor Agic was there and he must have told you what happened."

"Well, none of us is perfect," the colonel said philosophically. "Perhaps we all deserve to be arrested from time to time. You make a mistake if you think he's the only one . . . yes, someone told me," the colonel paused thoughtfully, "just who it was I can't, for the moment, remember."

"Signorina Marika," Captain Brambilla stated sadly. "Signorina Marika, my fiancée, informed you, didn't she?"

"You're right, Captain," the colonel said with a wave of his hand. "Really, my memory!"

"My fiancée no doubt also told you that Signor Malic has been distributing leaflets. He thrust a few under my nose as well. He claims that he speaks in the name of Free Montenegro and Revolutionary Europe, in the name of the International Communist Movement. He says that behind him stands the entire working class."

"Let him! Everybody's talking and putting on airs, why shouldn't he?"

"He's dangerous!" the mullah said, as if awakening from a

deep sleep. "You must punish him severely, or ban him from town. I'd be ashamed to repeat what he called me. While I was up on the minaret, too, in the presence of the faithful! He said they'd hang me by the tongue. Just think! And I've always been kind to him!"

"But this little Montenegrin also has threatened me with horrible things," the colonel interrupted. "He suggested that I join the Communists, and take along the entire Venezia Division. He threatened to have me castrated in front of the proletariat. I informed him by letter that his offer was unacceptable and that I'd make every effort to hang on to my precious balls for as long as I could."

Peduto's infectious laughter caught on. The colonel doubled up, his face was crumpled, his hands folded across his stomach.

"What can you do with him!" the colonel asked. "You can't even get angry."

"To the gallows with him!" the priest thundered, "I'll hang him myself! I ask you as commander and defender of this town to allow me personally to be his judge. Evil needs nipping in the bud!"

"I think so too," the mullah joined in. "Blasphemy needs severe treatment."

"I don't agree," the colonel said, "I'm not for any such gentle punishment."

They were all silent. The clock on the wall was ticking away.

"I'm for the severest punishment of all," the colonel said quietly.

"The gallows!" cried the priest. "The gallows!"

"No," the colonel said. "We'll punish him by not punishing him."

CHAPTER 2

"YOU MUST be brave, Malic. Clench your fists and look them straight in the eyes. It's high time you told them the truth. Raise your head higher. Let them see they are dealing with a true Montenegrin."

Malic's guests were drinking and singing. Throats swelled, eyes bulged, glasses were smashed.

"One more, *Montenegrino*," Augusto said, turning away from Pietro and the girls.

"Don't give him any more, *compagno* Malic," Barbagallo said. "He's stupid with drink."

Augusto was silent.

"Thieves!" Barbagallo said. "Thieves!"

Augusto's head turned toward the proprietor like a black sunflower. He gazed at the mass of bottles on the shelf and the obscene photographs on the wall. His face was prematurely wrinkled, tired and covered with bruises. He reached for a brandy bottle.

"Do you want me to beat you up again?" Barbagallo asked.

"Yes," Augusto said. "But I'll kill you afterwards!"

"Tell them you hate them," Malic mused. "Tell them to get out of your sight." Remind them of all the filth they've brought to this poor little town, and tell them to get the hell out. Begin with this and then your tongue will unleash. Don't be afraid. They can't do a thing to you. You're not alone any more and they know it."

"Pietro," Dana said. "You're a good boy. Come with me."

"No," Pietro said thickly, "you're no good."

"Pietro," the girl said. "Don't be silly. Your girl is a bigger whore than I am!"

"Leave me alone. Leave me alone!"

"And she has every infection under the sun," Dana said, stroking his chest. "I was examined yesterday and they gave me a clean bill of health. Pure as an angel. What's the matter? Let me give you a little kiss."

"Leave me alone!"

"I'll make you happy, Corporal," the girl said softly. "I'll never leave you. I won't deceive you. That awful Brambilla is her fiancé, don't forget. You come with me."

"Shut up. You've no right to mention her. Go away! Don't touch me!"

"You're mad and stupid, Corporal dear," the girl said tenderly. "But I'll wait for you; you'll get over it. *Compagno* Malic, a brandy! No, two. One for Barbagallo, my old love! Long live Barbagallo, long live all thieves and bastards!"

"Your turn," Malic decided. "Just wait till the crowd gets bigger and then let them have it! If they attack you, draw your revolver, take up a position near a corner. The time is ripe for open conflict. If they try to bind you or inflict any other form of indignity on you, pick up the grenade you've hidden among the bottles and hurl it. You mustn't surrender, not under any circumstances. What would the comrades from the movement say? Think of the words from the leaflets, and wait."

Augusto was singing.

"Soldiers!" Malic cried ceremoniously, seizing the edge of the counter. "Soldiers!"

Never had so many soldiers' and whores' eyes been fixed on him. The quarreling and singing ceased abruptly.

"Soldiers!" Malic repeated. "I've long been meaning to tell you that it's high time you returned to your homes! Your wives and children are waiting for you with tears in their eyes, your mothers and sisters wait while you, innocent but deceived, leave your bones in a foreign land!"

"Hear, hear!" cried someone from the crowd.

"They have convinced you that you brought us freedom. A hateful Fascist lie! They have brought a shameful slavery to a country which has never in its glorious history tolerated a foreign yoke! I assure you that Montenegro will never allow itself to be conquered!"

"Hear, hear!" several soldiers cried in unison.

"Poor Montenegro," Augusto Napolitano whispered, striking his guitar. "*Povero Montenegro* . . ."

"Not true!" one of the girls cried.

Malic stuck out his meager chest and flung back his head. He tried to recall the phrases he had spent days memorizing: their weight was frightening. Blood rushed to his temples, a strange blindness cast a net over his eyes. He heard the bustle around him, shouts, people pinching the whores who were opposing the idea that the soldiers should go home. Unaware that he was imitating that most eloquent of local speakers, Major Peduto, he went on:

"Therefore, in the name of this long-suffering land, in the name of the world proletariat and communism, I call on you to rise against your officers! Kill them, strangle them, and join us, so that together we may deal the final blow to the Fascist monster!"

"Christ, where did he get all those words from!"

"He's a Montenegrin. They begin making speeches the day they are born!"

Malic's head was buzzing. He no longer saw the soldiers cheering each other, glasses in hand; he no longer heard Augusto singing as loudly as his voice would carry him. Nor did he notice the prostitutes, gathered in a bunch, making signs to him to stop talking since he had already said enough to get himself hanged three times over. Nor did he notice the townspeople waving their arms and begging him to say no more because he would bring evil upon their heads.

He kept beating his sickly chest. He could no longer remember the booklet with the red star on its cover, nor its urgent summonses and threats of propaganda. He spoke of anything and everything, but especially of the need to liquidate the High Command and all its officers, to burn down the barracks, smash stores and give their stock to the hungry Montenegrin people, and march into a new and happier life, with a song on their lips and slogans in their heads.

Finally, he swung his right arm. The photographs of the royal family and of the army commander toppled down from the shelf, together with those of the women with legs spread wide open and naked bosoms. He picked them up, spat on them, tore them into shreds, crushed the newspaper clippings with their morale-building headlines. The level of noise made it impossible to hear what he was saying as he bounced up and down like a rubber ball. "Fascism," "death," "final victory," "blood," "happier future."

"*Bravo!*"

"*Bravo,* indeed!"

"*Cento volte . . .*"

"Hear, hear!"

"*Bravo, Montenegrino!*"

The soldiers rose to their feet and fell back again. They applauded and yelled and banged their glasses. The civilians stared into the tobacco smoke, the uproar, and the din. The whores were startled. They nudged one another apprehensively and talked of castration, ball-twisting, and various other forms of torture poor Malic might bring upon himself as a result of this outburst. One was moved to tears by his wonderful, majestic words, although she understood nothing.

"No response," Malic thought bitterly. "They have ignored your challenge altogether. Nothing can move this mob. You won't have to pull the revolver from under the counter. Nor the grenade. They've made a silly fool of you. Look at them! Shameless, that's what they are! They never even gave you a chance to finish your speech, and here they are grinning and yelping and barking. Calm down and think of other means of shocking them."

His chin shook and tears welled into his eyes. He held on firmly to the edge of the counter. Headquarters felt so small and insignificant, so weak and pathetic. He recalled the comrades in black capes and was overwhelmed with shame. He wanted to die: the only way to forget his disgrace.

"Come, Pietro, my love," Dana said as she drained her fifth glass of brandy.

Pietro shook his head. He looked at her, but didn't see her.

"Come, love," the girl said, sitting down in the armchair. "I've lots of lovely things to tell you."

Pietro's eyes were full of a strange, soft radiance.

"I'm good," she whispered parting her small, rounded knees, "and you're good. And your Marika's good. What I said about her before isn't true. Please, *Sardo*, forgive me! We're all good. Just unhappy! That's all. Come with me, *Sardo!*"

They brought her a sixth brandy.

"I'm not ugly, Pietro," the girl pleaded as she gulped down her brandy. "Look!" She lifted her skirt higher. She whispered something unintelligible in a thick warm voice and continued to lift her skirt. She had stopped whispering and was looking at Pietro. Her skirt went higher still, exposing her shapely white thighs. The skirt continued to rise. Men held their breath.

Malic stood at the same spot from which he had delivered his glorious speech.

"You're displaying yourself again, you bitch," he whispered to himself. His guests wanted to be served, but he had made up his mind that he wouldn't serve anyone that day. The soldiers helped themselves, flinging their money down on the counter. Malic gazed down at the floor. "Take it all, I don't care," he mused as he stood there anonymous in the crowd.

"I'm your own good girl, Pietro!"

Her skirt kept going up steadily, but more slowly. Everyone was watching her. Augusto's guitar sounded its highest-pitched and saddest strings.

"Se te la rompo, non te la pago . . ."[1]

All eyes were on Pietro, too, full of hatred and reproach. He acted as if he didn't see her. Still more slowly she raised her skirt.

"Don't you want me even now, my *Sardo*?"

Her long, gentle fingers raised the skirt above her navel. A few men fell on their knees to get a better view. They knelt there, not believing what they saw.

She lifted her small breasts, and looked through her lashes at the absent, preoccupied Pietro. Her eyes filled with tears, but her gentle well-shaped lips looked as if they were about to break into a pleasant smile or into quiet sobs.

A few people crossed themselves.

"In the name of God, let me out of here! Enough is enough," someone yelled. "By the holy Virgin, this girl is my own little sister, my poor, lost sister Ines!"

The silence grew more icy. The naked girl squeezed her breasts, proffering them, and threw her head back to hide her tears.

The lusty, terror-filled silence was broken by Augusto: he stepped out of the crowd and leaned over the girl and her dazzling black star and, obviously inspired, passed his fingers over all the strings at once:

"O povero, o povero . . ."

His voice was broken, but warm. He drew in his neck and thrust back his head. His large, inflamed eyes were still the eyes of a man seeking in the dense tobacco smoke on the low, filthy ceiling yet another star. His fingers caressed the guitar strings:

[1] If I break it for you, I shan't pay . . .

"O povero, O povero.
O povero Montenegro-o-o-o . . ."

The crowd joined in. Except for Gruban Malic, who stood alone, smaller and more insignificant than ever.

CHAPTER 3

THERE WAS A SILENCE AGAIN. The colonel tried to cheer up his guests by offering them cigarettes and saying nice things to each in turn. But the men looked at the floor. He began to speak Serbian, a long list of gruesome swearwords, in the hope of humoring the priest. This resulted in more nervous coughing. Then he gave up.

He sat down and grew silent. "I wonder who'll be the first to break this stupid silence?" The priest and the mullah began to talk. Mustafa Agic was restless. He turned to the colonel and whispered: "They're talking about Malic's speech."

"He is always making speeches. What's this one about?" the colonel asked.

"Punitive expeditions, *signor colonnello.*"

"Is that all?" the colonel exclaimed. "They have no sense of humor, do they?"

Colonel Allegretti recalled that Agic had at one time decried this "crazy red monster who is about to turn the world upside down," and recommended castration, tearing out the nails on his fingers and toes, or exile to Albania for life.

"I admit I myself am afraid of his threats, *signor colonnello,* especially the punitive expeditions that are so lacking in humor."

"In other words, you've no faith in me?" the colonel asked.

"We have unlimited faith in you," Mustafa Agic again showed his decayed teeth. "But who knows how long you'll be staying here. We live on your good will and your amazing good nature."

The priest boldly interrupted: the question was exile, castration, or Albania. He thumped the small table with his fist, his eyes bloody with anger.

"Gentlemen," the colonel began wearily, "considering that we have not come here as invaders, but as liberators, we dare not punish such barbarism with such rigor. This business with the balls, I maintain, is too much! We would not be worthy of our reputation as Italians if we were to deprive a man of something so essential. Exile to gloomy Albania is too much for him. Only the most hardened criminals are shipped there. Why not try reforming him instead? Her Majesty, our gracious Queen, is packing her bags to come and visit her native land. Her triumphant arrival will be the crowning glory of our harmony and our brotherhood.

"Other important persons from Rome will accompany her on this historic journey. His Majesty, King Emmanuelo II, may soon be paying us a visit. Someone, I forget just who, has already announced the exact day they will set foot on the soil of great and heroic Montenegro. . . ."

The guests remained impassive. He had no idea how he ever got involved with history, but he overheard himself listing important dates and turning points, stressing Italian and Montenegrin heroism through the centuries, linking all this with the priest and the mullah, with Malic and his threatened genitals. He was hopeful that the unforeseen interview was coming to an end. But the priest suddenly jumped up and thundered: "Just a minute! We aren't through yet. I want to settle a few more things."

The colonel was startled. He took a step back, and his hand automatically fell to his revolver holster.

"If you will neither hang him nor exile him, you must order him to go on selling . . . what he's always sold."

"To whom are you referring, *gentile* signor priest?"

"To that red viper, *signor colonnello*," said the mullah. "Think a little of us, dear commandant, and order him . . ."

"*Egregio signor muezzino*, in this very office, you personally protested against his trade. You and the signor priest. And now you demand that he be ordered to resume."

"Times are different, *signor colonnello*," the old man was embarrassed, "and we've learned a lot of sensible things from you."

"What is it you want him to go on selling," the colonel asked, "which of his wondrous specialties?"

"Those accursed rubbers," the mullah whispered, and blushed up to his ears like a small boy, "those French letters. More than half of my poor people are infected. If he doesn't make them available soon, my people are finished, *signor colonnello*. Who will then march shoulder to shoulder with Italians into a brighter future? And the priest can support what I say. People complain to him too, perhaps more than they do to me. There he is, let him say whether I'm lying or whether I'm telling the simple truth . . ."

The priest was shaking all over. "It's imperative this devil be ordered, in writing and with all the seals and signatures, to sell not only the condoms, but also the remedy all the women complain about, but which is nonetheless a good thing, because at the moment there's nothing else. His photographs are not essential, but if he has them, let people have them. I myself have a complete set of pictures and literature. . . ."

"You mean the pictures and magazines from Paris?" the colonel interrupted him.

"I don't know where they come from," the priest roared, "but they're good. When a man's lying down after lunch and studies such wonders, he feels . . . well . . ."

"He feels in the mood," whispered the mullah with a blush.

"That's it: he feels in the mood! At times such as these a good and happy disposition is of extreme importance. Not to let one's spirits flag, nor anything else, for that matter! Right, Mullah?"

The mullah folded his arms on his worn silk cummerbund and nodded like a boy.

"My dear sirs," the colonel cried, "I am delighted to be

able to state that we are now on the way to complete understanding and proximity of views. I must say that I am touched by your sincerity. I promise you, my dear friends, that in contrast to your first request, I shall, in all probability, be able to solve this one to your satisfaction."

"Long live our brave and excellent colonel!"

"May he live to the benefit of our long-suffering people!"

The colonel stood on the threshold of his office, watching them retreating backwards and still applauding.

"Yes, I will do all I can. But I must warn you that I cannot give him orders. Italy respects the freedom of individuals and forbids orders, especially if they are of a delicate and severe nature. I can negotiate with him, on the highest levels if necessary. I can ask him kindly. But my friends, you will remember that in the course of our conversation today I emphasized persuasion, enlightment, reeducation."

CHAPTER 4

"YOU MUSTN'T GIVE them time to breathe," Malic thought, as he ejected the crowd from his establishment. "Or to forget what you told them today. You must prove to them you're not afraid, that you're determined to go all the way. So, get going!"

Outside the troops were drawn up. Drunken officers uttered commands and obscenities. The soldiers were singing "*Vincere*."[1] Trumpets and drums blasted. Some of the units were moving out of town, leaving a cloud of dust in their wake. Malic was desolate. He stood in the middle of the street, alone, not knowing what to do. The sun grew stronger.

"They didn't dare come to grips with you," Malic thought, "they know who is behind you. They know you've been giving money to the movement."

[1] An Italian Fascist song: "To Conquer."

His finger was on the trigger of his revolver, but there was no one at whom he could aim. He stood there in the sun, listening to the commands, the swearing, and the songs fading into the distance.

He crossed the square, which he hated because of all the loudspeakers that bleated forth day and night. He loathed the dusty tank which was set in motion from time to time to intimidate the town and drown out the church bell. He passed the flagpole, whose banners hung limply in the heat, paused in front of the headquarters, and reached the tank. Blinking nervously, Salvatore Paolone was gently reprimanding a few young boys.

"*Ma perche?*" one of them said. "Why, *signor soldato?*"

"Because!" Salvatore was excited. "Because it's no good. Every day you piss on my tank."

"*Ma perche no, Signor Taliano?*" a scrawny little boy protested, pissing on the tank tracks on the other side. "Why not?"

"My boy," the soldier blushed, "it's no good. Go quick! Go piss on your own house!"

"I have no house," the boy said plaintively, watering the other side of the tank.

"I will talk with your father." Paolone was upset now. "We have another tank, so why piss on mine?"

"*I soldati* kill my father," the boy said. "A bomb went off and no *papà* or *mamma.*"

"Ah, my poor boy."

"I'm not poor."

"Come to me!"

The boy buttoned up his pants and went up to him.

"My poor child . . . *mio triste* . . . you come to me. . . . There, there. . . . I *tuo amico,* good boy, but don't piss on my tank."

"Why are you crying, *signor soldato?*" the boy asked, and moved away from him. "That's no good, *Taliano.*"

"You have no *papà,* no *mamma,*" the soldier sniveled, and handed the child some coins. "I killed your *mamma* and *papà.*"

"*Non è vero, Taliano,*" the boy objected. "Not true. *Altri soldati* dropped the bomb. I saw them. Two years ago."

"The same thing," Paolone said, and pulled more coins from his pocket.

"I don't like it when you cry, Salvatore," and he threw the coins into the dust and took off. He ran as fast as his rickety legs would carry him, his rags fluttering. An ugly little raven.

Paolone caught sight of Malic, raised his rifle, and coughed nervously. The thin face under the helmet expressed fear.

Gruban Malic drew his revolver.

Paolone bit his lips and stared.

"*Soldato,*" Malic said, "Soldier!"

Holding the revolver, he approached the tank, determined to pick a quarrel. But his voice lacked conviction. His chin trembled and his eyes were full of bitterness.

Paolone took one look at his melancholy visitor and wanted to say something warm and consoling to him, that the day was hot and that he would like to toss away his rifle and run off to the river. Instead, he just stood there gaping, in a state of mild anxiety.

"*Taliano,*" Malic said, and waved his revolver.

Paolone wrinkled his brows and pursed his lips: the face of a hurt, startled child. He understood that Malic hadn't come to fool with him, and he glanced around. The square was empty, the shutters on the colonel's office were closed. He couldn't call anyone and he was too bashful to fire his rifle. He began to tremble.

Malic looked in mournful horror as Paolone took cover behind the tank. Only his bayonet was visible.

"I won't harm you, *soldato,*" Malic said simply.

"I don't believe you."

"Don't hide, Amintore, I really won't hurt you."

"I'm not Amintore, I'm Salvatore. Salvatore Paolone."

"OK, Paolone," Malic said hoarsely, seeing the bayonet waver.

"I told you I wouldn't hurt you. My quarrel is with your superiors."

"Why bother me then? I'm on guard."

"Are your bosses at headquarters, Salvatore?"

"I am on guard and give no information. They are upstairs."

"Did you know, Salvatore, that I'm going to kill them all?" Malic was encouraged by his own question. "Every single one of them. Don't worry, I won't do you any harm. I'll help you join the movement."

"I don't want to join any movement."

"What do you want?"

"I want to go home."

"You'll be a witness to a great calamity, Salvatore! Come out!"

"That's your problem. I don't want to get mixed up with you, *Montenegrino*. Do what you want, but leave me alone."

"But, Salvatore," said Malic, going round the tank, "you must go and tell them. Prepare them. Understand?"

"I understand you, but you don't understand me," the soldier said in terror. "Do what you want, but keep away from me. Go, *Montenegrino*, go away from me and my tank! Someone might see us. Because, I tell you. . . . "

"Paolone!" Malic said, gripping his revolver firmly, "*Taliano!*" he added, moving toward the bayonet. "Have they ordered you to avoid coming to blows with me, have they?"

In the distance he saw a crowd of people approaching.

The priest was advancing in long clumsy strides and Mustafa Agic had to run to keep up with him and calm him down. The priest seized the white-haired mullah with his massive hands.

"A rotten commandant!" he shouted. "Weak. He refused to get that red devil! I tell him how the bastard threatens us and he raises his eyebrows and smiles like a whore!"

"Calm down, priest!" the mullah whispered, "or someone

may hear you and we'll have more trouble. In the name of God . . ."

"A rotten commandant!" the priest thundered, opening his large, bloodshot eyes. "What a commandant!" he added, striking Agic with all his might on the shoulder. "A Communist!"

"Priest!" the mullah wailed, "My poor, dear priest! O good people, stop him . . . hold him! Priest, my dear friend . . . if you go on like this . . ."

The priest pushed them both away and clenched his fists.

"The commandant is a Communist! Spit in my beard, if he isn't! I can sniff them out anywhere. . . . They're all alike! The Latin, the sly Latin, and a Communist and a whoremonger too! The worst kind! By God, a Communist defending his Montenegrin comrade! I tell you, tight as a pig's guts, working together!"

The priest was deaf to all reason. He ground his remaining teeth, tore at his crimson face, and raised both arms menacingly.

"But we'll see! I'll not let evil . . . I swore before God that I'd chastise unbelievers and sinners. Nor will I stop there. I'll go to the general, to the Queen!"

At that point, the mullah flung himself on his knees and, with hands clasped, cried in a pious and tremulous voice: "Priest, in the name of our mutual God, in the name of my faith and yours, I beg you to stop. We'll all end on the gallows, or in Albania! Our people will be left to corruption and disaster. Priest, my friend in misfortune and brother in adversity, I beg you once more . . ."

The priest's eyes turned glassy. He stopped and gazed like a madman over the mullah's turban.

The priest raised his arm and pointed through the heat, following the direction of his forefinger with a fanatic gaze. The mullah offered a prayer.

The priest's huge, staggering body shook. His eyes were filled with blood and darkness. In a voice rarely heard by human ears, he roared: "There he is!"

Everyone now looked in the direction of the priest's trembling arm. They saw the sky, the dust, the flag, the tank, and Gruban Malic. "Seize him!" the priest shouted, "Seize him at once! I'm going to castrate him here and now before everyone. That swine, that red blasphemer! Seize him!"

"I am not that easy to catch!" Malic said, standing between the soldier and the tank and twisting his revolver. "Just let anyone come near me! I'll blow him to smithereens!"

"I'll eat you, Communist!" the priest roared, towering like a mountain, "I'll eat you and your shitting revolver! Men, let me get at him! Brothers, let me trample him down! Let me. . . . "

No one held the priest back. "*Soldato!*" the priest yelled desperately, "Giuseppe, shoot! What are you waiting for? What are you gaping at, for God's sake! Kill him, shoot the Communist scoundrel! *Ammazzalo, ammazzalo, soldato!* Why are you standing still, Mario! Oh God . . . "

"*Signori* . . . you mustn't shoot . . . *signori cari,* you've no permission . . . "

"Then hold him!" roared the priest, "get him by the neck!"

The soldier blinked.

"Get going, Paolone!" Mustafa Agic ordered. "He's the enemy, Salvatore, our mutual enemy, Paolone! A Communist!"

"Call for someone else," Salvatore said.

"Get him now!" Mustafa Agic stormed, taking refuge behind the mullah, "*Adesso,* Salvatore! Get him from behind! And we'll get at him from the side!"

"I will, but first take his revolver away!"

The priest gave a yell and spread his arms in a gesture of helplessness. His companions caught him as he dropped to the cobbles. His mouth kept opening and closing, he was gasping for breath like some fantastic fish. As if wishing to abandon his awkward body, his hands dangling, his fingers touching the ground.

"That's right, die!" Malic snarled, "Die, you Fascist animal! If you don't die I'll tear your heart out with my own hands!"

They were now busy rubbing the half-dead priest on the

chest and behind the ears. The mullah prayed, alternately looking up at the dusty sky and touching the earth with his aged forehead. But the Almighty showed no desire to help the priest, who was bathed in the sweat of death and whose breathing grew more and more labored.

Salvatore ran over to the tank, crouched down, and took out a brandy bottle. On the way back he took a swig and handed the rest to Agic.

A woman walked up to Paolone and asked breathlessly, "Paolone, have you seen Pietro?" It was Dana.

"What Pietro, Signorina?" the soldier asked, absorbed in her heaving bosom, "I know a hundred by that name."

"Your friend, Salvatore, *Sardo*."

"I'm Pietro too."

"But you're not Pietro," the girl said in despair.

"Understand, Signorina, I can be Pietro, I have a guitar, too."

"A guitar's not everything, *Taliano*."

"All right, Signorina, I have other things too."

"The other thing isn't what's most important either," the girl said.

"I'll find the rest, *amore mio*," Salvatore said, measuring her figure. "I'll borrow if I have to."

"Oh you, Paolone, you Calabresian devil!"

"Perhaps you prefer goods? Shoes, blouses, coats? Anything you want."

She was no longer listening. She was after Pietro and Pietro wasn't there.

Once again the priest was miraculously revived with brandy. Mustafa Agic tilted the bottle and cleaned up the priest's matted beard, removed his shoes, and scratched his feet. The half-naked, airy, unwashed body soaked in the brandy like a sponge and began to show renewed signs of life. The mullah continued his prayer nevertheless.

"Those who refuse to join us in our honorable, superhuman struggle," Malic declared, glancing over the entire gathering, "will be considered enemies of the working people!"

No one was listening.

Soldiers came running across the square. They pushed their way through the crowd and placed the priest on a bloodstained stretcher. Six of them grunted under the weight of the priest's black mountain of a body. His head hanging backwards, his arms dangling, the priest caught sight of the large crowd, the flagpole, and the dome of his church against the sky. The cross on the Orthodox church looked more lopsided than ever. He wanted to be taken to that beloved and abused cross, to the peaceful old church whose fence the faithful were forever breaking down. His lips moved, seeking another drop or two of the sweet plum brandy.

The heavy, hot sky and the sad cross vanished from his view. The front of the stretcher was raised higher than the rear, and his head was propped up. He could now see the decaying roofs, the dirty walls, and the square-shaped heads of strange people. The stretcher was too narrow and his body overflowed its metal frame and his bony legs and long arms once more trailed in the dust.

Rolling himself off Marika, Colonel Allegretti rose to his feet and went to the window. Naked and happy, he opened the curtain and saw the two tricolored flags, the Italian and the Montenegrin, flapping in the wind, and the neighboring hills with their concrete fortifications and towers.

Stroking his hair-covered chest, the colonel caught sight of Dana below. She looked more shapely and provoking than ever. He knew her soft body, her flowing hair, and those frightened eyes. He even knew the tight dress of red silk that was almost pierced by the points of her breasts. What appealed to him now was her obvious distress. He pictured her beneath him, again obedient and unhappy, and began to feel excited. She was now talking to an officer who, in an attempt to grab her breast, broke her necklace. The string of false pearls scattered in the dust. Having earned a crisp epithet in place of a smack, the officer vanished in the crowd.

She turned around and bent down to gather up the pearls, making movements with her luscious, oval bottom. The colonel was by now panting. The girl groped in the dust, sobbing quietly.

Without altering her position, she looked around. In order to keep her balance she was forced to spread her knees. The colonel squinted, thought he had spotted something, but didn't trust his eyes. He grabbed a pair of binoculars: she looked soft, tear-stained, and exposed. She shook the beads from her bosom and counted them. The colonel stared between her legs and saw what he could never have enough of. Preoccupied with the sight that made him throb with excitement, he failed to notice Marika crawling on all fours to the window. Slowly she rose to her knees, put her arms around him, pressed her forehead to his side, and lowered her thirsting swollen lips to his organ.

He caressed her head with one hand and held the binoculars with the other. The girl suddenly spread her knees still wider, leaving the colonel overwhelmed with passion.

Having reassembled the necklace, Dana looked toward headquarters. She was pleased to see this hairy, broad, smiling man: he flung the binoculars on the bed and waved to her.

Gruban Malic stood next to the tank, snarling, holding the revolver which no longer frightened anyone. He trembled and wished the ground would swallow him up.

The priest was being hoisted onto the stretcher with difficulty. The six men swayed under the weight. Malic screamed more loudly than he believed possible: "Elephant! Montenegrin elephant!"

But no one took any notice of him. A woman burst out laughing and disappeared.

"Animals!" Malic shrieked. "Evil, wild animals!"

This brought no response either. They were all looking up at the window of headquarters, where the colonel stood, naked to the navel.

"My dear Mullah!" Mustafa Agic almost wept. "Look! Our colonel! Our glorious *colonnello*! Happy! Blowing us kisses!"

"Yes, happy . . . good . . . but why the kisses?"

"Out of affection, obviously, can't you see!"

"A strange affection," the mullah said softly. "I hope it isn't a bad omen."

"So long as he doesn't start shooting," the Montenegrin said.

"But why is he naked, my dear Agic?" the mullah inquired.

Startled, Dana fastened the necklace around her neck. "Priest!" Mustafa Agic called, and gently shook the bony shoulder on the stretcher. "Look at him! Isn't the colonel wonderful! He's forgiven you, he's forgiven us! Aren't we lucky!"

The priest frowned. He saw the colonel's torso framed in the window and was overwhelmed with contempt.

"A miserable commandant! And a Communist to boot."

Mustafa Agic and the mullah grinned broadly, and baring their rotten teeth, started blowing kisses too. Their faces were bright with joy, their eyes filled with tears. Others followed suit and before long the crowd was cheering the colonel loudly, waving handkershiefs, hats, caps, whatever they could get hold of.

The colonel saw nothing but the dark patch between Dana's legs. He was so excited that he kissed the glass and the curtain, the air, the sky, the sun. He almost fell out of the window.

"You're on your own again," Malic thought after they had all gone. "You failed to provoke them. Of course, they were afraid of the consequences: if they had touched you it would have meant trouble. It wasn't so bad after all. You showed them your revolver and you nearly killed that bastard."

He held the revolver awkwardly and wondered where to go now.

He walked over to the flagpole. His tired eyes rested on the tank and its sentry. Swarms of flies revolved around his green helmet and bayonet. A young boy was pissing on one side of the tank, the sentry joined him on the other. They looked at one another across the tank, two people with important things to say to each other.

"Why don't you say something, you devils, can't you see I'm alone," Malic cried.

CHAPTER 5

MALIC WALKED ACROSS the square. "First they insult me and then they all go away. A broken man! And it's hot! I should jump off the bridge and let the current take me to the very bottom."

Dana came running across the square and grabbed him by the sleeve. Her face was swollen with tears.

"Malic, *amico*, have you seen him?"

"No."

"*Amico*, where can he be? I've been looking for him for hours."

"Have you tried the front?"

"Oh, no, what am I going to do?"

"Go away, I've enough trouble of my own."

"But I love him."

"I can't do anything about it."

"You can," the girl said, wiping her tears. "Tell him."

"And what if he says nothing?"

"Then I have to work miracles."

"That's all right, but are you up to it?"

"What can I do, I love him," the girl wept.

"Try Salvatore!" Malic said. "He's wanted to marry you for two weeks now."

"He is common," the girl said, waving her hand in disgust.

But Malic didn't wait for her to finish. He went down a narrow side street that led to the river. He thought of people with red stars in their caps and felt better. "You go on fighting, comrades . . . I want to help you in your struggle. Today they humiliated me, but my finger's still on the trigger. They know we're in touch. They're afraid of us, that's why they've rejected my challenge."

He looked at the burning sky and at the smoke that circled around the distant stone peaks. The villages on the yellow slopes were on fire. The mountains were blue, with patches of last year's snow in their shaded gulleys. An eagle circled over the roofs, its beak full of dust, heat, and mournful cries.

He thought of Dana and her miracles. He hated these lusting women and their melodramatic love affairs. "A true Communist has no right to waste time with whores. A freedom fighter must keep his thoughts on the Revolution. Malic, my boy, watch out. We'll ignore what you did before. You were a poor unconscious animal. But now you must set an example."

He felt important. From time to time he pulled the grenade and the revolver from his pockets.

He ran into Pietro. "Put that damn thing away," Pietro said. "I've got something important to tell you."

Malic did not listen.

"Hide the revolver," Pietro said. "Someone may see you."

"Let them," Malic said resolutely.

"I wouldn't want them to kill you."

"Just let them try. I'll fill them full of holes! You're drunk again," Malic said, returning the revolver to his pocket with a practiced movement.

"True."

"If Marika . . . "

"Where is she? I've been looking for her everywhere. Tell me where she is: I'll go on my knees! I'll pray to her as if she were the Madonna."

"What are we going to do about Dana?" asked Malic.

"I hate those damned *puttane*. I loathe them! Where is Marika?"

"With the colonel, very likely."

"If I could only see her once more!"

"It's useless, *Sardo*."

"I'll kill her. And anyone who touches her!"

People stared at him. Women crossed themselves.

"We soldiers aren't like our leaders. We don't give in easily. We love! we love! Our word is our word. I told her I loved her. We Sardinians aren't like those swine from the north."

"I can't help you, Pietro."

"Ask her to have a picture taken with me," Pietro concluded abjectly.

"I have already. She says no."

"Do you have a picture of her? I promised my parents I'd send them one. They'll have it enlarged and keep it under the holy candles."

"I don't have her picture, but it's not hard to get."

"Then help me."

"Look, Pietro, it isn't hard to get her, let alone obscene photographs of her."

"I don't want obscene photographs, I want one with a wistful smile, with her skirt over her knees, and buttoned up to her neck. My parents and sisters don't like women who expose themselves. Especially my mother. She's says that the woman who marries me must be as pure as our Sardinian sun."

"Don't be a fool. Listen to me for once."

"Her picture, that's all I want. I don't want to listen. She is as pure as an angel! As honest as my mother. No one in this whole world is as gentle and understanding."

"Listen to me this once."

"I won't hear anything bad about her."

"Oh, *Sardo*!"

"They slander her because she won't sleep with them. She's saving herself for me! She wiggles her hips and shakes her breasts just for me. She's shy, my angel. I'm ready to die for her!"

"Don't, Pietro," said Malic. "We need people like you."

"Who does?"

"The common cause."

"What's that?"

"Communism."

"But our people say ours is the cause of justice."

"That's propaganda," Malic said sharply. "Fascist lies. We're fighting for equality, brotherhood, the universal love of mankind."

"Look, if I go over to your people, will Marika take me? Not to sleep with me. I'm from an honest Sardinian family. But her promise, that's all."

Pietro slumped against a nearby wall. The haughty Montenegrin departed, trampling and jostling everyone in his path. The sun burned Pietro's weary eyes. He gradually slid down the wall into the dust and into forgetfulness.

CHAPTER 6

MALIC ENTERED a narrow street with nice houses on both sides. Captain Brambilla and Fioravanti lived in one of them, in adjoining rooms. They were now engaged in an unusually lively conversation. Fioravanti always searched for his words and pronounced them hesitantly in a voice that rarely changed its timbre. Brambilla's voice was sharp, almost quarrelsome. Fioravanti was unshaven, in his shirt sleeves, lying with his dirty boots on the bed, whereas Brambilla was perfumed, dressed for parade. From time to time he would nervously stick the nail of his forefinger into his front teeth.

"That madman won't eat," Brambilla said.

"You mean the man the colonel thinks is Vuk Vukovic?"

"Yes, but Major Peduto and I have succeeded in disillusioning the colonel."

"He's quite a man, our commandant," said Fioravanti.

"Do you want me to tell him you said that?"

"Yes, but try not to embellish it too much."

Malic put his ear to the wall. He could hear the ticking of the clock and his own heart.

"Today's the fourth day he has refused food."

"That's his business," Fioravanti was adamant.

"And ours," Vittorio returned quickly. "What are we going to do with him?"

"Whatever you like."

"Hang him?"

"He's not guilty of anything."

"Then what?" Brambilla snapped.

"I'd let him go."

"I wouldn't!"

"Then ask the commandant."

"He has already forgotten the whole affair," Brambilla said. "I asked him the other day and he said I should deal with the matter as I saw fit. He was busy."

"He's got a new whore."

"If we send him to the gallows he'll struggle and refuse to put his head in the noose, kicking his legs and arms. Then a shudder and his tongue is out."

"We can't do that."

"We can watch him hanging half-dead, enjoying the last moments of his life! They say a man on the gallows has an orgasm!"

"I'd like to watch you hanging," Fioravanti said.

"Just think! He twists around and his expression changes. A hanged man changes his expression quickly! His head grows tiny and blue like a head of a cabbage; his eyes either bulge or retreat into his skull. But it's the tongue that really makes you sick. Sometimes it protrudes between the lips, ever so little, as if to lick something!"

"But he's innocent," Fioravanti said.

"Who cares?" said Vittorio.

"I do, you swine!"

Captain Brambilla was insulted.

"And the young men you allowed to run away into the woods, were they guilty?"

"They were guilty," Fioravanti admitted.

"Why did you let them go?"

"Should I tell the commandant about it?"

"If you wish. He's busy though and may not hear you."

"If he doesn't eat today, he'll die!" Brambilla said.

"He may not. He's amazingly strong."

"How much longer can he go without food?"

"Come on, let's have a bet," Captain Brambilla said. "I bet you he'll be dead by morning. I bet my watch. Or a bottle of brandy. That you can afford. How about it, Fioravanti?"

"I'll also refuse food if they arrest me," Malic thought as he went on his way. "I'll be brave like Rasko. Like all patriots and Communists. When they bring me food I'll shout: Death to fascism! Freedom to the People!"

He passed by the prison. A strong smell of mold and the sound of strangled groans reached him. Malic wondered where Rasko was kept. For three days a story had been circulating that under the blows Rasko had actually begun to speak. His first words were: "I refuse your Fascist food!" Then, louder than any normal human, he had broken into a titter. That morning he had again refused bread and soup and had told Major Peduto: "I am a Communist and will go on refusing food until you leave our tortured country!" Whereupon the major saluted him, sat down, and ate his portion.

"Well done, Comrade Rasko. We revolutionaries need people like you. Don't eat a mouthful. We'll soon liberate this town."

On the other side of the wire fence soldiers were making a lot of noise, shouting, beating on drums and on their aluminum mess tins. Malic walked up to the fence. On one side stood a bunch of children. With hollow cheeks, open jaws, and large eyes, they held out their bowls and stared motionless at the soldiers round the cauldron.

One of the soldiers rushed toward the children and

sprinkled them with brandy but they didn't move. The smell of bread and soup had mesmerized them. He spoke to them gently, urging them to crawl under the wire, but the wire was dense and spiky. A small boy began to cry and asked for bread.

Children begging, Moslem or Orthodox, were no unusual sight. They wandered through villages and along roads, went from shop to shop stretching out their skinny arms, or stood shivering in front of a mosque or the church. Older boys and girls helped children without eyes, legs, or arms, as well as crawling babies.

Another soldier, a short man with a mustache and a plume in his hat, hummed as he poured soup into the childrens' bowls. His eyes were filled with brandy, heat, and tears. The childrens' tousled heads and filthy hands were too far away for him to kiss and he kept whispering he would bring them "More soup, more and more soup . . ."

Malic jumped the fence, practically colliding with a few drunken soldiers. It was a strange fence: the stakes were woven out of willow twigs. Further on were the headquarters and the prison. In front a soldier crouched in his shirt-sleeves. It was Nino Bottoni, who liked fun and women. At his feet, just where the shadow of the fence ended, lay some ammunition belts. The cartridges that peeped from them were so yellow that an honest man might have mistaken them for gold. In the necks of the cartridges were bullets, skillfully set, narrow and smeared with poisonous paint.

Malic knew this giant of a man who loved the guitar followed a skirt as a sunflower does the sun. Nor was he particular. As a result his friends nicknamed him "the carrion." Today he was barefoot. Within easy reach lay his shoes and his helmet, full of flowers and red grenades, displayed for sale.

On the other side of the fence stood Ismeta, like a black-clad statue. The barrel of Nino's rifle pointed unwaveringly through the fence at her shins. There was something mysterious about that barrel's pupil-less eye, something icy in its horizontal gaze, that lay concealed yet sensed, that withstood and threatened and lay in wait to burst open and pour forth smoke.

Soldiers were calling Pietro, but he didn't respond. They looked for him all over to get him to eat and to don the sentry's armband. Curses and accusations echoed on all sides, but they failed to produce him. The sun burned. Malic approached the soldier and the phantom in black Moslem rags. He was beset by a sense of desolation and imminent disaster. His eyes turned to the filthy earth and the river beyond, gushing and impatient. He looked up and saw a dog and a bitch stuck together.

But the fence separated Ismeta and Nino. An unfinished letter lay at Nino's feet. "My beloved," the letter said, "I am always thinking of you and dreaming of you . . . I asked for leave . . . but they would not give it to me, nor will they until we win the war . . . they won't let anyone go home. . . ."

Nino pushed a willow twig through the fence and brought his breath closer to the girl. Something hot ran down the twig, it formed a circle around Ismeta's shins and knees, traveled up her thighs, and came to rest on her groin.

" . . . Our roads have been cut off and the town is surrounded by Montenegrin rebels. . . . We are all in danger and we go out only when we have to. . . . A few days ago they killed Valerio, Giangiacomo, Luigi, and my namesake who used to send you his greeting . . . they captured a major and tied him to a donkey. He died that same night, they say from shame, but he came from Turin and was always insulting or hitting Pietro and me. . . ."

Nino rolled up his sleeve and pushed his fingers between the slats. Blood ran hot in his veins as his hand felt the rounded knees and traveled upwards of its own accord till it reached the sweating, frightened bird and stopped.

" . . . said, *amatissima*, that the rebels don't torture our soldiers . . . we are standing firm and defending you . . . putting up tremendous resistance . . . sometimes we charge out into the villages and set fire to their houses. As soon as it gets dark, we retire to the barracks. Tell everyone I've been recommended for a medal, but I shall do no more charging, not for a whole sack of medals; what's the use of medals if I get killed and there's no one left to love you . . . ? Yesterday I was almost killed; terrible, the bullet hummed right over my head and struck a tree. . . ."

Yesterday, as on any other day, Ismeta felt his finger in her flesh. Huddled against the fence, she gave in to his strength, her knees shaking. The hollows of her eyes were filled with darkness, a darkness blacker than the soldier panting like a dog, a blackness deeper than the rags that shielded her face from the sun.

A sudden wave of noise reached them from the other side of the fence. A group of soldiers were escorting an unkempt man with bowed legs and bound hands to the prison. The man wept and swore he would never again steal from anyone, and certainly not from the Italian army. They struck him with their boots and whips, to Captain Brambilla's great enjoyment. He was walking beside them, casting an occasional glance at the thief who was all rags and blood.

Nino hid his head in the grass. He was more afraid of Brambilla than of any other officer. The haughty *Milanese*, as they called him, did not stop at jotting down their crimes in his notebook, he would curse loudly and threaten them with a court-martial. "I've had it if he's seen me," Nino thought. "He'll be after me for not having been on that patrol. It's all right for you, Nino, the captain'll say, making love to girls down by the fence, and then he'll start swearing. It's no good, though, my promising not to do it again."

Ismeta couldn't understand why Nino was crouching by her legs at the fence. She drew her veil aside and saw his pointed head and skinny neck, his shallow chest slowly rising. He smiled senselessly, and muttered what sounded like a groan; and what he said was warm, from deep down, from his very heart and soft as silk. His lips trembled. In her thoughts she kissed them and bit them and he no longer seemed ridiculous. She dropped the black veil back over her face, he went on whispering passionately.

She had a pretty face. Only the mullah's wife, whom he had seen without her veil two or three times, was so beautiful. Ismeta's face was as white as the silver belly of a fish, as the paper on which the unfinished letter was written, as the early morning sky. To Nino it stood for fate, for disaster.

Ismeta sensed something new enter her flesh. She swayed on her slippers. The dark-haired, muscular little man pushed still closer to the fence, which began to give way. Once more she swayed; the suffering vanished from her eyes.

"I love you, Signorina . . . I love. I can't live without you, *amatissima*. . . !"

The black-clad statue of flesh shivered and convulsively gripped the fence with both hands.

Pietro could barely stand, but the sentry's armband was put on his arm anyway. He was reprimanded, threatened. He half-listened, looking at the dusty tank and its melancholy guardian marching up and down, waiting for the relief that never came. "Paolone," Pietro said to himself, "don't despair! If they ever relieve you, we'll go straight to the bar and drink ourselves stupid." Then he tottered up to a group of soldiers sitting on a broken-down door and eating. Augusto was singing, a plate of soup in front of him untouched.

"Augusto, why do you always sing filthy songs?"

"That's life," Augusto said softly, "army life!"

"Sing of something beautiful," Pietro said, placing a hand on his shoulder. "There are clean things in the world."

"If that's an order, I refuse."

"It's not an order, Augusto, sing about something clean anyway."

"Look, I've got an infection again. It's the third time! I couldn't sing about anything beautiful or clean if I wanted to."

"If you're my friend, Augusto," Pietro said, swaying, "you'll sing my song for me. Please. Sing it! Why not? I'm not ordering you, I'm asking you."

"Mamma, ma la canzone mia più bella sei tu . . ."[1]

Augusto's chin and his lips quivered. He wanted to cry. The guitar responded and he began with a pained cynicism:

"O Lucrezia, non avrei creduto
Che tu avvessi avuto
Quattro peli sul buco del culo . . ."[2]

Pietro was angry and turned to go.

"Wait!" Augusto shouted. "Listen to me: I can't sing your song, Pietro, old man, I just can't! I'm diseased and loathsome and full of shame! How could beautiful words pass my lips! Forgive me . . . and stay with us!"

But Pietro would not stop. He was on his way again. On the square, he ran into Captain Brambilla, who barred his way. "You're drunk again," Brambilla thundered.

"Yes, Captain," the corporal confessed.

"You realize that you set a bad example to the men?"

"Yes," Pietro said with conviction," I am a swine that should be slaughtered! In front of everybody, as an example! I meant to tell you this a long time ago, Captain. I'm ready for it now. I've disgraced our army and I don't deserve to live!"

The captain gave him a long look. Pietro stood upright. "I've offended you personally, Captain," Pietro said. "You know what I mean. I wish to answer for that too."

"It could happen to anyone," the captain said in a conciliatory tone. "To all of us. You're young and you've got time to improve."

"I love her!" Pietro exploded. "And I can't live without her. Please kill me right now. Like a dog . . . a lousy filthy cur!"

[1] Oh Mama, you are my loveliest song . . .
[2] Oh Lucrecia, who'd ever have believed
That on your asshole you have four hairs . . .

"I hate her as much as you love her!" the captain said soberly. "We're in the same boat."

"Pull the trigger now."

"Why not forget the whole thing, Pietro?"

"I can't forget anything, Captain, and I'll grovel at your feet until you do what I ask. Aim at my heart or between my eyes. Tell my mother and sisters that I was cut to pieces by Communists and that no one knows where I'm buried."

Pietro sobbed. But he remained at attention with his hands by his sides.

The captain grew serious. "*Sardo,* I order you to stop this nonsense!"

"Here, Captain," Pietro said, touching a spot on his chest. "Here, between these two fingers. Here, I beg you. Have pity!"

"Enough, *porca miseria*! Attention!"

Pietro obeyed.

"Left, about turn!"

Pietro turned.

"Now, to the cauldron, quick march! Take a portion of soup and bread and report immediately to the cellar! Offer it to that madman! See if he refuses it again today. Now go! And then come to see me in my office!"

Captain Brambilla looked up at headquarters. The windows of the colonel's room were shut and the curtains drawn. He felt a sharp pain in the very spot Pietro had pointed to a moment ago. Suddenly he understood that he would never forget his shame or get over his love.

"You're wrong, Captain," Pietro thought as he went to the cellar with the bread and soup in an aluminum mess tin. "You should have done me in and had her all to yourself. If you won't, I'll go to the colonel and ask him to order someone to shoot me."

At the bottom of the steps he found himself faced with an ugly door and the cellar darkness. He recalled the brightness of the day outside, the soldiers singing, calling his name, Paolone awaiting his relief and swearing, little Bottoni tearing with the force of his passion at the ancient fence and at the living statue in black. And, before he had turned the key in the lock, he found himself wishing he were up there with them.

He was in the middle of the cellar. A column of light poured from the doorway and hung over his twin-horned cap. In the far corner, a man was stretched out on an army cot. His long legs and broad feet lay shivering on a pile of straw. Clutching the mess tin and the bread, Pietro bent down: the light was on Rasko's large knees and hollow face. He pulled up his legs, put his head on his knees, and uttered an inarticulate whine. His ankles were huge, the soles of the feet unnaturally broad and furrowed. Pietro touched him with the tip of his boot and pointed to the tin of soup.

Rasko grinned longingly, showed his few rotten teeth, and mumbled something.

"You've got to eat," Pietro said, much more loudly than he had intended.

Rasko rose from the bed and huddled against the wall. His arms dangled at his sides.

"You've got to eat this soup and bread," Pietro roared.

Rasko fingered his beard and uttered vague noises.

Pietro stepped into the crooked quadrangle of light and again pointed to the mess tin.

"If you don't eat, you will die."

The large, hunchbacked man hid his face in his hands and gave a sob. "*Montenegrino,*" Pietro said sincerely, "I don't want you to die. Eat. I am very hungry too, only brandy for me all day. I always give my soup and bread to children. Come, *vecchio*, let's eat. Like this."

Pietro broke off a crust of bread and began to munch. Rasko looked at him with hungry, frightened eyes.

"Have a little soup," Pietro said, drawing still closer. "*Macaroni italiano*. Good for me and for you."

Rasko mumbled.

"Live! live!" Pietro added, drawing away. "The officers want you to die, but I want you to live a hundred years. When the night comes, I will open the door and you can go. Go to your woods. No one will see, but you must keep quiet, because for this I could die. And I want you to live, to live and to love. . . .

"To live," Pietro thought, looking at Rasko's wide-open eyes. "To live, even if it's in hell itself, to live and do good. That's what matters. Open cellar doors, release prisoners, and give them bread, meat, and soup, and soothe wounds."

Pietro stepped back toward the door, which seemed a long way off. Rasko's jawbones protruded. His eyes burned insanely, two coffee-colored blobs, two burning points closely confined in the pits beneath his brows. His clawlike hands rose. Pietro had no time to be surprised. And no time to move. He clutched the bread and the tin and awaited the blow.

The cellar was sinking. No, it was rising up, hovering over the rooftops and hills. Pietro floated, holding on firmly to the aluminum tin and the round loaf of bread, wetting himself like a frightened child. Rasko's twisted face came closer and grew larger and darker than the blackness of the cellar.

Pietro gaped, opened his mouth wide into a smile, grateful and human. He gave a tiny, high-pitched, brittle laugh and then his smile turned into a look of surprise and froze. He raised his arms above his head. A stream of soup soaked his elbows. Fear, like a cloud of warm mist, hid his mother and Marika and he no longer knew whether he was between Marika's or his mother's knees, nor whether he was feeling the private parts of the girl he saw with the soldier by the fence, or one of his own swarthy sisters. More clearly than ever, he could hear the groans of a wounded prisoner from a neighboring cell as well as Augusto's singing. He sadly admitted to himself that he knew all Augusto's songs and that often, in sleepless nights, he whispered them lustfully to himself. In a quick prayer he mentioned his father and sisters, and swore to the Virgin he would guard and love his mother and Marika alike. But he had no time to retreat toward the door and his salvation.

Rasko mumbled again. With twisted face and clenched

fists, he hurled himself at Pietro. The boy's body fell to the floor. Then some mysterious strength raised it and gathered it in a circle of defense. Rasko's wrinkled neck flashed once more through the narrow ribbon of light and vanished. His cheeks were yellow and cracked like the earth.

Pietro, sprawled on his side, shrank into a pincer. The next thing he knew the giant had landed flat on his chest. He smelt his breath, putrid and dense as the cellar darkness. He felt a human hand between his teeth. Something sticky wet his lips. He tasted his own salty saliva mixed with Rasko's blood. The final blow stretched him on the floor, his arms by his sides. As the breath rattled in his throat he thought of the sun-baked earth, a song without beginning or end, and hard, vertical human pain. His eyes were shrouded in the blackness of deepest sleep.

Rasko stood up. He raised Pietro against the wall like a bag. The body began to writhe and emit a gurgling noise. The man grew afraid, and still grasping Pietro by the throat, vanished into the darknes. The aluminum mess tin rolled away, as if hopping from cobblestone to cobblestone, down a narrow street.

Rasko stood over the still body, looking at his own fingers. He was horrified. He had dented the mess tin and driven the spoon into the earth and the blackness of the floor. He dashed up the steps. At the top of the stairs he turned: stretched across the threshold lay Pietro's motionless hand, its palm filled with the bright light from the sky.

At the entrance to the yard Rasko collided with a soldier, who dropped his rifle and shouted for help. He knocked down two more sentries and dashed for the gate. He saw a tank and mule loaded with machine guns, and turned back into the yard. Captain Brambilla spotted him, took cover, and fired his revolver. He fired again and ordered that the fugitive be taken alive.

An entire unit chased after Rasko, their bayonets fixed, their red-painted grenades ready for use. Bent over, as if weighed down by a heavy load, Rasko overturned two more soldiers, upset a cauldron of macaroni and a row of dishes. He looked about him insanely, with clenched fists. No one dared come near him. With the adroitness and strength of a demon, he got away from several soldiers who had hurled themselves at his feet. Rasko was in the open; he saw the river and the distant mountains and his face lit up. With one leap he cleared the broad wire fence and dashed off across open country.

Captain Brambilla ordered the unit to fire.

Augusto grabbed his rifle and fired high over Rasko's head. The rest followed suit. The captain took out the machine gun. Bursts of machine-gun fire and explosions of grenades tore the air.

The wind carried Rasko right up to Nino. Ismeta gathered her black skirts about her and ran. Bottoni drove a bullet into the breech and propped his rifle on a tussock: the butt kicked his shoulder. Rasko gave a start: his arm was bloody and his shorn fingers had catapulted into the grass. He saw nothing and heard nothing. He ran down the slope, bent slightly forward, his head tucked into his shoulders, toward the wire fence and the gray stretch of the road and the dark forest on the other side of the river.

At Nino's fifth shot Rasko gave a jerk, stood upright, and turned in the direction of the smoking rifle, with bloody foam on his mouth. Panic-stricken, Nino watched him running toward him with his arms outstretched, his eyes wild.

Bottoni stopped him with the sixth shot. Rasko turned his back on all of them and set off in the opposite direction. For a moment he stood upright, dead on his feet, and then, doubling up as if balancing along a beam, fell on his face and buried it in the dust.

The soldiers fired no more. They ran along the fence and watched as the large body slithered down the slope, gaining momentum on the steep bank of the wild-foaming river. Rasko's body rolled off a rock and splashed into the water.

Part Four

CHAPTER 1

GRUBAN MALIC stood on his doorstep and watched the soldiers marching, in full gear, in the direction of the mosque, pushing their way through the dust and the deafening song. Their bayonets glistened in the sun. Beggars and children followed, trying to keep step with the army.

A large crowd had gathered in the square by the fountain. Marika was talking to Mustafa Agic, the chief of the local agents. Clad in a light-blue vest with short sleeves, officer's trousers, and low-heeled shoes, she kept shaking her head. Agic's flabby lips parted in a grin, but Marika remained adamant. In desperation Agic pointed to Malic and passed his hand across his throat. Captain Brambilla joined them as Agic drew the outline of a gallows in the air.

"I think my fiancée, Signorina . . ."

"Shut up!" Marika snapped, pushing the captain's perfumed hand aside with a gesture of loathing.

"Signorina," the captain stuttered in embarrassment. "Don't forget that we are engaged."

"What do you mean, the gallows!" she said to Agic. "You must be mad."

"You are defending a Communist criminal," Agic said, closing his left eye. "A dangerous tyrant!"

"Nonsense," Marika said.

"Maybe you're in agreement with his perverted ideas," Agic flared, putting his forefinger to his nose.

"Yes, I'm a Communist," Marika said provocatively.

"In God's name, Signorina!" Brambilla said.

"*Tonto!*" Marika retorted. "Fool!"

"That's no way to talk to your fiancé and liberator," Agic whispered, striking his forehead with his fist.

"I don't give a damn for liberators and fiancés! Particularly not for a fiancé like mine!"

The captain bit his lip. "An exotic, wild Montenegrin," he thought. "The more she loves, the more she ridicules."

Still arguing, the three of them started toward Malic's establishment. Malic was at the door, his hands shaking, a black lock of hair covering his scowling brow.

"Let us in, you Montenegrin fool!" Turiddu cried. "We want to drink and sing! We're celebrating victory on land and sea, *compagno* Malic. In the air too. Especially in the air! Long live our wings! Give us some brandy!"

For a moment Malic stood undecided. He wanted to hurl a torrent of abuse of them, but instead, he trembled and clutched a roll of paper. "Show them you're a thousand times stronger . . ." he thought feverishly, "show them now . . ."

The blood beat in his temples as he slowly unfolded the roll of paper and spread it out: large, colored letters under a five-pointed bright red star. He placed it over the doorknob. Captain Brambilla's hand dropped to his holster.

"There!" Malic said, backing away from them, his hand on the grenade in his pocket. Captain Brambilla blew his whistle. The two-horned caps swarmed round the poster and its star.

Malic stood alone, waiting for their attack.

But no one took any notice of him. They were drawn to the poster.

"I was right!" Agic cried. "And I told you, *signor capitano*! If you'd only listen to me. . . ."

"I want you to translate it for me," the captain said, "word for word."

Agic wiped the sweat from his forehead and read, first in Serbian and then in Italian:

I REFUSE TO WORK FOR THE ENEMY! I AM CLOSING THE SHOP FOR POLITICAL REASONS. I AM EVERYWHERE.

"Very interesting," Captain Brambilla said.

"Outrageous," roared Agic. "I was right, of course. We must act immediately, before he escapes."

"Strange handwriting, too."

"Yes, the letters are red!" Agic yelled.

Gripping the grenade by its ring, Malic prepared to defend himself. His breath failed him as he heard Agic mention gallows, matches, and gas. He wished they would attack: he imagined a mass of human flesh, bullet-pierced skulls, and scattered brains, a mountain of empty cartridges and broken weapons; beneath the smoke and noise he lay, looking upon the motionless battlefield, blood flowing from his dust-covered wounds, yet feeling no pain.

But Captain Brambilla and the soldiers calmly walked past him. There was nothing for him to do but curse: "The bastards won't let me show them my courage. . . . If they go on tormenting me like this, I'll have to perform a miracle."

Malic walked over to the mosque. A group of the faithful, eyes full of heat and terror, were staring at the minaret. Malic glanced upwards into the blinding light. His eyes searched the sky. An eagle was slowly circling: the entire space above the roofs was filled with its ravenous, exhausted cries.

He kept walking, attracted by the smell of food and the sound of singing, and reached the mullah's gate which was guarded by a sentry. He had spotted a gathering in the yard. Unbelted and unarmed, Colonel Allegretti sat at the head of the table. He was toasting the priest, who swayed at the other end of the table.

"Friends!" the colonel said in Serbian, getting to his feet. "I drink to you and to us . . . and to our friendship," and he drained his glass. Suddenly the mullah climbed on a three-legged stool and bleated:

"My dear *kum!* I thank you a thousand times!"

Glass shattered and brandy spilled. The air was saturated

with a smell of mutton and sweetmeats. The little mullah spread his arms and spoke warmly:

"My excellent *kum!* You are the sun that shines upon us! For a long time now I've waited for this hour. I knew it would come."

Holding a sheep's head in his hands, the colonel leaned over to his neighbor: "What's this *kum* anyway?"

"I can't translate it for you exactly, Colonel," the man said. "The brandy's gone to my head and my brains have gone to sleep. In any case," he went on, gnawing at the sheep's shoulder, "in any case . . ."

"It isn't derogatory? Or ambiguous . . . ?"

"No, Colonel, I don't think so."

"It isn't political, is it?"

"No," the man replied. "It means godfather."

The colonel looked at the mullah happily and began to pull the sheep's head apart.

The army chaplain, a small man with a low forehead, dull blue eyes, and long arms, was also present. A sour, impertinent smile played between his thin mustache and his brown beard. He was explaining something to the priest who, spattered with drink, was roaring with laughter and stroking the small, flattened head of the *padre*. The blood rushed to the *padre*'s temples and ears and he glanced sideways at the colonel.

"*Padre*!" the colonel suddenly came to life. "Where's the child?"

The chaplain wriggled out of the priest's embrace, tidied his tunic, tightened his belt, and vanished, followed by Major Peduto. Before long Nidzara, the mullah's wife, smiling but sad and for the first time appearing without her black veil, walked in bearing her son in her arms. She was accompanied by Mustafa Agic, Major Peduto, and the *padre*. They reached the head of the table, and the *padre* said formally: "Colonel, we are here!"

"Good health to you!" the colonel said, throwing the sheep's eyes and the brains into a large dish.

Nidzara stood in front of the colonel. Despite the military

songs and the distant gunfire, the child was not crying. Slyly she cast her eyes over the guests. There was no sign of the glorious aviator, Corporal Turiddu Barbagallo, and she was overcome by a quiet, insinuating sadness. The infant stared at the colonel, the sky, and the mountaintops.

The priest put his huge arms round the mullah and the *padre*: neither of them came higher than his chest. "My friends, my friends! We must not part. . . . We have a common enemy!"

Dressed in baggy trousers of the finest red silk, Nidzara stood in front of the colonel, who was staring into her heavy, milky-white bosom. It wasn't until he was given a pair of scissors that he realized what was expected of him. He was about to approach the mother and child when the priest, suddenly releasing the mullah and the *padre* and clutching his hand to his heart, cried: "Friends, he's here . . . I feel him . . . He's here somewhere! *Veramente*, the viper's somewhere around!"

The priest swayed. The colonel stared dully at mother and child.

"Get him for me today, get him!" the priest rasped. "I'll do him in right here!"

"Who?" asked the colonel, looking at the young mother.

"Malic!" the priest howled. "Gruban Malic, alias the International!"

The guests stood silent. To break the uncomfortable silence, the colonel went up to the mother and clipped several locks of the child's hair.

"And now give him a name!" the priest hollered. "A name, *signor colonnello*, or have you forgotten?"

"Ah, yes," the colonel said in Serbian. "But I don't know what name the parents want. I know only three Moslem names for women and two for men."

"The child shall have your name, an Italian name," said the priest, standing between the mullah and the child's mother.

"How about it, *signor muezzino*?" the colonel asked, "I only want to do what you wish."

"I'd like the child named Muhamed," the little mullah ventured. "Like my late father, who was also a mullah."

"Impossible!" the priest roared, gripping the colonel by the arm.

"Priest," blinked the mullah, "the child's mine, not yours."

"That's of no consequence," the priest said angrily, showing his sparse teeth. "The child's a child, God's gift, and may it prosper! What's most important of all is the name."

"Well," said the colonel, grinning.

"The child must bear your name," the priest said, squeezing the colonel's elbow still harder. "Let it be a token of our affection for you."

"But the child's mine," the mullah wailed.

"I hate sadness," the colonel said. "I prefer compromises, *signor muezzino*."

"I love and respect our colonel too," the mullah said. "We should erect a monument to him. I probably have more affection for him than you do, priest. But I'd like the child to bear his grandfather's name. He's my only son. My first wife's children all died."

"How dare you deprive our excellent colonel of the honor which we wish to show him! It's a shame and a disgrace to speak as you do! In the name of our common God, Mullah, watch what you're saying! You are lucky he still thinks you're joking!"

"Muhamed is mine," the mullah said softly, wiping the tears on his sleeve. "And you can't take him away from. . . ."

Realizing that he had gone too far, the priest said in a somewhat calmer voice: "How about giving him two names: one chosen by you and the other by the will of the people?"

"That is a good idea," Agic was relieved at this compromise solution.

"His first name must be his grandfather's," the mullah said with a snivel, "and his second can be anything you wish."

"Don't shame us before this heroic man, *muezzino*," the priest blasted again.

"Let him have his way," Agic said contemptuously. The old man was beginning to cry again. *"Prego, signori amici!"*

The guests drank and shouted, hurled dishes, bones, and sheeps' eyes into the air. The colonel kept firing at the sun with a revolver drawn from a gold-mounted holster, until he fell under the table. He emerged to drink the health of the little "Muhamed Spartaco, who must not and will not become a muezzin, like his aged and honored father, but a great Italian admiral, an explorer and conqueror of the South Pole and other unknown and impassable wildernesses. . . ."

The mullah wept. The priest sang Serbian Church songs and obscene Italian ones. The well-built young wife was showered with brandy and compliments as she cast a sober eye in search of Turiddu: she wondered if he had gone swimming and, like the soldier the day before, would drown. Her strong legs astride, she looked at Augusto as he struck the strings of his guitar and, with fear and passion, hummed the obscene words into the colonel's ear.

"They're having a good time," the sentry commented, shouldering his rifle.

"It won't last long," Malic replied, firmly.

"Heh, who knows?"

"I do, I know for sure."

"The mullah's got a lovely wife."

"The whore!"

The soldier motioned him to be quiet and to follow him. Looking around cautiously, he whispered: "Why do they call you the International?"

"You'll find out, *Taliano*," Malic said, and set off again.

"Well, good luck to you," said the soldier, and returned to his post.

Malic interpreted the uproar in the mullah's yard as the beginning of the end. Revolvers cracked, drunken shouts and curses echoed. The priest sang "*Giovinezza.*" Major Peduto shouted at the top of his lungs, which was altogether unlike him, and Agic, irritated with the celebration, looked anxiously at the mullah's child and beat himself on his forehead.

"You just go on singing," Malic thought. "Go on yelling and screaming, you black, senile bear. And you, too, Colonel, I'll have your balls in a rattrap before long. And yours too, Peduto, you swine, and yours, Brambilla! I'll capture the lot of you and hang you by the feet, so just go on singing and drinking to the health of that little bastard and his whore of a mother!"

He walked for some time, not caring where he was going. Soldiers passed, silent and depressed, burned brown by the wind and dark with sorrow, dragging themselves through the dust. He gripped the sweaty grenade in his pocket, played with the trigger of his revolver, and followed the soldiers like an evil shadow. "Follow them," he whispered to himself, "because your place is wherever there's pain and suffering."

The soldiers turned into a side street. Malic caught sight of Dana at the far end of a yard, on her back, her head thrown back, her legs apart. The sun baked the scratches and bruises that covered her body. A group of soldiers took turns: her naked body offered no resistance to the impassioned male force. It twitched and quivered. A brandy bottle was passed from mouth to mouth. An assortment of children and beggars stood by on the dry grass.

In spite of himself Malic joined the crowd. The earth seemed to give beneath the fragile, doubled-up body. The hollow beneath the tree bore the imprints of her small spine and ribs. As he drew near her he saw her face; the scratched cheeks, her hair shorn in mourning, her eyes vacant. She was cuddling somebody's boots, and whispering to them in a tender, childlike voice.

"They cheated you, my sweet Pietro. They put you to sleep. Open your eyes and look at your little sister. You've forgotten me. Don't run away, little *Sardo* . . . Why don't you defend me, my dark-eyed hero, I hurt all over. They've pulled my insides out, Pietro, they've burnt me alive."

No one listened. They pulled her arms apart and tried to bite off her lips. Her lips avoided them and spoke of pain, the dust, and the sun.

But still no one listened. More soldiers arrived, some bandaged, others in full battle gear. They neither sang nor spoke. They simply took turns.

A large crowd had gathered around the soldier by the tank. His bayonet high above his helmet, his lips cracked and blue, and his eyes full of tears, Salvatore could have taken a turn too. He didn't want to. But he didn't want to go either. He watched them plucking at her, pulling her apart. He watched like someone enjoying his own agony. There was no sign of relief for him, no one to pull him by the sleeve and tell him to get the hell out of the sun and out of that damned yard. Salvatore stamped his feet, like a true sentry, ignoring his burning helmet. "They'll destroy her."

"Shut up, Salvatore," Malic said.

"She's been there all night, she doesn't recognize anybody. She keeps scratching her face and talking about Pietro. I told her I was Pietro, but she didn't listen. I called for our priest, but he won't give her confession, because she isn't a Catholic. He says he hates the Orthodox like poison because they're all Communists. 'This poor thing too?' I asked. 'She too,' he said. 'The devil who's under her skin is a red one.' 'But I love her,' I said. 'Does that mean I too have wandered from the path?' 'If you haven't, you soon will,' the *padre* said. 'I am crazy because I'm always in the sun,' I said, but he didn't hear me. I said it again and again. But he didn't answer. I turned to your priest, but he wouldn't listen. He is never sober; the devil's in him too. I offered him money, but he wouldn't do anything. I talked with the mullah. He kept playing with his beads like a child and spitting; and I hate people who spit."

"Guard your tank," Malic snapped.

"I just couldn't make love to her. I stood there with my trousers unbuttoned and those bastards laughed at me. A rotten trick!"

"Be careful," Malic snapped again, "or someone will walk off with your tank!"

"You're right," Salvatore agreed, pushing his helmet onto the back of his head. "Thieves are everywhere. How about you and me picking her up? Don't worry about the cost, I'll pay."

"Oh, Salvatore!" said Malic.

The sky was cloudless. He decided to leave Salvatore because he simply couldn't stop talking. He turned and shouted: "Salvatore, hurry up: the devil got into your tank! You'll be court-martialed. And you'll end up in hell. Your tank, your tank! Look: another devil is getting in! Run!"

CHAPTER 2

MALIC PAUSED at the fountain. A few soldiers stood by idly. Whores raised clouds of dust with their skirts and their motorcyclists. Malic had a splitting headache. He cooled his forehead and aching eyes with a splash of water.

In front of his saloon a group of soldiers stood singing, jostling one another, waving to Malic and greeting him in both Serbian and Italian. They wanted him to let them in. They tried to force the door, but then hurried off to find brandy and song elsewhere.

Malic felt betrayed and deserted. Clouds of fine dust rose with the wind. Suddenly he pictured himself charging into the battlefield. Companies of twin-horned caps running for dear life, green knapsacks falling, blood, brandy, and shattered genitals gushing from them. He was in the forefront of the combat, pursuing the colonel, the priest, and the mullah, with a drawn knife. One more step and he will stab them through the heart! He is accompanied by two figures in black capes and sunglasses. He decided to test his military prowess by driving his bayonet through the fat bottom of Colonel Allegretti himself.

He was so angry that he would surely have shattered Allegretti's heart, had it not been for Marika. Dressed in officer's riding breeches, whip in hand, she strolled over. Startled out of his reverie. Malic looked at her sternly.

"*Amico,*" Marika said. "Why so sad and gloomy?"

Malic said nothing.

"Now look at me," she said provocatively. "Look how well equipped I am. All I need is a revolver and some medals. Come on, look at me!"

"I don't want to talk with you," Malic said, moving away. "A man like me shouldn't be seen talking with a traitor; what would the comrades say?"

"What are you talking about?"

"You know very well what I am talking about. You're just pretending. But I tell you again, I can't waste my time with someone who has betrayed . . . "

"Who's betrayed what?"

"Who has betrayed her country," Malic said, "her brothers and fathers who are shedding their blood out there for our happier future."

"But *amico,*" Marika said, touching his shoulder with the tips of her breasts, "I don't understand."

"You're always with the Fascists," Malic said contemptuously. "And don't forget that we Communists never forgive. We punish such offenses very severely!"

"I'd like to know what you've got to do with communism?" Marika asked excitedly, waving at an officer.

"You've seen the proclamation," Malic stated, "you translated it for them, didn't you?"

"I did, so what?"

"Take another look at that star. It's red and has five points."

"So?"

"That means: the whole world. That's me! I'm everywhere!"

"That's something," Marika put in quickly to stop his invective.

"Yes," Malic said triumphantly. "I've broken with my old, negative life. I am thinking of mankind's highest ideals."

"You mean, you've given yourself over to communism," Marika concluded.

"I don't know if you've hit on exactly the right word," Malic said, "but the Revolution is the only thing that has meant anything to me for some time."

"Well, yes," Marika said half to herself, "everyone has to have something. But, for God's sake, why choose that?"

"I told you you were stupid and didn't understand," Malic said, sprinkling his face again.

Marika glanced over Malic's head at Lieutenant Riva, who was singing.

"You're an incorrigible whore."

"I'm not. I am getting married."

"You mean like you did the last five times."

"No, it's different now. Why should I leave Brambilla?" Marika said. "He's patient and good, and he's never reproached me for having my photo taken with Spartaco. He suffers in silence. And Spartaco is kind and gentle to him: he has recommended him for a decoration. The medal's been in our drawer for the last two weeks and we will get our promotion when the general comes or when we go to Italy."

"When are you going?"

"When Spartaco lets us."

"You'll never get out of Montenegro alive!" Malic said, glancing at the surrounding hills. "You little fool, don't you know what you are doing? We are not easy to deal with."

"Who is we?"

"We Montenegrins, we're vipers! Don't forget we butchered Turks for five hundred years. And then Austrians. In Nineteen fifteen, we killed twenty thousand of them in one day."

"But they really love me!" Marika sighed with delight. "They die for me! They caress me and call me little pussy and they lick me all over, just imagine what it'll be like when I go to Italy. Perhaps Spartaco will marry me. He says he won't give me up."

"You make me sick!" Malic said. "In such hard times you think of getting married! And to a dwarf like that."

"You are crazy," Marika said, and waved her handkerchief to Lieutenant Riva. "I'll send you packages from Milan. First I'll send you a suit. You need shoes too, your shirt's patched and you've no winter coat."

"I don't want any Fascist rags," Malic was red with anger. "I'll hang your Brambilla and take his clothes."

Lieutenant Riva walked up to the fountain. He passed his forefinger through his thin, tidy mustache and offered to help Marika carry water in a large earthen pot. He ordered his two escorts to stay behind.

"You Italian devil!" Malic said.

"I like to carry water," Riva said.

He put his arm round Marika's waist. She giggled and blew them all kisses.

"Listen, you shameless bitch!" Malic roared, "I'll try you, you Fascist bitch! You and him! I'll have your head shaven and I'll hang him by the balls! Go and tell your Brambilla and Spartaco I'll have their hide for sandals! I am not going to move from here, not for love or money, not even if that deformed King of Italy were to beg me . . . "

Malic was standing by the fountain, holding his revolver and the red grenade. Two officers were nearby. reading the poster. One of them photographed the church, the mosque, and the little café. They were clean-shaven, with white teeth and clear eyes.

Malic walked over to the bridge. From the mullah's yard came the sound of singing and revolver shots. His throat was dry with melancholy. He passed by old acquaintances who pretended not to recognize him.

He caught sight of a tall peasant with a large head and a long mustache, dressed in a shirt made from an Italian tent, in trousers of faded homemade cloth, and a round Montenegrin cap on the back of his head. He was talking with Corporal Barbagallo.

"How are my mules?" Barbagallo asked.

"Bad," the peasant said. "One has a cough and looks like it's going to go any minute. The other is lazy as a clod of earth. You've swindled me, *Taliano*!"

"I've got another, you can't find a better one in our whole stable, perhaps not in all of Italy."

"You know why I've come this time," the peasant said softly. "We'll talk about mules later. But don't swindle me again."

The peasant's small nag swished its tail, fighting off flies. From the packsaddle hung sacks and half-dead chickens covered with blood and dust.

"You're asking too much," the peasant said again, counting on his fingers, "much too much."

"It really is an excellent cannon. Almost new. And as you know our artillery is the best."

"Still and all, you're asking a lot, *Taliano*. We are poor and it isn't easy to part with that kind of money."

"But I'm giving you the best gun in the world," Barbagallo flared. "To say nothing of the risk I am taking. I'm poor too! All I have is my life and I could lose that any minute."

"You should," the peasant retorted. "Why the hell did you come here in the first place?"

"God knows, I didn't want to."

"Be that as it may, you'll die," the peasant said, putting a hand on his shoulder. "Just let me catch you in the open. I'll do you in like a hare! Like a hare, *Taliano* . . . ! That's how I'll get you!"

"I know I'll die soon," Barbagallo said. "So why should I give you the cannon for nothing?"

They continued to argue for some time. Barbagallo wrote down some figures on the wall.

"We'll pay your price but in installments," the peasant said cunningly. "Installments, my man, installments. Over a ten-year period. What do you say to that, Corporal?"

"I don't like installments. Ready cash only."

"You don't trust me?" the peasant changed his tactics. "If there's no trust between us and no love, there's no point in talking."

"I do trust you, but. . . ."

"You say you're going to stay here for ever," the peasant said, "so what's ten years? Come on, Corporal, let's seal the bargain!"

"But if I'm going to die soon," the corporal said slyly, "and you yourself said you'd do me in like a hare, who will collect the money? That's why I want it in cash."

"Oh, *Taliano*," the peasant said.

"Oh, *Montenegrino*," said the corporal.

"Look here, my boy, we must have the gun. We need it tonight. Lower your price and let me go."

"I've always hated deferred payments," Barbagallo repeated. "I'll lower my price, but I'll only take cash or nothing doing."

A few *Carabinieri* were approaching. Barbagello thrust a grenade into the peasant's jacket, grabbed a chicken from the packsaddle, told the peasant to meet him the next day by the church, and dashed off down the street.

Tall and upright, his face hard, the peasant stood like a statue at the edge of the road. Malic felt himself weak and insignificant by comparison. He decided to scare him. "What are you doing here?"

"I'm selling poultry; eggs, too. They just love them! They prefer a good chicken to a lamb."

"Is that all you come here for?" Malic asked, as it were, confidentially.

"I also come to buy things from soldiers."

"Don't you know that's strictly forbidden?" Malic asked.

"Everything is forbidden," the peasant laughed sarcastically. "Living's forbidden, but we still go on breathing. Just tell me where you'd get food today and then we'll talk about things being forbidden! They've got it coming to them," the peasant said and gave a wink.

"What do you mean?"

"Just that," the peasant said, laughing at his own joke.

Malic stepped away from him, switched his revolver from one pocket to the other, and said sternly: "How dare you say such things?"

"I've said nothing," the peasant protested.

"Do you realize that you could be arrested for what you said?"

"Yes, I know," the peasant said, "but I thought you were one of our people."

"I could have you in chains at the drop of a hat," Malic said, grinding his teeth. "And someone else will buy the gun. In chains, I tell you!

"But I won't," Malic said, striking a pose of one who forgives easily. "I'm sick of all these arrests. Don't be afraid, I really won't hurt you. I'm not bad, but people don't understand me. Next time take care. You're on thin ice. I'd only have to move a finger and my people would come, various agents and troops, and put you against the wall."

The peasant gave him a long look and then asked: "Is it true that officers also sell things?"

"Listen to this!" Malic said. "I spare his life and he talks about goods!"

"Our children run around naked. Mine and my brother's. My brother was killed this spring. They say officers specially . . ."

"Leave me alone," Malic said. "Be off, and hide those grenades: they're sticking out of your shirt! Be off, I tell you!"

But a group of soldiers, in full battle gear, leaped out of a dusty truck and surrounded the peasant. They plucked feathers from the chickens and stuck them in their caps.

"How much for two eggs?" asked a young soldier, holding a bloody bandage to his forehead.

“Goods, goods,” grumbled the peasant. “Coats, shirts, shoes. Things like that. Yes, bandages too.”

“Have you got any cheese, good Montenegrin cheese?”

“Yes, *Taliano,* one egg, one lira. Two eggs, three lire. What's money these days, it's worth less and less!”

“I have no money. I will take three eggs today and pay tomorrow.”

“No,” the peasant said, spreading his arms wide. “Take off your coat, and you can have fifteen eggs.”

“No, one shirt for ten eggs.”

“No, *Taliano,* not if I have to go naked.”

“How much is your little horse?”

“Not for sale, folks.”

“Are you a Communist, *Montenegrino*?”

“Me, a Communist! Look at me! Heh, *soldato,* leave that rooster alone, or give me your shoes.”

“A Fascist then?”

“No, but maybe.”

“You've got a revolver, grenades, ammunition? What do you have, *Montenegrino*?”

“Nothing, *soldato,*” the peasant said. “Heh, you there, take the rooster! Go on, soldier, take an egg each. I know what it is to be a soldier. Go on, take some cheese, and let me get home to my old woman before dark. There, that's it, take it all, and pay later. No, I've no weapons. Our dear and beautiful Queen Helena is your Queen!”

They leaped on him from all sides. He shouted, begged them to let him go, but they searched him anyway.

“Here are some weapons!”

The peasant pushed the three soldiers to the ground, took cover briefly behind the horse, and then dashed down the road, followed by a cloud of dust.

Suddenly, like an evil spirit, Captain Brambilla showed up and ordered them to fire, to run after the peasant, to take him alive. He fired the revolver several times and ran down the road.

The whole company charged after the peasant, firing their

rifles. He never looked back, running as fast as his legs would carry him, crouching and rising, skillfully weaving his way toward the river. He dived into the river and swam across.

The road was soon deserted, except for Malic and the peasant's horse.

"I'm hungry. I haven't touched a thing since yesterday, except for water and fruit," Malic said to himself, as the smell of freshly baked bread reached his nostrils. "If you don't stick something down your gullet, you'll collapse in the dust and nobody will pick you up."

The sun blazed in its zenith. His eyes ached with the light and the dust. The scorched earth smelled and the filthy, crooked walls and old roofs were falling apart. The drunken singing of the soldiers spread all the way to the bridge and the river. Malic dragged himself along the uneven road. The stench of his unwashed army shirt was unbearable. "You mustn't fall," he told himself as his knees gave way. "You mustn't fall, ever," and he clenched his fist.

He remained standing by the fountain for some time, splashing his hands and forehead, but he still felt nauseous. His temples pulsated. His brains were boiling. Red-hot dust filled the sky and hovered over the narrow square. "I won't give in," he whispered, clinging to the tap like a drowning man. "I won't die alone, like a dog. I want to win!"

Paolone's head emerged from the little tank. On his shoulder hung a rifle like a withered branch. "I feel sick," Paolone complained.

"I do too," Malic said, again wetting his hands and forehead.

"Terrible heat. I just threw up."

"That's good."

"You've no idea how my head ached. If they don't relieve me, I'll kill somebody. I'll shoot at the first person I see."

"Why not a bullet through your own temple?" Malic said. "That's a sure relief."

"I haven't the strength."

"You're a real Italian coward," Malic said.

"I don't know what I am, but I know I want to be relieved, get rid of this rifle and get under the shade."

"You want a lot!"

"Be a man and ask them to relieve me. Tell them I'm seeing things. If you're my brother and friend, go help Dana; she's still lying under the bridge."

"But I'm not your friend or brother," Malic said. "We're enemies."

"That's what you think."

Malic was on his way. He paused at the door of his saloon. He was at the end of his strength. Through the heat came the squeak of a solitary trumpet and the sound of *Carabinieri* curses.

He reached in his pocket, drew out a piece of red chalk, and scrawled across the door:

THIS SALOON . . .

He leaned against the wall. The heehawing of donkeys drowned out the trumpet and the *Carabinieri*'s curses. In his daze he clearly saw a lop-eared ass and was afraid. For some time he had felt that he was not really the man people called Gruban Malic, but a donkey. His head dropped, his forehead scraped the doorpost. And as the sound of the trumpet receded and the dust settled on Salvatore's tank, Malic grew a tail. The torn army boots on his feet were ill-shod ass's hoofs. His belly suddenly grew hairy, rising and falling rapidly with the filthy air and undigested thorns. His ears were already long: he could clearly hear the eagle crying above the rooftops and the sentry coughing by the tank.

. . . BELONGS TO A COMMUNIST RAT . . .

His arm fell to his side. "A donkey," he whispered, feeling himself behind the neck. "You're turning into a donkey, your ears are growing and they're full of rotten hairs and black fat! A donkey," he whispered, "a common Montenegrin donkey, that's what you are. Stubborn suffering monster pissing words against walls! How can you live among the people you've always wanted to be equal with; your tail will make tracks in the dust, your braying will make children laugh. You don't know who you are, or where you're from, what you want, or how you've come to change your form . . . !"

He felt sick. His donkey's sides heaved. "Don't give in," he told himself, "until you are through writing your sentence:"

. . . WHO SHOULD BE LOCKED UP . . .

The letters reminded him of a donkey's worn hoofs, of the heat that melted the brains in his skull. He dropped the chalk and glanced at the words, sorry he had not completed the writing or embellished it with quotation marks, underlined it and put circles round it, and then collapsed. "Half man, half donkey," he whispered, "a vision to amuse and frighten people. Ass, where's your packsaddle and halter, and why aren't you overloaded and beaten, as you should be. No, don't heehaw: stand up straight against the wall and look at your donkey's words, your stupid donkey's challenge. That's it, take a deep breath and tell those who have gathered that you'll turn back into a man, and as soon as you lose your tail, they can bind you and drive you out of this stinking, hateful town!"

Shriveled and exhausted, he fell on his knees like any other man. His head hit the wall, his hands clawed at the dust. He did not feel the blood that poured down his face. He heard whining nearby: soaked in blood, he began to wail.

A large crowd surged into the square. Major Peduto had his arm round Captain Brambilla. The mullah bleated like a child. The priest groaned from the stretcher, speaking of communism at the end of the world. Agic pushed people aside with a stick. He was furious with the colonel. The colonel was carrying the child. The diapers stank, little Muhamed Spartaco kicked and struggled. The commandant was singing the "*Giovinezza.*" The shapely mother, alluring despite her coverings, strode next to him. They reached the fountain.

The colonel laughed; he laughed so loudly that he almost dropped the child. The crowd was bewildered.

"There! My friend," the colonel said, pointing to Malic.

They saw the red sign and laughed nervously. The colonel wanted everyone to go so he could put the neck of a bottle to Malic's bloody, caked lips. People massaged the priest's neck and chest. Gazing at the drunken sky, he groaned and swore he would not die till the red dragon's back was broken and its head crushed.

Malic lacked the strength to remove his hands from the dust. Nor could he speak, although he no longer imagined he was a donkey.

"Major Peduto," the colonel said, "the general is coming from the south. Evidently he wants to surprise us."

"I understand, Colonel," Peduto said with a smile.

"We must have the houses on the streets to the south whitewashed immediately. Only the facades, of course. The fences and the tree trunks, right up to the foliage, the latrines, too. That's important."

"What do we do with the triumphal arch at the north end?"

"Leave it there, Major!"

"We don't have enough whitewash," Antonio said.

"I know. Buy some from the Communists."

"They only have red paint, Signor Colonel," said Agic.

"Water it down," the colonel said.

"They charge too much, Signor Colonel."

"The general is coming from the south," the colonel said, walking in front of Malic's saloon, "and this street is full of shit."

"Our guardian's commands shall be obeyed," Agic whimpered. "The town must be cleared of suspicious people, too; I'm thinking of drunks as well as of subversive elements. Do I have the authority, Signor Colonel?"

"The general is coming from the south," Allegretti repeated, "and generals are strange people; they like order and cleanliness. Especially General Besta."

"So we can start interrogating at once!" Agic was ecstatic. "To start with, why not arrest him?" he added, pointing at Malic.

"Everyone except my friend," Spartaco said, plopping the

baby into Peduto's arms. "My improbable, brave, unhappy friend," he added, stretching his arms. "We're a lot of swine! We drink and have a good time and the poor man must be hungry and thirsty. . . ."

"My dear colonel, the godfather of my child," the mullah said, "we are concerned about your life. If anything happens to you we shall be carried away by the filthy Communist flood."

"Give him some brandy," the colonel ordered.

"And bread and meat!"

"And poison!" The priest stormed from the stretcher. "Rat poison or broken glass, and make him drink it! Oh God, let me get on my feet!"

"Paint the whole square," Allegretti said, grabbing the bottle. "The fountain has stopped working again. And decorate that stinking road with flags, hundreds of them. This stuff's real alcohol! Give me some more! My friends . . . Long live the crazy Slavs, long live my second fatherland, Montenegro, the land of heroes and geniuses . . . give him some brandy too. He's thirsty . . ."

The child was howling in Peduto's arms. The commandant cursed in Serbian. The mullah stopped both his ears and his wife looked for Turiddu with a watchful eye.

The crowd moved off toward Malic's saloon. Sensing the proximity of brandy and the enemy, the priest yelped, as if wounded. When he got to Malic, the colonel paused.

"Drink!" he ordered, handing him the bottle.

Malic smelt the brandy and the angry crowd. He heard the colonel's heavy wheezing, toasting his health in both languages.

Allegretti seized him by the hair. With his other hand he thrust open his jaws and put the bottle in his mouth.

"Now let them say we're inhuman!" the colonel exclaimed.

The brandy gurgled and Malic's famished body jerked and shrank. He fell flat on his face in the dust. The commandant took the child from Peduto and, singing "*Giovinezza*," led the mob across the square.

The general is coming from the south. His mouth was full

of blood and brandy. *The arch of triumph and the streets full of shit.* He realized he was disgraced, they had made him drunk. *The crazy Slavs* and *Long live my second fatherland.* The colonel's hands were soft and moist. The mob was swaying and laughing; all of it lost in the vague mist of drunkenness. Salvatore Paolone stood upright in the bitter darkness.

CHAPTER 3

MALIC STRUGGLED to get to his feet. He flailed his arms, tried to prop himself on his knees, but collapsed again. He looked around. The sun was so bright that he could see nothing.

"We should help him," Salvatore said to Augusto, wiping the tears on his sleeves. "You take one side and I'll take the other."

"He'll manage," Napolitano said.

Malic spread his arms wide in another attempt to get off the ground, but this time landed on his forehead and sobbed violently.

"Stop sniveling," Augusto said to Salvatore.

"I've got to do something," Salvatore said. "I've watched him lying there for two days."

"Well, you suffer too," Augusto said.

"I'm different, I dream. And that's something."

"Always the same dream?"

"No! I have a clean shirt and Dana is well again, and she doesn't crawl on all fours. She stands up straight and says it's hot and it would be nice to have some rain. I kiss her filthy hands and she seems more beautiful than ever."

"Do you sing to her?"

"No. I've no voice. But I love singing and make up words: my village is waiting for me, I see my mother and sister, I am free of weapons for the rest of my life. That's my favorite."

"I could arrest you for singing that song."

"I'm already arrested. Look at me and this tank: the tracks are full of shit and so am I."

Malic turned on his back and muttered something. A spasm twisted his lips.

"Augusto, why do the bells ring so often? People can't be dying all day long?"

"The bellringer is drunk. He has a few drinks, runs up to the belfry, and rings."

"But is he allowed to?"

"You're a bore, Paolone. Shut up."

"You're right, Augusto, but things aren't easy. Imagine: two weeks without being relieved."

"Always the same, Paolone."

Malic beckoned to them.

"Who made me drunk?" Malic whispered, his eyes still closed. "I thought it was night. Full of stars."

"It is night," Augusto said, "a dark, cloudy night."

"What is shining then?"

"The moon."

"I always thought the moon was cold."

"We're freezing."

"Is my writing still up there, on the door?"

"Of course," Augusto said. "But hardly anybody stops to read it. People just laugh."

Malic groaned, shaking his fist in the dust.

"Signor Colonel has been here twice this morning," Salvatore said. "He photographed you and your writing."

"Did he say anything about arresting me or hanging me?"

"No," Salvatore replied sadly. "That's too much trouble."

"*Au revoir*, gentlemen," Napolitano said, passing his finger over the guitar. "All will end well, and we'll be singing again. I'm off to get something to drink, because the general is coming. From the south."

With the guitar slung across his shoulder Napolitano staggered down the narrow street. He felt a quiet happiness. He approached the bridge and the river. He sat down by the roadside and drank. He wanted to sleep, but instead his eyes turned to the dark hills and the flame that stretched to the heavens. The air was burning. He rested his aching eyes on the mountain, where last year's snow was still white in the gulleys. He longed for its freshness.

Motorcyclists suddenly turned up from round the corner, furiously firing in all directions. Herdsmen rounded up their flocks.

The last motorcyclist came to a sudden halt. In the low sidecar, disheveled and half-naked, sat a woman. Augusto took a swig from his bottle.

"Why didn't you salute us?" the rider asked, pushing his goggles over the helmet.

Augusto lifted his bottle high.

"Is that the way to salute Blackshirts?"

"This is how I salute the whole world."

"Come here," the Blackshirt said, shutting off the engine. "I'll show you how to salute."

Augusto stepped forward. The soldier in the side seat felt the woman's breasts. Her bare arms and shoulders were blue with bruises. She giggled and threatened that if he went on pinching her she would pee. The soldier was intrigued by the idea and mercilessly tugged the tips of her breasts.

"You can't even stand up," the soldier said to Augusto, dismounting from his machine.

"Communist," the woman shouted, the soldier's hand between her legs. "He's a Communist, Roberto! Not with your fingers, Carlo! Give him hell!"

"You will salute the Blackshirts as is proper," Roberto said, and struck Augusto across the face with his whip. Augusto didn't budge; a strange smile twisted his lips. He was struck again and again. Blood streamed down his cheeks. He licked his lips. Carlo got on his knees by the sidecar and flung himself onto the woman's body.

"Maybe you are a Communist," Roberto said, and the blows

poured down on Napolitano and the pain rang through his bones. Wounds, old and new, but he didn't cry or beg for mercy.

"You just sing, don't you?" Roberto said, pushing him aside.

"Yes," Augusto answered without hesitation, his mouth full of broken teeth and blood. "Yes," he repeated, crazed with pain, "I just sing."

"Sing now!" Roberto demanded, pushing back his helmet.

Augusto was silent. Blood covered his brows and lashes. His feet astride, Roberto quivered with rage. But Augusto was no longer afraid of anything, not even the pain.

"Sing, you bastard!" Roberto yelled, kicking him on the shin.

Augusto fell on his knees and groaned.

"Good, Roberto!" the woman cried, as he swung the whip. "That's it, he must be a Communist if he won't sing!"

"Sing, Commie!" Roberto cried.

Bent double across the sidecar, Carlo was trying to catch the tips of the woman's breasts in his mouth. She kept begging Roberto to continue and Carlo to be gentle. Impaled rapidly, and not for the first time that day, upon a horn of flesh, the woman kicked her legs. She groaned and asked them both to continue.

Irritated by the human heap in the sidecar and disgusted with the blood that had soiled his whip as well as the sleeve of his tunic, Roberto screamed and kicked Augusto with his boot. Augusto fell on his back. He had never been hit so hard.

"Oh, Carlo," whispered the woman. "Oh, my crazy Carlo. Oh, *amore mio* . . . my Carlo, my *Romano* with balls of lead . . . oh, my love, no one like you! . . . Not even Roberto."

Roberto trampled Augusto, who didn't once try to defend himself: whenever he was beaten he told himself it would pass and that he would again live to sing to his heart's content. But this time it might not be easy to get back to his feet and seek out his guitar. Roberto danced on him and shouted: "Don't you know our songs, you Communist swine! Or don't you want to sing them! Eh, you . . ."

Augusto lay with arms and legs outstretched. He couldn't

see Roberto, but he wanted to tell him that he knew every song under the sun. But he couldn't move his jaw.

Roberto put a boot on his neck.

"If you don't sing '*Duce, Duce, nome benedetto*,'[1] I'll kill you! I'll strangle you, Commie! Come on, sing!"

"I can't," Augusto mumbled. "I sing only my own songs."

"Communist!" the woman screamed. "We know what their songs are like! Shoot him, Roberto! Please Roberto, shoot him! Oh, Carlo *mio*! Oh my mad *torro*, I'll have you too, Roberto, if you finish him off."

The Blackshirt leaped at Augusto, and crushed his stomach and chest.

"Sing something! Come on, stop squirming! Open your mouth! Sing, anything. . . . I can't stand looking at you like this!" Roberto shouted.

Twisting his neck, Augusto whispered:

"*Se te la rompo. . . .*"[2]

"I said he was a Communist!" the woman cried. "They are filthy! Are you finished, Carlo! Ah, my little Italian cock . . . you poor little cotton balls! Now let's have you, Roberto, but first spill his brains in the dust!"

Her breasts bare, skirts lifted, the woman's head was tilted back. She was taking a swig from a bottle and shaking. Carlo was seated on the motorcycle, looking at Augusto.

"Have you had enough?" Roberto asked, adjusting his helmet.

"I hate you," Augusto whispered. "I hate you!"

Roberto started the motorbike, and with a burst of speed, rushed right over him.

Augusto's body lay motionless. Carlo struck the woman on the neck and said the infantry were the worst soldiers in the army. Roberto said he had lost faith in the artillery too. The woman remarked that soldiers often deserted to the Communists in the

[1] Duce, Duce, oh blessed name!
[2] If I break it for you. . . .

mountains. Roberto ended their conversation by saying that this was the way to treat Communists and ran over Augusto's head and stomach at full speed. The woman screamed. Then, rapidly, the motorcycle disappeared. Augusto was alone at last.

He tried to open his eyes, but they were full of blood and dust. "Strange," he whispered, "he has broken my legs and arms and ribs and pushed my teeth down my throat, yet he had gentle almond-colored eyes. And that Carlo on top of the woman with the soft thighs and flat stomach. A jolly trio taking their pleasures on the road! Everything will be all right again. My bones will heal, and I will live to run my palm and fingers over the guitar strings again. I should think of something nice, or something that happened yesterday, think of the sun.

"A good thing too, you didn't sing what they wanted you to sing," he whispered. "No, don't ever sing '*Duce, Duce, fiore nostro bianco,*' "[3] he sobbed. "Sing your own songs. Promise me never to sing for any leader. Give me your word you will always hate that fat fool, who drives us poor little singers to glorify him."

He wanted to feel his guitar but the pain spread through his arms like a plague. The guitar was smashed, its strings lost in the dust. He thought of the mountains and the gleaming snow. And of Salvatore by the tank. "Ah, Salvatore," Augusto whispered. "Why are you here? To tell me that you haven't been relieved and that you would like to change your shirt and your skin? Go away, Salvatore, and hang onto your rifle. Don't blame the motorcyclists. Tell everybody it was an accident."

Salvatore departed, pulling the bloodstained muddy tank after him on a thin wire. A lot of soldiers and midgets followed him.

"Let that monster roll down the hill," Augusto whispered, "or it will burn your hands. And get out of my darkness! Please let me close my eyes and sleep for a long time on the white snow up there."

But the mountains and the peaceful blue sky quickly van-

[3] Duce, Duce, our white flower.

ished. He felt the hard earth heave beneath him. He felt his toes and fingers beginning to freeze and the darkness from the forests settle on his chest. His heartbeat slowed down, his throat contracted. Somebody was singing one of his songs and he wanted to weep. "Who is that man with a motorcycle wheel round his neck?" he wondered. "Pietro, throw the tire in the water and help me. Don't let the water carry me away. Don't let the fish eat me. Sing something, anything. Mother!" Augusto thought in cold darkness, "I would like to sit in your lap because I'm sick again. But I can't say your name. I have no lips. *O Bolognese, o sole!* Ah Augusto, you mustn't disturb her. Let her be. Don't ask her to lift you from the dark. And tell your friends the truth: you have never been in Bologna and the girl lives only in your songs. She doesn't exist, Bologna doesn't exist. Oh, Roberto, I want to hang onto your whip. I don't want to be felled by it."

Cattle trampled on Augusto as he lay on the road with legs outstretched and his arms twisted under him. His face was as calm as the earth. The day was hot. There was not a cloud in the sky.

CHAPTER 4

SOLDIERS WERE CLEANING up the square, whitewashing the cracked walls and old doors, the poster columns and trees. They sprinkled the cobblestones, the air. They grumbled and sweated. Everything was white. But the water went on flowing, cold and muddy. The men sang military songs as well as songs about a better future. They fought with their brooms and brushes. A few passers-by asked to be whitewashed as well. The small clouds that drifted across the sky were white too.

Meanwhile Balestra and Porta were feeding Malic macaroni, meat, and bread. Feverishly Malic swallowed everything they gave him, coughed, and asked for more. He spoke incoherently, vomited macaroni and lime, and tried to get up on his feet.

"You're white from head to foot," Salvatore told Malic as he gave him a hand. "Funny, eh? Everybody is white except for me. I'm as black as a raven. The general is coming from the south, they say, but I don't believe it. He will come from the west."

Unsure on his feet, Malic staggered down the street.

Suddenly, the commandant's plane emerged from the hills. It flew right above the rooftops, over the square, and scattered leaflets, informing the town of the general's imminent arrival. Corporal Barbagallo waved to Paolone, as he flung him a handful of colorful paper.

"Barbagallo is my friend. He never delivered my complaint to the colonel," Salvatore thought. "He is the most cunning soldier in the Italian army. He sleeps with the mullah's wife who wants another son, and he has a lovely Gypsy, who is also big with child. He's a good pilot and, before he came to Montenegro, he was in Albania, Greece, and Abyssinia. I'm nothing," Salvatore thought dryly as he watched the corporal turn the plane on its side and disappear.

"Dana must be dead," Paolone thought. "No one can find her. But I don't care any more. She probably went down into the river with the fish. I have another dream now. I don't know her name. She lives in Bologna and was once in love with Augusto and since she can't love someone who isn't there, I will take over. Her feet must be small, her knees rounded. I never really look at them because I'm in a hurry to go higher up between her thighs. That's a country to itself, broad and spacious like my Calabria! If I live long enough, I'll drag myself into that shell and stay there till the authorities pull me out by the ears. I'll beg my fat-assed angel's forgiveness that I can't sing, I will tell her stories about Augusto and make her believe he died for her sake. I'll promise her a wonderful future with lots of children. . . ."

He was distracted from his reverie by Nicola Riva, who was unbuttoning his trousers and shouting: "This is the third time

I've had gonorrhea since I came to Montenegro and the fifth time since I've been in uniform, a combination of Montenegrin-Greek or Albanian-Abyssinian!"

Balestra and Porta looked around in fear and embarrassment, but dared not move. Riva drew his revolver from its holster, looked along the barrel at his flaming penis. "I'll shoot . . . I'll kill the bastard that's robbed me of my promotion for the last two years."

The bugle was blowing: Balestra and Porta turned to go. But Lieutenant Riva gripped his cock's neck and roared: "Bring that donkey with the load of firewood over here . . . you bastards! That's the lieutenant's orders. And all the other female donkeys in the area. I'll show them how the Italian Lieutenant Nicola Riva can slaughter! Bring me anything female, on two or four legs! Today I'm going to sow love and disease! You bastards! Don't leave me on my own in the middle of the road!"

"I'm here, Signor Lieutenant," Salvatore said.

"I don't want you," Riva said flatly, returning his revolver to its holster.

"You said you didn't want to be alone," Paolone said softly. "And button up your trousers, Signor Lieutenant."

"Listen, you Calabresan bastard!" Nicola Riva roared. "Bring me Augusto's Eleanora and get lost!"

"I'd rather be relieved," Salvatore said.

"Bring her to me, you swine!"

"She belongs to me alone, Signor Lieutenant."

"Why you? Nothing is yours alone, or mine alone. Everything's everybody's."

"Augusto and I were good friends. We shared good and evil. Eleanora belongs to me! And I ask you, Signor Lieutenant, to promise me . . ."

"You are mad."

"I beg you not to touch her!"

"I'll not touch anyone and I won't promise anything, but I order you to stop sniveling."

"If you touch her, I'll tear your throat out with my teeth! I'll drink your blood. Do you hear, Signor Lieutenant!"

Nicola Riva stood still on the road, his eyes glazed, his jaws set. The soldiers carefully whitewashed him from head to foot.

CHAPTER 5

"BRAVO!"

The military police desperately tried to disperse an angry crowd that had gathered in the square, as a bulletproof car, surrounded by motorcyclists and a personal escort, roared into town. A dozen leather cases were carefully tied up on the roof. They bore labels from hotels in Nice, Monte Carlo, and Biarritz. The dust and the wind raised the branches that camouflaged this steel monster, and revealed skis and ski poles, a sporting gun in a cover made of fine leather, and some fishing tackle. The car moved on, hooting wildly.

"*Bravo!*"

Suddenly the music died down and the crowd fell silent. Some fifteen photo reporters pushed their way through the crowd. The car came to a halt. The general jumped out like a puppet, and struck up a pose. The cameras promptly recorded the gleam of his false teeth and the white glove with which he saluted. Colonel Allegretti returned the salute cordially, the high-ranking officers shook hands and grimaced appropriately. They engaged in conversation, looking straight at the cameras. They turned to inspect the guard of honor and the music boomed again.

Salvatore climbed onto the mantle of the tank. Viewed from above, the general appeared much smaller: his neck was wrinkled, his chest narrow. Notwithstanding his ribbons and decorations he was nervous. A white stallion trotting in front of them docked its tail, raised its member, whinnied, and grazed the earth with its silver mane. The general paused in brief embarrassment but, like a good actor, recovered his composure quickly, grabbed the saddlebow, and put a foot in the stirrup. The cameras clicked and, once more, he showed his regular teeth, but didn't mount. He merely raised his right boot to the stallion's flanks. Then he quickly crossed to the other side and tried again. This time the boot reached almost to the stallion's crupper. The great commander remained in this position for a moment, then leaped lightly to the ground, turned to the crowd, and said something. The stallion was led off and the general and the colonel began their inspection.

The general was a man of about fifty, with good-looking eyes and a thin mustache under his Roman nose. He marched in front of the company, trying to look vigorous, carefully brushing the dust from his shoulders.

Major Peduto made his report and joined the general and the colonel. He raised his gloved hand. Everyone followed the gesture. The three commanders saluted the company that roared: "Long live Italy and her invincible power! Long live the unbreakable brotherhood of the great Italy and gallant little Montenegro!"

A group of local people, some thirty of them whitewashed from head to foot, raised their white hands and shouted greetings to the general. There were a few merchants and craftsmen among them, but for the most part they were tramps and idlers who hung around the barracks. One was a procurer, one a thief. The thin one, with a head like a horse's, was Mustafa Agic's favorite spy. He had seven children. Facing the sun and shouting to a point of exhaustion, they stood still, the whitewash dripping from their jaws and their raised fists.

Duce, Duce, chi non sapre morir . . .
Quando tu lo vuoi, gagliardetti al vento, tutti, verremo a te.[1]

[1] Duce, the eternal Duce . . .
We shall come at your call, with banners waving.

From the nearby hills came the roar of guns. Red grenades exploded on all sides. The sky rocked; the earth cracked. The bells of the Orthodox church announced the arrival of the guest of honor. The mosque had been whitewashed and decorated right up to the tip of its crescent moon. People opened their windows and showered the general with flowers.

"Only in Sicily have I had such a welcome," the general said, saluting the whitened rank of men, "and that was many, many years ago."

"They love the army and its weapons," the colonel said. "In fact, they're a lot like the Italians."

The companies filed past them in full battle order.

"Long live our friends!"

The leader of a long line of women threw a bouquet of flowers at the general's feet. She was a huge woman, with a mustache and whitewashed down to her waist. High over her head she held the Italian flag. Next in line was a short-necked girl, carrying the Montenegrin flag on a long pole and singing the "*Giovinezza*." The seventh and eighth were twins in Moslem trousers, their heads bound in embroidered scarves. The general was impressed by their thick braids, decorated with false jewels and Italian coins.

"Long live our friends!" cried the monster at the head of the procession, and her companions took up the cry. "And may God and King preserve them!"

The general collided with a new column of women. A photographer aimed his camera: female faces grinning from ear to ear, a sight which made the general want to order their mouths shut. He said something, but it was lost in the shouting and applause. Some thirty women filed past, all of them whitewashed, bow-legged, ugly. Most were Gypsies: one, with a belly up to her teeth and a face black as soot, yelped: "Long live the fathers of our wonderful children!"

The pregnant women took up her cry. The dark-eyed, large-headed children joined in. Colonel Allegretti and Major Peduto caught some flowers that had been thrown to the general, and departed quietly. The general wiped the sweat from his brow with a perfumed handkerchief and asked for a glass of water.

The *Carabinieri* and the Blackshirts parted the crowd. Trampling the flowers on the whitewashed carpet, the general walked toward the rostrum. He gathered his strength, and with a couple of light steps reached the rostrum. The crowd shouted, "Long live the bravest and most lightfooted Italian commander, General of Infantry, Giovanni Besta!" The great commander smiled cunningly.

With some difficulty Major Peduto followed the general's footsteps and took his place beside him. Captain Brambilla made it after two attempts. The steps were too high and his trousers too tight. He tripped and fell into a trough of limewash. He was extricated with much effort and hoisted onto the rostrum. He groaned, shivered, and swore.

Colonel Allegretti was terrified. Standing on the bottom step and holding onto his medals, he stretched out a hand to Peduto, who pulled him up and set him next to the general. The guns boomed.

"Long live the powers of the invincible Axis!"

Accompanied by Major Peduto, the general greeted the Orthodox priest and took note of five Italian medals fixed to his black mantle. Colonel Allegretti introduced the mullah to him, who soaked his own eight medals in tears. The general addressed a few encouraging and consoling words to the transparent hierophant and caught a whiff of unwashed skin. The stiff Montenegrin in uniform squeezed the general's hand and made him squirm with pain, asked after the health of Her Majesty Queen Helena, his distant relation, tapped the general on the shoulder, and displayed his metal teeth and his recently acquired bronze medal.

Mustafa Agic fell on his knees and kissed the general's feet. The general kissed Agic's head.

As Mustafa Agic was getting to his feet, the general counted his decorations: he had thirteen.

"You've one more medal than I!" General Besta remarked, "And I have been a soldier all my life. You've got the *Medaglia d'Oro*![2] That's remarkable. Congratulations! Congratulations a thousand times!"

Agic promptly burst into tears. The music blasted. The general drew a paper from his pocket and began to read. The paper was white, the words were white, the general's tongue was white and damp.

CHAPTER 6

MALIC TRIED to pick a quarrel and provoke a few people in the street, but they whitewashed him all over again and ran to the rostrum. They carried banners of colored paper and flags.

Malic set off down the street, gnawing on a crust of bread.

It was impossible to escape from the general's whitewashed speech; it echoed in the remotest and filthiest side street.

A woman's scream made him pause. In a cellar nearby a few soldiers were smashing bottles, beating a barrel. A woman panted and swore in Italian. Malic recognized her voice and spat to one side.

"Oh, Umberto," she yelled, "you Neapolitan devil! Not there, that's my bottom . . . Not there, I've never had it there."

"That's what I want, my love," growled Umberto, breaking the junk around him.

The woman felt the flesh enter her and fell onto her belly.

"Where's the hose?" someone asked. "Where's the sheep gut? I want a drink. The gut, you cannibal!"

"My hose is busy, Franco," Umberto roared.

"You shit!" said Franco. "You southern shit! Showing off, aren't you?"

[2] The gold medal—the highest Italian decoration.

"What's his name?" Umberto asked angrily.

"Whose name?" the woman's voice asked from the darkness. "The general's?"

"Piss on the general!"

"Good idea, but what's his name? I'll hold you like this until you remember."

"OK," the woman answered from under him. "Let it come out of my mouth! It's good to be alive."

"General Giovanni Besta. *Conte di Tirano*. Piss on his title! Tirano is a piddling little town between Montenegro and Switzerland."

"I didn't know he was a *conte*. Tirano: I know where that is. When I was young I had a girl there . . . a girl like you," said Franco.

"My little gray Franco, say I'm good! If you don't, I'll never let you between my knees."

"Leave the man alone!" Umberto said.

"Franco, come here and give me your hose," the woman said. "Your old soft hose. Come on, *caro*!"

"I'm a family man," Franco said drunkenly, "and I must look after my gut. You mind your own business, child."

"I piss on you and on your stinking gut," the woman was hissing. "You worn-out old nag!"

"I am busy drinking," Franco said. "You listen to the general."

"Your general wriggles like an old whore," the woman said.

The earth and the cellar's darkness shook with the noise of gunfire.

"Darling Umberto, please! *Napolitano mio*, fill me right up and close me, beat me. I'll burst like a bomb and die. . . ."

Malic went on his way. Round the corner Branko's wife was waiting for him. She was a slender woman with tiny mustaches that quivered shyly. Holding her hands to her breasts, her skirt just barely covered her knees, her eyes burned with shame. The wind ruffled her dark hair.

"Why did you call me?"

"Important business," Malic said, taking her arm. "We've got to hide somewhere."

She walked beside him, obedient as a lamb. They entered the cellar. She asked why he was covered in whitewash.

"I am cunning," Malic said, putting his arm around her.

She huddled close to him as they sat down on the straw. On the other side of the thin wall, Umberto was wailing that he would soon be dead.

"Have you listened to the radio?" the woman asked.

"No, but I know our people are advancing rapidly, too rapidly. The war will soon be over. We're great fighters, we do everything but use our teeth!"

"If they were all like you, the war would be over in no time," the woman said sarcastically.

"You are wrong," Malic said. "I am a great fighter, a Spanish revolutionary."

"Why are you here?"

"Special duties, espionage and so on."

"Aren't you afraid they'll catch you?"

"It's not that simple," Malic said. "They are afraid."

"Well, you be careful."

"Why should I?" Malic said. "*They* are looking after me."

"Ah," the woman cried, falling on his breast, "I am so unhappy."

On the other side of the wall Franco was grinding his teeth. He cursed Umberto, swore, and finally threw his tunic, boots, his belt and his revolver over the wall.

"Why did you bring me here?" the woman asked softly. "It's hateful."

Malic caressed her bosom.

"They are torturing Branko in the camp," she said.

"Somebody's got to be tortured."

"Poor Branko."

"Poor Branko."

"He hasn't betrayed his comrades," the woman said.

"Of course not," Malic said. "He is a good Communist! A strong character! We're all the same, to a man!"

Malic took Franco's belt and buckled it round him, adjusted the holster and the revolver.

"If only I could go and see him," the woman said. "It would be easier. Especially for him."

Malic caressed the dark, firm tips of her bosom. The darkness in the cellar grew deeper. He lifted her skirt, she flung her head back and whispered: "Someone'll see us! . . . Oh God, I'm married! . . . I need someone to love me, a true friend. I don't know anyone in this town. Except for you. Why are you in espionage, tell me, why? I'm so hot; take everything off, that's it. I'm still too hot. There! You're so good, so hard, like a donkey, you are. That feels good. . . ."

The military music was powerful and beautiful. Both parts of the cellar were flooded with light.

"How do you spend your spare time?" the general asked, catching a bouquet of flowers with the skill of a goalkeeper.

"We don't have much time," the colonel said, "between training and political education. Political education isn't going too well. Our men are great fighters, but they're individualists. They would rather learn this strange Slavic language than study the history of our wars."

"Do they sing?"

"Oh, yes," the colonel said, wiping the sweat from his forehead. "We had a Neapolitan who was capable of corrupting an entire division with his pornographic songs."

"I'd like to hear him," the general said, jumping to catch a fresh bunch of flowers.

"Unfortunately, he committed suicide the day before yesterday," the colonel said. "His fiancée left him and he shot himself through the temple. You know what emotional people we southerners are."

"Make sure his suicide isn't interpreted politically."

"His farewell letter makes his motive clear. Generally speaking, it is best to blame such things on love."

"You're right, it's a broad field," the general said, photographing a group of pregnant girls. "What do the troops do for entertainment?"

"They're not very keen on propaganda films," the colonel said, standing in front of the general's lens. "Crime and love is the thing. Musicals too. Operas."

General Besta caught sight of a motorcycle. Marika was on it, riding with dignity in soft boots and officer's trousers, with a blue ribbon in her hair. He gazed at her oval bottom which covered the saddle. She passed by the troops, as if carrying out an inspection. Then she opened the throttle and a dense cloud of dust rose, obliterating the motionless heads and the melting helmets of the soldiers. At first she rode slowly, then fast, and then faster. She charged between the companies, testing her brakes and the power of the engine, with headlights on and the hooter blasting. Bent forward, her marvelously divided rotundities still more emphasized, she dashed up to the rostrum. The general managed to photograph only the whirling dust, a strand of flying hair, and the palpable shadow of a thigh.

"So?" the general raised his brow. "Who was that?"

"My greatest discovery," Colonel Allegretti smiled nervously.

"Her name is Marika, she is Captain Brambilla's fiancée. He is at the other end of the rostrum talking with local intellectuals. I find that she has some amazing characteristics. Major Peduto promised he would write a novel about her. In fact, she is quite phenomenal. A danger to one's health, perhaps to one's life as well."

The *padre* showed up on the rostrum, altogether unexpectedly, and shook hands with his old friend. In a state of general excitement he embraced the army chaplain as well as the mullah. The colonel was in flowers up to his neck. Major Peduto tried in vain to make an important point to the distinguished guest. The rostrum joined in the women's song: "*Tu sei la viva stella.*"[1]

The troops marched past in perfect order: the general and the colonel saluted them. The earth shook, the bayonets flashed. "*Per il Re, per il Duce, alala,*" the Blackshirts sang. The general scattered flowers over their helmets and their hunched knapsacks. Like a row of automatized puppets, the soldiers drew level with the painted women and executed a sharp turn. The dust rose thick. The general took the colonel by the arm:

"I gather some of your people write."

"Yes, Signor General, several. One composes marches and hymns exclusively. He has already written more than a thousand. I've released him from all military duties. He composes and we sing. He has no ear, though, which is unfortunate."

"Do you remember any of his lines?"

"But of course, Signor General. I know many of them by heart. Most of his songs begin and end with:

> '*O Italia, o mamma mia,*
> *Tu che conosci soltanto la vittoria.*' "[2]

Mustafa Agic brought in a bottle of brandy and a few glasses on a copper tray, but the colonel motioned him away.

"Not very impressive, Colonel, is it? Commonplace, I call it."

"But humanity is commonplace."

"True," General Besta said, "but the verses of your genius lack fresh metaphors, and depth. You know, I used to write poetry. I still do, now and again, at friends' requests. . . . Ugh, this dust! Our soldiers don't use epithets sufficiently."

"Epithets are a Communist privilege," the colonel said, feeling the general would concede the point. "You see, Signor General, I like these songs; they are factual. 'Oh Italy, you know only victory,' makes me tremble with excitement."

[1] You are the shining star.
[2] Oh Italy, my motherland,
You who only know victory.

Mustafa Agic again brought in drinks. Major Peduto reported that a group of children and a teacher from a local school wanted to pay their respects to the general and ask for his permission to name their school after him.

"You are a writer, Major," General Besta said, "aren't you?"

"Yes, Signor General."

"Prose or poetry?"

"Poetry," the major said shyly.

"The theme?"

"Man and his fate. Man and defeat."

"Not our man and our defeat?"

"Man and defeat in general, man faced with the impossibility of choice."

"Another examination of freedom?"

"Freedom's finished, of course," Major Peduto said with sincerity.

"What's left, in your opinion?"

"War and pornography. In fact they're one and the same thing. I never understood why there were two words for the one concept."

"That's a fine beard you have!"

"It's utterly pornographic, Signor General," Antonio Peduto said.

"I'm glad we've met once again. Colonel Fabiani, whom I saw in Athens three weeks ago, is a great admirer of yours. He pleaded with me to send you down there. Are there any other writers here?"

"Two people," the major said, "Adamo Balestra and Tilio Porta. There's also a *cocaro*,[3] but he's a vulgar *bel canto*. And a huge woman with a mustache, one of the locals. Her husband was killed while committing a robbery, but she gets a widow's pension as a victim of communism. She writes patriotic verses in Italian, I write pornographic poems in both languages."

"Wonderful material for a war novel," General Besta said,

[3] A peasant from the neighborhood of Rome.

flashing his eyes. "We are reforming a primitive society with our arms, our culture, and our spirit. Why not begin a novel tonight, Major?"

The major cast a gloomy eye over the crowd. The soldiers' helmets, their bayonets, and aluminum mess tins glistened in the sun. "*Salve a populo d'eroi,*"[4] sang the monstrous, pregnant women. Hungry children with spindly legs and large heads pushed their way between the ranks of green-clad soldiers. To the rear loomed a somewhat more orderly group of men and women and, still further away, a multitude of posters, banners, and a huge heap of lime. The central public lavatory, which had been built some two weeks before, was decorated with thousands of flags; so was the prison. The Duce's image was present everywhere, on walls that bulged and leaned forward like outthrust jaws, in tiny shopwindows crowded with colored paper and dead flies. The Duce frowned out of picture frames, glass-covered or simply glued to paper, open to the dust. "*Per Benito Mussolini eia, eia alala,*" echoed from the skies.

White had always made the major's eyes ache. He lowered his glance and saw Salvatore: a rough face burned to a cinder. The only signs of life were his large eyes with their Calabresan expression of surprise. Beyond the tank was Malic's saloon. "*Alala*" echoed once more; Peduto shuddered.

The general squinted and reached for his binoculars.

"What do you see, Signor General?" Peduto asked.

"New ideas everywhere, Major. Our new order. In short; a rebirth!"

Umberto and Franco were still quarreling and toasting General Besta. They splashed in puddles of brandy and threatened one another. The woman told them both they were shit—soft, flattened Italian shit that could not satisfy a simple drunken Montenegrin whore.

Malic helped Branko's wife to her feet. She shook the dust

[4] Hail, land of heroes.

and wisps of straw from her skirt and fell into his arms once again.

"They saw us," she said, sobbing. "What am I going to tell Branko? Oh, what have I done? My poor Branko, my poor boy. . . ."

"Tell him we composed leaflets," Malic said.

"He won't believe me."

"If he's a real Communist, he must believe you."

"Even so, he'll never forget this. I'll have to throw myself off the bridge."

"We'll think of something else," Malic said. "Don't cry."

"I'll go off to the right," Branko's wife said, as she crossed the cellar threshold. "You take good care of yourself."

Malic grabbed her under the arm.

"You said you'd follow me through fire and water. Now you talk of turning right. That's treason!"

He embraced her and told her he loved her almost as much as the movement, picked up a can of liquid whitewash, and set off down the sunlit street. She walked next to him, whispering she was married. Somebody would see her. Head held high and collar unfastened, Malic pushed his way through the crowd.

"What have you got there?" the woman asked. "What is it?"

"Poison!" Malic said, and marched into the square.

The band played wildly. The soldiers were singing to the Duce, the general, the colonel, and the major. The general was pleased; he reached for his binoculars and focused them on the crowd. The rostrum swayed, the mob roared: "*Italia, o mamma mia.*" The general again caught sight of Marika on her motorcycle. He twisted the ring on the binoculars and brought her rounded bottom into focus. She waved at the gathering on the rostrum.

Then he saw a man, carrying a can of whitewash, pushing his way through the crowd. People made way for him and laughed. He paused in front of a door, set down the container, drew a white five-pointed star on the door, and a hammer and sickle, and looked across at the rostrum.

"Who is that?" the general asked.

"A representative of the local opposition," the colonel replied, and told him Malic's story. The general smiled and summoned Major Peduto.

"A local hero," the major said. "His last name means *little*. He wants us to arrest him. But Signor Colonel refuses to give him the satisfaction. I am writing him up."

"Is he really worth it, Major?" the general asked.

"I have five hundred pages of notes on him," Major Peduto admitted. "I think I could spend the rest of my life writing about him."

"Such stories aren't written much these days, still less published," said the general.

"No one would dare publish what I have written," Major Peduto said.

"Why don't you write about yourself, Major? That would make more sense," concluded the general.

Going at full speed, Marika made circles round Malic and his saloon, including a company of soldiers within her perimeter. The general glanced again at the girl with gleaming teeth and long hair, and held his breath. Meanwhile, holding the woman by the hand, Malic moved to the rostrum.

"Down with traitors!" Malic cried, cutting through a company of soldiers who made no effort to stop him.

Everybody on the rostrum gathered about the general.

"Down with the betrayers of the great Montenegrin people!" Malic roared.

Both remarks were translated for the general. He asked the colonel where the girl with the motorcycle had gone. The priest was shouting and grinding his teeth. Major Peduto explained to the general that Malic was the priest's greatest enemy, and that the word communism invariably sent him into a frenzy of excitement.

In horror the general looked at the priest's bulging, bloodshot eyes. He spoke of bombs and knives and was so angry that several people had to restrain him.

"Down with fascism! Up with communism!" Malic yelled.

The white paint and flowers filled the air.

"Sounds good," the general said. "Well composed, indeed. So simple, yet so stupid and frightening."

"I'll give you a photo copy of his slogans as a souvenir, if you wish, as well as his messages and letters," said the colonel.

"I'd rather have his photograph," the general replied. "With you in it, Colonel. And you, Major."

"Thank you, General," the colonel said.

Finally Captain Brambilla, accompanied by three soldiers, marched up to Malic and ordered him to leave the woman alone. Malic swore at the woman, who burst into tears and challenged them all to combat.

"What are they doing to him, Colonel?" the general asked.

"Training him for further contests!"

The soldiers separated Malic from the woman, who never once raised her head. They held his arms but made no attempt to stop him from shouting his favorite slogans. Captain Brambilla pulled out handcuffs and skillfully locked the woman's hands.

"Take me, not her, you Fascist bastards!" Malic screamed from the depths of his belly. "I'm dangerous, not her! I'm preparing death for you, complete liquidation! Lock me up, if you dare, you Italian cannibals!"

They led the woman away and pushed Malic aside. Malic tottered and fell over, the can of limewash splashing his legs. His head struck the ground, his puny body shook. A crowd gathered around him, and broke into song.

"And that, Major, is what you call a theme," Giovanni Besta said. The major couldn't take his eyes off the small, whitewashed body. Taking the major gently by the hand, the general led him to the colonel.

"Major, write a novel about our colonel," the general said. "About the soldier who has gained yet another child in the process of reforming this wild Balkan people."

"You must be joking, Signor General," Spartaco Allegretti gasped.

"Our descendants are no joking matter, Colonel. In any case, the child was a boy. Another soldier."

"Signor General!"

"Major, why not write about me?" said the general. "Forget your enemy, let him gnaw the earth and swallow the dust. Just this once, Major, I beg you, leave him alone. Gentlemen, don't you think our time will be known as the time of glory?"

"The time of glory or the time of shame," the major thought. "The time of Italian lies and Italian horror."

In the major's eyes the whiteness turned to black dust. He glanced once again at the flattened figure of the Montenegrin hero. A sluggish breeze blew over his head.

Salvatore Paolone could hardly keep on his feet. "You mustn't collapse," he thought, "the general will see you." The ground disappeared from under him. He fell into the dust by the tank.

The general took a bottle from Colonel Allegretti and had a drink. Everyone on the rostrum applauded. Except for the priest. His hand was on his heart. A grenade was concealed in his bosom. The general greeted mankind, the surrounding hills, the burning sky, and the mob that shouted "Long live the brave and handsome son of eternal Italy." Moved by the noise and the echo of the Orthodox bells, the general pulled out his revolver and fired into the sky.

Leaning on his elbows, Salvatore shivered. His tank moved, shook the dirt off, and skidded to the left.

To the accompaniment of trumpets and the beat of drums, the general descended from the rostrum. Dust and the flowers were up to his knees. Supporting himself as if wading in a fast-flowing river, he made his way through the crowd. The general spotted Malic and said. "Montenegrins are indeed a strange people!"

"They are brave too," the colonel said.

"That is how they are like us," the general remarked, wiping his forehead with a handkerchief.

"Bravery is their basic complex, Signor General," the colonel went on, watching Malic's body shaking with tears. "They have a love of glory that I find irritating. To Major Peduto, they are like the ancient Greeks."

"They fight, by God," Peduto said. "And they die like flies. They're typical Slavs."

"Crazy Slavs!" the colonel laughed.

Salvatore saw the tank run over Malic. No one defended the small man as the tank revolved on its axis several times, burying him in the dust. The steel monster turned around, dispersing the soldiers like withered stalks of maize. Malic groaned. Someone told him to be silent or go home.

"This brandy is beginning to go to my head," the general remarked jokingly. "Colonel," he added, "Order my compass and maps brought here. I should know exactly where I am. Bring the barometer too. From the blue case. Ugh, this brandy. I'm beginning to understand why they're so brave."

Corporal Barbagallo speedily returned from the general's car. "The blue case, Signor Colonel, is full of the finest quality women's underwear . . ."

"Shut up, you fool," the colonel said. "Take two sets and get lost."

"I've already done so, Colonel," Corporal Barbagallo reported.

"The compass and maps must be in the green case," the colonel said.

"I'm delighted to have met you again, Major," the general said. "Your views on the war, of course, don't please me. But the writing on our provocateur's saloon is brilliant. By the way, why not introduce him to me?"

Still unable to get to his feet and take refuge in the shade, Salvatore saw the tank effortlessly climb on top of the general's horse. The steel insect turned in the saddle and snorted at headquarters. It leveled the sentry and his bayonet to the ground and struck the wall. The building shook, but withstood the blow. With the agility of a beetle, the tank climbed over the wall, smashing window frames, grinding glass. Its gunbarrel, bent by the heat, broke down telephone wires, tore the rotting flags, combed through the lime trees and pines. It crawled over the roof like a child, hurling a shower of slates. For a moment it hid the sun, casting a brief but cool shadow. It set off across the roofs, bridging the gaps between the houses as if they were holes in the earth.

Salvatore heard shouts and concluded that the general and his escort were close by. He wanted to die. "They'll shoot me anyway," he thought, "because I let my tank go." With a tremendous effort he raised his head and saw several people standing over him and laughing.

His head spun. They sprinkled him with flowers and once more he fell on his face. "I'll suffocate," he whispered, and dug his teeth into the earth.

The general put his boot on Salvatore's hand. Salvatore felt a sharp pain, but remained motionless under the flowers. The general crushed the fingers of the hand. Salvatore grit his teeth, as bouquets of flowers heaped higher and higher on his shoulders.

"You said something about thefts, Colonel?"

"Yes, Signor General. As the war draws to its end there's more stealing than ever."

"A medieval custom."

"Our army is worse than the local population."

"Southerners again," the general said.

"On the contrary, our worst thieves are from the north," the colonel remarked respectfully. "They have a gangleader."

"A gangleader?" the general stuttered. "Unheard of! Arrest that maniac who's written a thousand hymns. When I was a boy

I had a friend who wrote poetry. He was an incurable kleptomaniac. Arrest anybody else who writes. Including the woman with the mustache. Before dark I want to see them all in handcuffs. Every single poet, except for Major Peduto."

The general moved off.

Salvatore raised his head from the flowers. The tank was on its way back. Jammed with telephone wires, cables, and weeds, its caterpillars came to rest. Salvatore whispered: "Thank God you've come back!"

The songs continued unabated, the companies continued marching. The soldiers' faces were vacant.

"They've been marching a long time," the general said. "Perhaps they should be dismissed."

"Oh, no," the colonel objected. "They like it. They love it!"

Salvatore drew himself up with difficulty. As he was slinging his rifle over his shoulder he thought he saw his bayonet growing. It glowed like a stem of Calabresan wheat. He resumed his position by the tank. "If the general came by again, I'd ask him for a little water," he thought. "My relief must come soon. I don't want to disgrace myself in front of the general. I'll stand at attention, salute him, and request a clean shirt," he concluded, tapping his feet on the burning flowers.

The white rostrum collapsed under the weight of the flowers, the heat, and the dust. The companies were leaving the square. Their place was taken by beggars and whitewashed women. Children shouted and sang in Italian. Grabbing him by his arms and legs, several people dragged Malic to his saloon. They flung him down in front of the door with the star and the hammer and sickle on it.

The general was fiddling with his camera. He photographed Malic's saloon, first from a distance, then a closeup of the star and the inscription in red. Malic covered his face with his hands and wept. Colonel Allegretti and Major Peduto were by his side. The weakened and exhausted body was ready to drop but they kept propping it up, removing his hands from his face and pushing the hair from his forehead. They tidied his shirt and his tunic, adjusted his Spanish revolver. The general's swift camera caught every movement.

Suddenly Marika and her motorcycle entered the general's picture, as if driven by the wind. For the first time he smiled. She returned his greeting with a flash of teeth. Colonel Allegretti squeezed her shoulders and frowned. Major Peduto, noting the colonel's jealousy and the general's blushes, laughed softly.

"Would you like to be photographed, young lady?" the general asked, looking at her over his camera.

"Yes, but not here," the girl said, passing her long fingers through her hair.

The general looked into her damp bosom and down the rift of her breasts. He fixed in his memory the freckles on her neck, the provocative smile on her upper lip, and the dimple in her cheek.

"Where?" he asked.

The general got into the sidecar of Marika's motorcycle.

"Spartaco," Marika said. "Come on, join us. But no room at all for you, Antonio."

Colonel Allegretti sat behind the girl and caught her round the waist. Marika opened the throttle and dashed across the square. They flew past the armored car. The general caught sight of his suitcases and thought he might be robbed. Spartaco shouted: "Long live the Axis powers, Italian motorcycles, and Montenegrin women!"

"Let's go to the country!" Marika cried. "We've got blankets!"

"To the country!" echoed the general. "If it isn't full of Communists."

Major Peduto released Malic from his arms, letting him fall again into the dust. Marika's motorcycle disappeared round a corner. The major looked at the bloodstained Malic and went to the fountain: his own arms were filthy to the elbows. He paused: it was a waste of time to wash his arms. He looked about him: the day was hot, the square utterly comic.

Part Five

CHAPTER 1

GENERAL BESTA laughed. Bravery and heroism bored him to death. Marika placed him on the bed and undressed him, as she had done the day before. The general first miaoued and then surrendered.

Marika leaped on top of him, seized him by the groin. Through half-closed eyes, the general looked at her smooth, firm body. A shiver went through him as she kissed his naked chest and stomach. He abandoned himself to the afternoon heat and her skilled hands, lacking the strength to embrace her, or draw her close. He gazed up at her, mumbling a few hurriedly learned Serbian phrases.

"Nanni, my only Nanni, tell me we'll never part," she said.

"You have guessed my thoughts," the general said. "Beautiful. That's just what I was thinking."

"Only death do us part."

"Not even that," the general said, stroking the points of her breasts.

"We'll have lots of children. At least five sons."

"More, darling."

Marika thrust his arms aside and lay across him. Her long, perfumed hair covered his face. Firm and oval, she rolled on top of him, biting his lips and his ears. The general imitated a tomcat and rubbed himself against her flanks.

"What worries me is that you agree to everything," the girl said, tickling him under the navel. "My little naked, Italian snail, are you sure you're not a fraud? Tell me, Nanni."

"But I am!" General Besta said with feeling. "A real Italian fraud, my love!"

"You always agree to everything?"

"I'm in no position not to give my word," the general whispered. "It's my second favorite weakness," he miaoued.

"What is your first?"

"Catching butterflies."

"What about the promises you made the day before yesterday, the day we fell in love. . . . Are you going to keep your word?"

"Oh, I do love you, my savage princess. You smell of the woods and the ferns and the moss . . . oh, my princess!"

"I'm no princess, I am Marika," the girl said, pulling him by the ear. "Forget the moss and the ferns. We were talking about promises."

"I'll try to keep my word, because I'm an Italian, and a high-ranking officer to boot. We'll have lots of children. Why not? Five, six, ten! Who cares? Yes, you can give them any names you like, Montenegrin, Italian, Japanese. I can't tell the difference between day and night anymore. This war, you know. All I can think of now is your scented bosom."

"I've never seen so many suitcases before. You must be very rich, *primitivo*. Look: eleven of them!"

"Military matters," Giovanni Besta said. "I have eleven more. They're still in Albania, in Tirano. One doesn't go to war empty-handed."

"How wonderful to meet a soldier with so many beautiful, unnecessary things. Those skis and the net for killing butterflies."

"Not for killing butterflies. For catching them. I must tell you that your *primitivo*, I like your calling me that, your Nanni is a remarkable man. I'm like a rare butterfly which, to the joy of us entomologists, still exists in certain places. I'm probably the only general in the world who . . . how warm you are and how happy I am under you!"

"Let's have a little ride," the girl said, taking him by his soft neck. "Who'll ride whom?"

"You me, of course," said the general. "It's tiring and puts one under an obligation."

General Besta was on the floor. Marika mounted him. He set off on all fours. She caressed his neck, pulled his ears, and giggled.

"You're divine, unforgettable," the general said. "You ride wonderfully, you have a lovely damp, swollen froggy. I feel it on my neck. Oh, what a country! What a people!"

"I've never ridden a general."

"And you won't again. Other generals ride only round their headquarters or through public squares."

"The minute I saw you I knew I was going to ride you," Marika said.

"How?"

"I don't know, but . . . but I felt it. You are a real Italian, and a general too. With you one can do anything. Any other Italian in this position would start talking about his conquests and exploits."

"What would our Spartaco say?"

"He'd kill himself," the girl said, "or somebody else. But I'm so much in love with you. Love knows no shame. Right, Nanni?"

"True. And what would Major Peduto say?"

"War, glory, and pornography are finally together in one place! 'Long live everlasting warm and perverted Italy!' "

"Idiot," the general said. "A nice idiot."

The girl ordered him to carry her to the window. The general pretended he had not heard her. His neck was hot and wet and he wanted to go back to bed. The girl kicked him. The general set off unwillingly. At the window she ordered him to raise himself a little.

"What's happening on the square?" the general asked.

"Major Peduto," Marika cried, pushing aside the curtains. "He really is wonderful, my *pazzerello russo*, my Antonio! He is standing in the middle of the square, by the spring, laughing like a madman. He's spreading those wicked hands of his. *Dio mio*, he'll burst."

"A writer," the general said contemptuously. "He has a beard too! Hm! I would send them all to Africa, to the Abyssinians! Let them laugh there. And then they could leave us in peace!"

"He's still laughing, *primitivo*. Oh, *che matto*!"

"I must tell him he has been made a colonel. That will really make him laugh. The cretin! The fool!"

"They say he's brave, that when he charges he sings."

"Brave or just mad?"

"Brave," the girl said, caressing him. "You're a great people."

"Great nations never charge. That's for savages. For maniacs. I'm sick of heroes and heroism! I'm beginning to shiver. Cuddle me, my love. Who else is there?"

"Malic," Marika said. "*Compagno* Malic. He's greeting people and embracing them. He has a revolver. Look!"

"He is marvelous," the general said.

"He has two revolvers," Marika said. "Like you, *primitivo*! Aren't you men funny, sometimes!"

"Perhaps Peduto is laughing at him," the general commented.

"No," Marika said, "he's laughing at himself. He often does that."

"Take me to bed," the general said weakly.

"First you must shout 'Long live Italy!' Come on, *primitivo*, shout!"

"I can't," the general said, "I'll choke."

"Long live the great Italian people that knows only victory! Go on, shout. I want to hear you say the word victory!"

"What victory!"

"Go on, shout!"

"I will not. The Russians are advancing like madmen, the English and Americans too. Madmen! They never rest, do they? We are finished. We might just as well have a good time."

"It's impossible to conquer Italy," Marika said sincerely.

"Let's go to bed," the general pleaded. "And please don't bring up that soldier by the tank again. He'll get his relief. He is a soldier. Let him wait!"

Marika caressed him all over. Blood rushed to his temples.

"Tell me, Nanni, that no woman has ever ridden you before," Marika begged.

"I'd like to, but I can't. An Albanian woman rode me early this spring. But she had her head shaved and was ugly."

"I'll die of jealousy!" Marika blurted, stretching herself next to him. "Not an Albanian! A greasy Moslem! I've been deceived and shamed and betrayed!"

She covered her face and pretended to cry. He looked at her and decided he had never seen such a beautiful female body before.

"My Nanni, kiss me all over, if you wish me to forget that horrible Moslem. Everywhere, my little Italian snail, the father of my child. Come . . . I'll die if you don't."

General Besta drew out from under his pillow a flat gold cigarette case, a gift from his mother for his twentieth birthday, opened it, and extracted a soft, rubber appliance from the talc. Swiftly and skillfully he fitted it over his tongue and pressed his cheek against Marika's groin. The girl shivered, feeling the man's breath at her openings.

The day was hot. Her body lay still.

Major Peduto got up from the dust. He waved his hand and told Salvatore that he had brought a tortoise from Greece that was suffering from starvation.

Salvatore pointed to his bayonet, which continued to grow. He looked at the major respectfully, but said he had not understood the metaphor. Peduto promised him relief. The soldier spread his arms. His rifle was seven and a half yards long and still growing.

CHAPTER 2

MALIC PACKED all the grenades that he had bought that morning into a large military haversack. He wrapped the revolvers up in old Italian newspapers and the cartridges in some linen. "This is all I can carry", he decided, hoisting the pack with difficulty.

He opened a couple of windows. The saloon was full of flies, dust, and pornography. "I must get away from here," he said to himself, wiping the sweat from his forehead. "I will return with the Communist troops."

As he was carefully checking the sack with grenades, the comrades from the movement came in. "Shut the window. We must not be seen," the fat one barked.

"We are being followed again," the red-haired one said, locking the door.

"They can't touch us," Malic said. "We will fight. This sack is full of weapons. We will fight like true Communists."

The fat one waved his hand in a gesture of disdain.

Malic closed the shutters.

"You were good the other day," the fat one said, "a true revolutionary, as the saying goes!"

"I'll do better still, comrades," Malic said. "I am working hard," he added, pointing to the sack. "Thirty bombs and five revolvers. The rest is ammunition. Some medicine too. I'm leaving this afternoon, tomorrow at the latest."

"We know," the fat one said. "The whole town knows, in fact."

"Are they angry?" Malic asked.

"Some are and some aren't," the redhead said.

"What's the attitude of the army?"

"One can never tell," said the fat one. "The Fascists are cunning. They'll do what they can to stop you."

Malic looked at the hunched, red-haired man, who nodded.

"They may shoot. The exits have been blocked since this morning, and the guards have been reinforced. Agents are everywhere."

"At last!" Malic was ecstatic. "I give you my Communist word of honor that I will fight to the last drop of blood!"

"Not so loud," the redhead said. "Don't forget we need revolutionaries now more than ever. We don't want you killed."

"But we must win," Malic said.

"Victory will come of its own accord. First we've got to stay alive."

"I don't want to stay alive!" Malic flared. "The battle calls us, comrades!"

"The movement wants you to stay in this town. You must go on collecting money. The movement needs money, Comrade Malic!"

"Life here is unbearable," Malic said.

"And who will look after the underground?"

"You, comrades," Malic said, his eyes full of fire.

The two men looked at one another in surprise.

"We trust you're not going to leave the movement without a contribution? You can't go away and leave us at the mercy of the Fascists!"

"This is all I have, comrades," Malic said, drawing a large wad of bills from his inner pocket. "I gave you my silver the other night."

"To whom?" the redhead almost jumped, "Are you sure it wasn't a Fascist provocateur? They'll stop at nothing to impoverish the movement. Who was it?"

"Several comrades from the 500th Montenegrin Division,"

Malic said softly. "Two men and a lady who sang our battle songs till late into the night. We all got drunk. I gave them everything. They are now waiting for me out there in the liberated territory."

"Still, how could you give them everything?" the fat one banged the table heavily.

"They told me the movement was in a crisis and that the needs of the proletariat were great. I asked them about you. They roared with laughter and said you were from another party cell. We all got drunk."

"You are still drunk," the fat one said.

"Yes, I am," Malic said, "with joy. I shall soon be crossing into liberated territory. Come, comrades, take half of these bills!"

The redhead took half the wad. He was obviously upset. Malic offered them each a packet of contraceptives.

"How dare you?"

"It may be useful. Mankind is full of infections," said Malic.

He accompanied them to the door. They didn't bother to shake hands.

"I'm going," Malic said, fastening his pack. "The Italians have finally understood that I am dangerous. Just let them point their rifles at me and blood will flow in rivers! They will never take me alive! I must go. If I put off my flight till tomorrow, they'll forget about me again."

Malic shouldered his pack and walked off, leaving the door wide open. No one was in the streets as he walked to the mosque. The mullah was proclaiming the onset of the evening hour.

He caught sight of Captain Fioravanti, standing in the middle of the square. A drunk and disheveled prostitute was smacking his face. He made no attempt to defend himself, unaware of what was taking place.

"The child is yours! Yours! You Mussolini bastard, you monster! . . . Swine, Fascist pig! I'll spill your drunken brains if you don't admit it's yours!"

"Where are you going?" Salvatore asked Malic.

"To join the Partisans."

"Join the Partisans? God! Now, in broad daylight?"

"Yes," Malic said." That's the whole point!"

"Don't you know that all points of exit were mined?" the soldier asked. "Except for one. I don't know exactly where it is. If you wait till dark, I'll tell you. I don't want to see you killed. You're innocent."

"In this town and in all of Montenegro, there's no man more guilty than I," Malic said proudly. "I will rush the main exit. Let them shoot if they dare!"

"They will shoot."

"What do you think I've got in this bag, Salvatore?"

"Food. And water."

"Grenades!" Malic said, hoping everybody would hear him. "Grenades!"

"O *mamma mia!*" Salvatore wailed. "What if they all exploded on your back?"

"Goodbye, Salvatore, go on guarding your tank until I get to the top of the mountain. I won't miss, Communists never do."

"We'll never see each other again," Salvatore said. "Never! I feel it . . . think kindly of me and forgive me."

Malic looked at Salvatore's thin face and his large, sick eyes under the helmet, shouldered his pack, and waved.

Salvatore was alone again. A dense cloud of dust and stench screened him from passers-by.

"Where are you going?" Mustafa Agic asked Malic.

"To the Partisans," Malic replied. "The load I'm carrying isn't a pile of newspapers either. Grenades and revolvers."

"If you see our Dojcilo," said an old man.

"What Dojcilo?"

"Dojcilo, you remember Dojcilo. He spent a lot of money in your saloon."

"He is probably just an ordinary Partisan. I am going to the headquarters of the 501st Montenegrin Division."

"Straight to the headquarters!" exclaimed the old man. "How's that? He's been in the woods for eleven months and I'll bet he has never seen the headquarters."

"Well, there's a big difference between an ordinary Partisan and engaging in espionage," Malic said. "There's even a rank waiting for me up there," he added, pointing to the snow-covered peaks.

"Tell him to come back," an old woman begged. "They said at the headquarters his crime wasn't serious. They won't punish him or anything. If he doesn't come back, his wife'll run away with the colonel's pilot. He knows him well: they used to do business together. She tries to speak Italian, even with us! I beg you, Malic, like a son, I beg you tell him to come home."

Other mothers and fathers followed Malic. They gave him messages, asked him to take letters, confided methods of code-writing.

"He is going to the main exit," someone whispered in admiration.

"This is a trap, a swindle!"

"Maybe it's just a provocation?"

"Everything is a provocation!"

By now a mob of people was following Malic. The wooden bridge in the distance was guarded by soldiers in full battle gear. Several Blackshirts stood by, looking down the barrels of their camouflaged machine guns. A prickly calm reigned on the bridge.

"They say he will jump the barbed wire."

"Impossible!"

"He may!"

"The weapons in his pack are too heavy."

"They will kill him!"

"He is a hero!"

Suddenly Malic stepped off the road. Actually, Balestra and Porta had pulled him into a patch of beans. Covered with foliage, Malic unbuttoned his trousers and pissed on a few pumpkins.

"They're after us," Porta said. "The patrols are looking for us again."

"They beat us with canes and with wet ropes too," Balestra added.

"Soldiers beat us with anything they could lay hands on. At the end of the ranks the general was waiting for us, General Giovanni Besta. He spat on us. 'Poets!' he cried, 'Artists! Scum!' He pulled us by the ears and said we were shit-eaters who should be hung by the testicles. He had us beaten with dung-covered hoes. This was really bad. Stinks too."

"What are you going to do?"

"Preserve the pride of poets," Porta said.

"Living off grass, roots, and cucumbers, we shall wait for the capitulation. Do you have any bread?"

"No, just weapons," Malic said. "A grenade each?"

"No, thank you," Balestra said. "We threw our own weapons away. We will never shoot at humanity again."

"That's what I want to do now," Malic said, "and to defend mankind as well, shoot straight at fascism."

"Good," Porta said.

"But be careful up there in the mountains with all those wild animals," said Balestra.

Malic waved to them and went back to the road. Casting a provocative glance at the crowd, he buttoned up his wide army trousers.

"A truly brave man!"

"A true Communist! They say sometimes they don't bother to button up their trousers at all!"

"They may not have any, naked beggars!"

"Poor Malic!"

Malic approached the bridge and the thick fence of barbed wire and dense weeds. On both sides of the wire there were army motorcycles and trucks with machine guns protruding from them. All weapons were aimed at Malic.

Malic stepped onto the bridge. The crowd grew silent. A donkey heehawed. Malic shuddered. He remembered the time he thought he was losing his human form. The donkey heehawed again. Malic wanted to choke it and hurl it into the stream.

He saw nothing but bayonets and helmets. He feared nothing. Machine-gun barrels peeped from the ridiculous bunkers. Malic clenched his jaw, breathed more quickly, gathering his strength. Mustafa Agic's forefinger slipped to the trigger, while other barrels were swung in Malic's direction. Malic adjusted the pack on his back and switched Franco's revolver from his hip to his groin. Still nobody approached him. He was tired. The fence was high and dense, and the pack hot and heavy. Pain had curled his lips. Again Malic saw the scabby donkey and banged his fist on the white-painted fence.

At that point Major Peduto suddenly emerged from the mass of uniforms. Laughing nervously, he lifted the barrier and said: "Signor Colonel Allegretti has granted you permission to leave unharmed! Italy grants you your life this time! The glorious and eternal Italy does not desire. . . . Oh, my excellent and ridiculous country . . . wonderful country! . . ."

The mob groaned. Some cursed Italian softness. Mustafa Agic struck himself on the forehead and swore. Pleased to have avoided bloodshed, soldiers banged on their aluminum mess tins, on the machine-gun barrels, on helmets. The Blackshirts sang "*Duce, Duce pace noi vogliam*"[1] in powerful voices.

Raising the barrier, Peduto added loudly: "Both General Besta and Colonel Allegretti congratulate you on the rank which awaits you at the headquarters of the 501st Montenegrin army! I too congratulate you, my friend! Write to me as soon as you reach your destination, Comrade Malic. Look at me! Honor me with a glance!"

Malic reached the middle of the bridge, and then looked back. The gunbarrels retracted like snail's horns. He took another look at the noisy crowd and felt sad. He heard a donkey

[1] Duce, Duce, we want peace.

braying and once again he thought he had a tail, hoofs, and a speckled belly full of grass and Italian flags.

Darkness was decending gradually. The mob was grumbling against Italy and her easygoing laws, and Peduto was screaming: "Bastards! Rats! Go home! Or to work! Or to bars! But let him be, you sons of whores! Clear out or I'll order you shot!"

The crowd now fled headlong, knocking down fences, trampling gardens. Peduto waved his revolver and laughed.

He glanced at the bridge. Malic was still there, bent double under the heavy pack. "I don't want anything to happen to my most cherished metaphor," Peduto thought. "Malic must go on living to stun this stupid pornographic humanity. I will save him from destruction with my notebook."

He couldn't take his eyes from the fragile figure that was leaving the bridge. "We'll never be parted, you and I. We are two sides of the same misfortune! Still it would be nice if you turned your head back to look at me."

CHAPTER 3

MALIC REACHED the river and looked back. The darkness had gathered about the bridge and the white barrier. The crowd had dispersed. The echo of obscene songs mingled with the sound of the stream. Darkness had enveloped the arches of the rickety little wooden bridge and the last reflections of the tormented day had faded. He heard someone calling him. He turned off the road and saw a man in the bushes. A wounded man. He asked Malic to bend down.

"Can I trust you?" the peasant asked.

"Why shouldn't you?" Malic said. "When were you wounded?"

"Last night," the peasant said, showing a few large teeth.

"We were mining the bridge. Two of us fell into the river. I can't understand why they didn't find me."

"Can I help?" Malic asked. "Are you still bleeding?"

"I bandaged myself up with rags. I'll lose my legs to above the knees. Still there'll be something left. Legs aren't all that important. My arms are all right. My eyes too!"

"Tell me what to do," Malic said, seeing the peasant's broken, crumpled legs.

The peasant propped himself up a little. "Can you see the bridge? Good. And the approaches? Very good. On our side, by that white stone on the road, there is a fuse that has to be lit. That will show them. The foul Italian dogs! Oh, God, it hurts!"

Malic set off. The peasant warned him to be careful, but Malic paid no attention and went straight up to the white stone. The peasant waved a massive arm and vanished into the darkness.

For several seconds Malic looked up at the broad, ugly bridge that linked the steep banks and the helmeted soldiers marching up and down in boredom. Below the river was in a hurry, carrying its noise and foam away into the darkness. Malic swore at the sentries who were passing one another indolently. He thought of his saloon and of Major Peduto and of Colonel Allegretti and of the general and Captain Brambilla. He was seized with fury. He spotted the end of the cord in the sunbaked grass and shuddered with excitement. He thought of the peasant with his drooping mustaches and smashed knees, and put a flame to the cord.

The writhing flame vanished in the grass. Malic was afraid the cord had been broken and that the flame would not reach the dynamite. He adjusted the sack on his back. The skeleton of the bridge and the noisy surface of the water were suddenly lit up. Beams and planks flew into the flaming sky, obliterating the stars and the steep riverbanks. A dense darkness descended on Malic's eyes.

He was brought to his feet by the searchlights, great jets of light that came from all sides from the concrete bunkers, from the clusters of barbed wire, from the sky. They lit up the unsightly ribs of the bridge, the icy foam of the river, and crossed on Malic's forehead. Blinded, he walked along the road. Heavy machine guns hammered, bullets crossed above his head, but he was radiant with happiness. "You Italian bastards, you can't kill me! You foreign shit, you green lizards, I'll destroy all your bridges . . ."

A shell knocked him down. He stopped to swear and threaten. The shells continued to burst. He was covered with earth. He thought he had been hit and was delighted.

He shook the earth off, realized he was unhurt, and felt disappointed. The searchlights combed through the bushes and the steep bank that led down to the river. He wanted to stand up and march along the road straight into the machine-gun barrels. Then he heard the peasant's rough voice: "This way! Crouch down, I tell you! You will get killed, you fool! Quick!"

Followed by a swarm of bullets, Malic crawled into the bushes.

"Let me embrace you. Look, no bridge! I don't mind dying now. Oh, the pain! Both my knees are smashed to bits!"

"I won't let you die," Malic sobbed. "I won't let the Fascist dogs kill you! I want you to live. Open your eyes! Please! I'll carry you away from here!"

"I am heavy," the peasant groaned. "You are small and weak. Leave me and run. Go on, do as I ask. We need people today more than ever."

"They don't need me," Malic said.

"Yes, even you. Everybody. Large and small."

The bursts of gunfire grew more frequent and shells began to rain. Malic tried to lift the wounded man.

"Be off, brother," the peasant wailed. "Tell them where I died. Tell them they never took me alive, never dishonored me! Oh brother, go, go, go!"

"Put your arms around my neck," Malic said, "I can't lift you. I'm weighed down with ammunition. But we've got to get away!"

Malic crawled on hands and knees, dragging the peasant and his heavy sack behind him. He wanted to get to the riverbank. The wounded man was dropping off to sleep, whispering as he did. This was his seventh bridge since the Italians entered Montenegro. He had no regrets. He gave his name and the unit he wanted informed of how he had died.

Malic crawled like a snail. He reached the edge of the steep decline from where he could see the river. The peasant was no longer whispering. His hands were cold and solid, like claws. The large head, hit by several bullets, dangled on its limp neck. Malic closed the peasant's upturned eyes and set off down the bank.

At the edge of the river he freed himself from the peasant's grip. He arranged the mutilated head and legs, and turned the face toward the East. Then he heard the sound of soldiers and dogs. The guards were calling to one another and the dogs were rolling down the decline and sniffing along the riverbank. Malic waded into the water. From the road and the approaches to the bridge, soldiers were shooting and tossing grenades: bullets plopped into the water. He got caught in the current and was afraid the load on his back would get wet.

Soaked and bruised, Malic reached the far bank. Utterly exhausted, he fell on the ground shivering with cold and misery. The sky was full of searchlights and stars, reeds and water, from which came the barking of dogs and the vision of mustachioed, mutilated peasant heads.

CHAPTER 4

"THIS IS UNHEARD OF!" General Besta said, banging on Allegretti's table with such force that the flame of the petrol lamp wavered. "It is disgusting!"

"I am altogether baffled," the colonel said, steadying the

map of the area. "I guess anything is possible in this country. A wretch like this damned Malic, an utterly ridiculous type . . ."

"Are you surprised too, Major?" the general asked tartly. "Or simply pleased with the work of your hero?"

"I can't say I am sorry another ugly bridge is gone," Peduto said. "Besides, it's not the first bridge we've lost through fornication."

The general stroked his mustache and caught Marika's scent. He held his fingers under his nose.

"I'll bet you call this pornography too. This business with the bridge."

"It's our fault, Signor General," Peduto said softly. "If we had arrested him, we would now have both him and the bridge."

"Is this the end of your story about him, Major?"

"No, Signor General, the end of the first half."

Colonel Allegretti opened the door. Captain Brambilla stepped across the threshold: "The current carried away the third span too, Signor General. The fourth is holding, but it won't last long. I tossed the peasant's corpse into the river. The red bandits are singing on the far bank, up in the woods, and they are lighting fires."

The general spread the map out and began to study the terrain. The woods on the far bank of the river were dense and intersected by streams. Suddenly he saw Malic, his sack on his shoulders, striding across the map, singing Communist songs. "Strange man, your hero, Major! It just occurred to me how suspicious his background is. Circus-artistic! Only artistic scum are capable of giving one such surprises!"

The blood rushed to the major's head, but he managed to remain calm.

The colonel spotted with horror the scratches on the general's neck: they were Marika's traces. He wished the ground would open and swallow him up.

"Of course, he must be caught," the general said. "I refuse to leave this place until I've had the satisfaction of killing your hero, Major. All my life I have struggled against the perversion of poetry and have killed many metaphors. I still don't know how to deal with yours. But I'll think of something. We must resort to all methods: hostages, rewards, decorations, and public recognition."

The officers were silent. The general's eyes were full of mist: "But we must catch him. If we don't destroy him, he'll destroy us! He will dig out your eyes and slit your throat, Major. He will castrate the colonel and me. Horrible! We can't allow this to happen!"

All four of them stooped over the map. The river was fast, and bridgeless, and the forests dark and endless.

"Miaou!" came from the general.

"I beg your pardon, Signor General?"

"We've got to catch him, I said."

CHAPTER 5

"HELL MUST HAVE broken loose in town," Malic thought. Searchlights illuminated the sky and the surrounding hills. Variegated rockets and shells burst among the stars. Malic swore at fascism and spat in the direction of the distant roofs. He parted the branches and looked at the moon that suddenly grew steadily large and red. He thought of the river whose bridge he had destroyed. He heard the distant barking of dogs and the thought of life warmed his heart. A fresh wind blew from the mountains. Through a plum orchard he approached a peasant's cottage. Sheep bleated. Footsore and blind with fatigue, Malic tried the door.

"Halt!"

"We've halted," Malic said, looking at a dog dancing in a circle.

"Who are you?" the voice asked.

"One of your own people," said Malic.

"The password!" growled the voice, and a bayonet peeked out of a haystack. "Quick! The password!"

"Malic, Gruban Malic."

"The password, or I fire!" the deep voice threatened. "What you gave me is no password, it's your name. Stay where you are. Don't move!"

Malic raised his hands.

"Take him inside."

"Comrades . . . "

"Shut up," said the man. "Or you will alert the enemy!"

"Where's the enemy, comrades!" Malic said. "I'll charge, you follow. I've got plenty of experience. Just tonight I blew up a bridge!"

"Inside with him! He must be drunk."

"I am not," Malic said, his hands still above his head. "I've given up alcohol. I decided to join the freedom fighters. . . ."

A soldier grabbed him by the shoulder and led him into a spacious, dark room full of weapons and tobacco smoke. A man with mustaches so long he could have tied them together behind his neck dropped a pencil and grunted: "Not another one! You can't get a moment's peace."

"Yes, another spy," the soldier said. "Shall I get rid of him."

Malic's eyes filled with tears.

"So, you've learned your lesson from the Italians?" the commandant said with a grimace. "Tears! Now show us a picture of your wife and children and go down on your knees. Sit down!"

Malic obeyed. He placed his hands on the table like a schoolboy.

"How long have you been a spy?"

"Ever since the Italians arrived."

"Do they pay you well?"

"Pay me?" Malic gave a start and raised his hands above his head. "But . . . I'm your spy, that is, ours!"

"Don't talk nonsense," the commandant said. "We know everything. Confess now. We won't torture you much."

"I've been sending reports for two years," Malic said, placing his hands on the table.

"To whom?"

"To liberated territory," Malic said, "and for months I've been supplying the intelligence department of the 501st Montenegrin Division with money."

Loud laughter shattered the half-darkness.

"Who are you?"

"I'm an ex-proprietor of a saloon, a former lover of vice. For a long time now I have been the heart and soul of the movement. The Italians called me the International. They didn't dare kill me. And they knew where all my money went."

The commandant rose. He saw Malic's torn, bloodstained jacket and the pack weighing heavily on his weak shoulders. "One of us is mad! Tell me who you are or I'll kill you!"

"Gruban Malic. The notorious Gruban Malic. The man who on this very night destroyed the enemy's most heavily guarded bridge."

"Who destroyed the bridge?" a peasant leaped out of the corner and grabbed Malic, "you or I?"

"I did," Malic said.

"Say that again and I'll strangle you," the man roared.

"Maybe we both destroyed it," Malic said, feeling the peasant tighten the grip on his collar. "I lit the fuse . . . maybe you set it . . . "

"Don't you take credit away from me," the peasant hissed.

"Maybe we both did it at the same time, from both sides of the river," Malic suggested. "In any case, there was a man there, one of our . . . "

"But that was me, you swine!" the peasant cried, "don't you remember?"

"The man I was with was killed. He was wounded and I dragged him all the way to the river."

"Fool, that was me," said the peasant. "I pretended I was dead. Sit down and shut up!"

"Can't you see I'm covered in blood? Look!"

"That's hen's blood," the peasant bristled, "hen's blood!"

The commandant unslung the pack from Malic's shoulders, undid the many knots, and took out the ammuniton. He distributed the cartridges to those around him. He tossed the red grenades to the peasants, who caught them as if they were apples. He stuck two revolvers in his belt and kicked the empty sack under the table. "A strange spy," he said, chuckling.

"Comrades!" Malic said, "I am a spy, but your spy. I worked for the 501st Montenegrin army. I can tell you here and now that I know the entire order of battle of the Italian forces. I know what everyone is doing under fascism. I could go on for days telling you about their shameful behavior. There are people down there who have shamed our history, and we should wreak justice on them!"

The peasants chuckled.

"Is the headquarters of the 501st far from here?"

The commandant's lips stretched into a smile.

"He'll go on till dawn if we don't stop him," said the commandant. "We've been on the march for more than twelve hours and we clashed twice with the Italians."

"How many Fascists were killed and how many taken prisoner?" Malic interrupted, glad that the commandant had dropped his sarcastic smile.

"We'll tell tales later," the commandant said. "Stick him in the barn. Tomorrow we'll find out what he knows and who he is working for. And don't wake me unless necessary. I'm sick of spies and tedious trials!"

A moment later the commandant had turned down the lamp and dropped his forehead on his folded arms.

Malic was left alone in the barn. Horse collars and plows scared him more than machine-gun barrels. He fell onto the straw and was afraid he might not be able to get up again. In the far corner was a heap of Italian helmets. He picked up one that wasn't full of bullet holes and put it on his head. He felt important. He climbed onto a pile of sweet-smelling hay and thrust his head out of a small window. In the distance were the hills and burning villages. Around the barn was a field of rye, silver in the moonlight. A dog was barking at the flames that reached to the sky.

"This must be the headquarters of the 501st," Malic thought. "They are afraid to tell me now, but they will tomorrow. Reddy and the fat one will give them all the information. Ah, Salvatore, my poor unhappy *Calabrese,* if only you knew! You didn't believe me, did you, you stinking swine! But what if this isn't the headquarters of the 501st?"

Malic broke into a cold sweat. Rolling around in the hay, he came across a belt. He put it round his waist. From a heap of footwear he chose a pair of boots and hung them round his neck. "Now I look fierce!" Using a dismantled machine-gun barrel, he broke down the door. "Run," he told himself, "because you've landed in the headquarters of a division that's never heard of you." He straightened his helmet and set off along the path. He bypassed the headquarters with its sleeping sentry and reached a copse. The dog was baying at the moon.

With the first rays of sunlight he came to a crossroads and sat down on a treestump. Before him were several paths that vanished into the woods or dropped into valleys full of dew and peace. In the distance was his town with its two churches, two mosques, and the river now liberated from its ugliest bridge, rolling its wild and icy waters. He was hungry, but he convinced himself that it didn't matter. He studied the area and listened to the thunder of the guns.

He saw a peasant and a little horse with a packsaddle of firewood. The man was barefoot and looked familiar. He must have bought cheese and brandy from him at some point. The peasant greeted him as he passed by. Malic adjusted his helmet which shielded half his face from the sun and stopped him.

"Where are you going?"

"You can see for yourself, soldier," the peasant said. "To

town. To sell this wood. I've been without salt and paraffin for ten days."

"You shouldn't go down there," Malic said. "Last night we destroyed the bridge. They're mad as can be. They're making arrests and killing people too."

"They won't touch me," said the peasant, pointing to his tattered leggings and bare feet. "Look at me. A scarecrow!"

"Go back, old man," Malic said. "We need people these days more than ever."

"It's the first time I've ever been told I was needed," the peasant said, with a cunning smile. "I'll be back soon. I've no salt either! I know about the bridge. We Montenegrins mean business. That's what I tell Italians and they ask for eggs and milk. Strange people. How many Fascists were killed?"

"A lot."

The peasant looked at him disbelievingly.

"Unload and go home, old man."

The peasant obeyed. He removed the logs that smelt of dew and stroked the little horse's mane. Malic put on his army boots. They were too long and too wide for him.

"You won't let me earn myself a little money!" the peasant said in mild reproach. "Eh, the army!"

"If money is your problem, we can easily settle that," Malic said, taking several banknotes from his pocket. "Take it, old man, and stop cursing the army, especially ours. Take it, why not! It's our duty to help one another in times like these."

"It's too much," the peasant said in mock protest, and mounted his horse.

"I am giving you money, not beating you," Malic retorted, pushing the helmet onto the back of his head.

"Have you ever beaten anyone, soldier?"

"Yes, I have," Malic said.

"The army!" the peasant said. "That's the army for you; you can beat anybody you like and as much as you like!"

"Especially the enemy," Malic said, and noted a green forester's uniform on the peasant's lap. "How much, old man?"

"It's too big for you."

"Too small, you mean," said Malic. "Throw it to me and don't worry about the money."

Malic opened up the blouse: it was wide indeed.

"See, old man, it fits me perfectly," Malic said, popping another note into his hand. "Made for me . . ."

"That's the army for you! Again you've given me too much, soldier. What can I do for you?"

"Well," Malic said. "When I pass through your village with my division, give me a handful of decent tobacco. How is that?"

"What division are you with? The Dalmatians?"

"Get going, old man," Malic said. "Don't ask too many questions."

"An excellent helmet you have there, soldier, excellent!"

"A souvenir of last night's clash," Malic said.

"Eh, I'm sorry it's a souvenir!"

"Why?"

"I'd like to buy it, soldier."

"What would you do with it?"

"I have no pots left. I would use it to boil milk or broth."

"Catch!" Malic said, throwing the helmet to the peasant.

"But it's a souvenir."

"The needs of the people come first."

"Thank you, soldier," the peasant said, not knowing what to make of it. He pulled the helmet over his large head and set off down the road. The sun was gathering the dew from the foliage and from the burned grass near the road. Malic wondered if he would be able to walk once he made up his mind which way to go.

All morning he followed a Partisan unit, trying to pursuade its commander to let him join up.

"Let me come with you," he pleaded with the captain.

"No," the captain replied, casting a worried glance at the wounded. "We are busy."

"Comrade, I've been dreaming of this meeting . . . please let me come with you!"

"I said we were busy," the captain snapped, taking up his position at the head of the column. "We've got a long way to go."

But Malic wouldn't be discouraged. He told the captain who he was, he told him he had destroyed the bridge. He spoke of the redhead and his fat companion, of the headquarters of the 501st Montenegrin Brigade that was expecting him. The commander turned on him abruptly, as one would on a dog, and told him to go home.

Malic was alone again. The column departed, followed by a herd of dogs. Malic took off his new jerkin and placed it under him. He folded his arms behind his head and wondered where he was. He gazed into the distance, full of fire and thunder. He was hungry.

The next unit that passed by was not a Partisan unit. The men all had beards and wore cockades in their caps. Malic didn't talk to them. He wanted to buy a piece of bread from a wounded soldier, but the soldier was whisked away, leaving Malic with the memory of a round peasant loaf and the wounded man's crazed eyes.

Soon he met a large man in rags, barefoot, with knees the size of a sheep's head, carrying a Yugoslav flag on top of a long staff. He was followed by a goat. The man smiled broadly, exposing rotten teeth and blue gums. His hair was full of lice.

"Who are you?" Malic asked softly.

The man waved the skirts of his coat and raised the flagpole still higher.

"A Yugoslav major who guards his flag like his own eyes," he said. "I've been carrying it for two years and I'd rather die than allow anyone to defile it!"

"Why don't you give yourself up?" Malic asked.

"That's the trouble," the man replied, "I've no one to give myself up to!"

"Montenegro is full of Italians."

"The Italians aren't serious enemies," replied the man, and rammed the pole into the moss. "They aren't worthy of this honorable flag. People who eat cats eat shit. And people who eat . . ."

"Surrender," Malic cut him short.

"I can't surrender. I've already strangled a dozen of them with my own hands. An Italian isn't worth a bullet. Look at my hands! What army would dare come within reach of them! I grab a man and strangle him like a chicken." He picked up his flag and set off after his goat.

"Where are you going?" Malic asked.

"To find a worthy enemy." The man made his way through the branches and vanished into the gloom of the woods.

Malic decided to go to the nearby village. On the way he ran into another Partisan unit. They told him they were not the 501st and that not even the Russians had that many divisions. He replied they were ill-informed and that the number of Montenegro's armies was a carefully guarded secret. The leader of the group told him to go to hell. Malic had no choice but to go back the way he had come.

In the next clearing he came across a group of fugitives. They told him there was fighting on every side, but they were only interested in plundering. They took turns pinching the neck of a large, swollen woman, then all five of them raped her. The sound of a tuneless song was interrupted by groans and cries. Malic reached the edge of the village. He walked up to a woman who stood on the threshold of her house and asked her for some bread. He told her he had not eaten since he blew up the bridge. She gave him a long searching look, her infant seeking the tip of her breast; her breast was full of tiny blue veins and milk. Malic said he was thirsty too, but would not drink brandy.

"We Communists don't drink," he said.

"There is very little food about," she said, "and no milk."

"I know," he said as the stench of soiled diapers reached him.

"No food for officers, never mind the ordinary soldiers," the woman went on, thrusting out her soft belly. "All gone, soldier."

He was pleased to be called a soldier. He gave her a military salute and went off into the nearest thicket. He took out a few pieces of red cloth from the pocket of his new blouse: badges of rank. He decided on a ribbon and two stars for each sleeve: a lieutenant. He thought of the woman, her milk and the child's stench, and was on his way. Soon he reached the cemetery.

Children were jumping over the graves and playing hide-and-seek among the crosses. Cows grazed the grass on the mounds, and goats nibbled at the flowers and greenery. Sheep licked away at the headstones, obliterating the slanting Cyrillic letters, the dates of birth and death.

"Here, children!" Malic called, waving his rank at them.

"Here, Lieutenant," one of the boys replied, fingering the firm goitre in his neck.

"How do you know what rank I have?"

"I can see," the boy said. "I see a bar and two stars. If you sew on one more star, you'll be a captain," he concluded, holding his throat.

"Whose village is this?"

"The peasants'," replied another boy.

"I mean is it for the Partisans or for the traitors?"

"For neither. For fugitives and thieves."

"That white house there with a thatched roof, whose is that?"

"Jovan's. He is dead."

"His poor wife, how is she?" Malic asked. "How does she manage with the children?"

"The children steal. They don't give the village hens time to lay their eggs in peace."

Malic said goodbye to the children and decided to look for Jovan's widow. "She must be in deep sorrow," he thought, remembering Branko's wife and the cellar. A warm shudder went through him and he longed to be between a woman's legs. His shoes no longer hurt him. Jovan's house drew nearer and nearer.

He was awakened from his musings by a cow mooing. He reached for his revolver, but seeing the frightened face of a woman holding the cow, he stopped. She was large, with plaits wound around her head, her lips moist, her eyes full of blind fear. The cow tugged at the rope, the foam flecking its broad nostrils. The woman was trying to hold it back, beating it with a hoe.

"Stop . . . the devil's got into you!" she hissed.

The cow continued to pull the plump woman. Malic gazed at her bare arms and knees, at the folds of her tight skirt which rose every time she bent to restrain the mad cow. She fell with her feet apart. The cow stopped tugging at the rope. Malic was dazzled by the whiteness of the woman's thighs.

"The devil's got into you," she said to the cow. "The same devil's in us both . . ."

"Don't do anything," Malic told himself, "wait till the cow is gone." He took in the misty eyes that begged and reproached and the soft skin around the knees scratched by brambles, and continued on his way. The bellow of the cow and the woman's groans accompanied him until he had reached the top of the hill. "Plenty of bulls round here," he thought and with a self-satisfied smile added: "But we males grow more scarce by the day."

He was in front of Jovan's house. A woman with full breasts and round green eyes smiled at Malic. Malic smiled back with half-closed eyes just as Antonio Peduto used to do when seducing local beauties. He wanted her to notice the rank on his sleeve, and his new boots.

She saw everything. Feet apart, hands on her stomach, she waited for him to speak, or simply pull her into the grass.

"Your roof leaks," Malic said, "the fence is broken, the locks don't work."

"There's no one to do the work," the woman said, "not even the ploughing. There isn't a man in the village, Captain."

"I'm a lieutenant," Malic said, drawing close to her. "I'm not a captain yet."

"You soon will be," the woman said, taking his hand. "War brings quick promotions."

"True enough," Malic said, stroking her hair.

"There will be plenty of fighting," the woman said, "whether we like it or not. Hard times, Lieutenant."

"You're right, Marija," Malic blurted, gently taking her by the arm.

"How do you know my name, Lieutenant?"

"I was poor Jovan's best friend," Malic said. "We knew each other before the war, when we were engaged in illegal action. He was one of my best soldiers. He was killed at my side."

"My poor Jovan," the woman burst into tears and flung herself into Malic's arms. "My poor husband who left me to mourn him for the rest of my life! Oh God, I'm unhappy! . . . Come in, Lieutenant, and sit down."

"Where are your sons, Marija?"

"In the village, Lieutenant."

"What are they up to?"

"Playing."

"You've three. Jovan used to speak of them with pride."

"Three wonderful boys," Marija said. "But where do you come from?" she added.

"I don't really know," Malic said. "Montenegro is a big place."

"Anyway, I'm glad to welcome you here," the woman said, feeling the tips of her breasts tingling, "in my beautiful village."

"I'd be glad to eat and drink," Malic said, "if there's anything left by the enemy. Lieutenant Malic has been fighting the Fascists for three days and four nights and hasn't had a drop of water in all that time," he concluded, drawing out of her bosom a cheap chain with a cross.

"I'll be right back," the woman jumped up. "You will have some food, Lieutenant. Oh God!"

"Don't mention God in my presence," Malic said flatly. "Your husband died for communism and you wear a cross round your neck! You should be ashamed! Throw it away, Marija!"

"Oh, yes, I will," said the woman. "Here's some bread and cheese and brandy. You're right. I should throw the cross away, even if it was a gift from Jovan. You just eat and then take a little rest."

He ate and gazed greedily at her knees and ankles. She lowered her head, and complained about the drought. She gave him a deep wooden dish whose contents he quickly emptied.

Darkness from the straw roof enveloped the cornfield and the withered grass as far as he could see. Outside the window the branches of a plum tree weighed heavy. Malic held his hand between Marija's knees, feeling the heat spreading up her thighs. He knew that she would soon fall and he didn't feel like saying anything to her. The darkness around the bed grew thicker. The woman seized his cunning hand, kissed it and wet it with her tears. Malic suddenly said: "Where are your sons, Marija?"

"In the village. Playing."

"What, at night?"

"Yes, and how."

"Have you tossed that cross out of the window, Marija?"

"Yes," the woman whispered passionately, pressing herself to him.

"I wouldn't let you near me with it," Malic said. "The movement would object."

She was now undoing his shirt, his trousers, whispering how much she loved him, how masculine he was, how strong . . . He urged her to rave on. Pushing apart her burning knees, he admitted he didn't know what she was talking about.

The woman laid herself bare to him with a groan. Her belly, broad as moonlight, lay naked. Malic touched the tips of her breasts with his naked body and decided he had never before lain on a firmer heap of flesh. Feeling a blunt, hard fire enter her, a fire that grew, reaching to her very throat, the woman dug her nails into his flanks.

" . . . Oh, my dearest, forget your revolver, it's here somewhere, no one's going to touch it: go deeper, don't spare me, there's plenty of me. What a fine revolver, my lieutenant, my colonel, my general! . . . You say your name is Gruban, the best name there is, my commissar, my stern commander of a division! No, my sons aren't here, my love. Don't worry about your revolver or your rank . . . you're so much better than poor Jovan, who always had stomachaches."

Marija's sons arrived just before dawn, decked in feathers and poultry. They said they had found them on the road. Marija gently reproached them and sent them off to sleep in the barn. She went back to her room and dropped her head on Malic's arm.

Morning showed pale in Marija's hair. She was asleep and frowning in her sleep. She had tiny golden hairs on her lip, white eyelashes, upturned brows, and a well-cut forehead. Her neck was covered with his toothmarks. He felt no desire to uncover her further.

CHAPTER 6

"MIAOU!"

"I agree, Signor General," Colonel Allegretti said.

"And we'll get him. My intelligence service is quite phenomenal."

"I think it would be an excellent thing to get him," Major Peduto said, throwing a heap of rolled paper onto the colonel's desk. "Everything that can be done has been done. But don't forget, if he's made up his mind to escape, no one will catch up with my Montenegrin. A legendary hero like Malic will be protected by the people," the major concluded, certain that General Besta had not noted his sarcasm.

"Are the photographs ready?" the general asked.

"Our superhuman efforts have borne fruit," Peduto said, unwinding several rolls of paper. "Let this Communist bastard know that we aren't nearly as naive as he thinks."

The first picture showed Malic with a knife between his teeth; on his belt, in addition to the revolver, there were some dozen grenades. Slaughtered people lay around. The Cyrillic sentence underneath read: THE MOST NOTORIOUS MONTENEGRIN AND ITALIAN CRIMINAL. In the second picture, piloting a Russian heavy bomber, Malic was depicted destroying Rome's church towers. Malic, the intrepid Montenegrin pilot with flying gloves and earphones, was laughing satanically at the exploding landscape. General Besta remarked that the plane was of American, not Russian, design, but that made little difference at that point. In the third picture Malic's head protruded from the hatch of a tank, calmly watching the tracks crushing the citizens of Sicily. The general reached for a bottle of brandy. MONTENEGRIN BROTHERS, SEIZE HIM. WHOEVER DELIVERS HIM DEAD WILL RECEIVE 10,000 ITALIAN LIRE IN GOLD, the large bold letters read. IF DELIVERED WOUNDED WE OFFER 20,000 LIRE. Colonel Allegretti asked the general if he thought the sums attractive. ANYONE DELIVERING THE GREATEST ENEMY OF OUR FRATERNAL PEOPLES ALIVE WILL RECEIVE A GOLD MEDAL AND 100,000 IN CASH! WHOEVER APPREHENDS HIM WILL BECOME RICH AND FAMOUS OVERNIGHT!

"To tell the truth I would prefer to catch him myself," the general said, "and not just for the glory of it either, Colonel. The photos are excellent, Major! You are a true poet. But don't forget to put AND OUR MOST FAITHFUL MUSLIM BRETHREN next to Montenegrins. At this point we need them. They fall into ecstasy when anyone calls them brothers. Major, I'm pleased with your efforts!"

"I hope the five hundred copies will do," Colonel Allegretti said jealously. "The only man who can catch this damned Malic is Major Peduto here."

"If you get him, Major, I'll write a story about both of you," the general said, smiling sourly. "Imagine, the author has succeeded in catching his hero not just by the tail, which is often the case, but by the throat. An excellent theme! Major, I can already see you with a gold medal, and a general's rank!"

"My hero is sly," Major Peduto said. "I just may get demoted instead."

"Cunning is the mark of a hero," General Besta said, "I won't hang him; you will. That'll be wonderful! The writer kills the hero whom he has created, and physically at that! I'll photograph it. Thrilling, isn't it, Major?"

"Thrilling indeed," Peduto retorted.

"Aren't you sorry for him?" the colonel asked, "or perhaps a little disappointed?"

"Both," the major said.

"Gentlemen, the bulk of our business is done," the general concluded. "He is as good as caught. The posters are excellent, the rewards enticing. The populace, and especially the Moslems, are loyal to us. Ten, twenty, a hundred thousand lire! My God, what sums! Who wouldn't cross the river to catch him for us? I am tempted to do it myself. I am suddenly in a good mood: miaou, miaou, miaou!"

"No ordinary day, today," Peduto thought, crossing the square. "Utterly mad. The sort of day you don't forget." He dropped a pile of posters on the tank and said, "There's Paolone!"

Salvatore Paolone was talking to himself. He spoke of Augusto and of Pietro, he called their names again and again. There was no answer. He begged them to give him a drink. He scratched the hot steel tank and recited in a dry voice:

"O povera, o povera,
O povera Italia-a-a . . ."

"Still croaking, Salvatore," the major said. "You may be hoarse but the words are pretty. Where did you hear them? Salvatore, stand up and answer me! Don't you recognize me?"

The sentry crawled up his rifle, which was already some twenty yards high. He looked down on the major, who was putting up a poster on the tank. "I knew he was a pilot, but I had no idea he could drive a tank," Salvatore commented.

"There's no skill he hasn't mastered," Peduto said.

Salvatore looked bewildered. He counted the posters and wished he were Gruban Malic. Then, suddenly, he wept, right under the bayonet that glowed hot.

"Sing, Salvatore. Sing, my good Paolone. Let's sing together: *O povera, o povera Italia.* The tune is not important, it's the words that count."

Salvatore gave him a dull look.

"When I put you here and ordered you to remain without relief, I didn't realize you would turn into an ape that weeps and laughs like a man. My poor, ugly little monkey."

Salvatore suddenly seemed alert. "Signor Major, what's happened to Malic? I hear odd things. Has he been promoted again? Signor Major, can you see me? It is marvelous up here! Except for Malic and the tank, everything looks so insignificant! Signor Major, am I weeping or laughing? Do you have tears in your eyes, or pearls? Oh lord, *o sole, o Bolognesina mia,* I've prayed to you instead of to the Virgin. Don't be angry with me, Signor Major, because I stink. Wait, I beg you, tell Eleanora, my golden doll, that I sometimes think she is this rifle and that her milk will flood all of Italy and that when I kiss the barrel I imagine I'm kissing her breasts. Signor Major, you are my only friend, you're not listening! Oh my hope . . . stay!"

"I will neither stay nor go, Salvatore," Peduto said to himself, "I don't want you to see my tears. There will be no relief for a time yet, but then you will have your peace. And I, selfish, evil dog that I am, will be satisfied. Come down now and grovel in the dust. You will have to stay on top of that indestructible rifle."

Major Peduto put one poster by the fountain and another on the door of Malic's saloon. He looked around and realized that he was being followed by Mustafa Agic. Agic's right ear was five times larger than his left. "Oh, good," the major smiled, "I thought something like this might happen. Still, I wish your ear would stop growing!"

He turned a corner and glanced at Agic. He felt better. He decided to call on Brambilla and Fioravanti, and walked to their house.

"You're right, I am a swine and a cad, but try to understand, Lorenzo, please," he heard a frightened voice.

"Admit it!" Lorenzo said.

"I do. I admit I've been denouncing you ever since we came to this stinking country. I don't know why. I was lonely and in love, and I thought it might help me to get promotion. Yes, I did send reports to the command, but they may never have left the colonel's desk! I kept watch on you. As a result I've been promoted and twice decorated. You look so big, Lorenzo. I only reach to your waist. I am so tormented. Don't come near me, just go on drinking. I have spied on other people too, on Major Peduto who is hateful and bad and a great friend of all the local cretins and whores."

"Don't move," Lorenzo shouted.

"I won't. Let's sit down and talk," Brambilla pleaded. "Do you need money, Lorenzo? I'll give you all you want. Take my watch too, my binoculars, my gold-plated revolver. Take it all, I want you to have it. I'll bet General Besta himself hasn't got as many houses as I do! Spare my life and I'll tell you what to do. Run away now. Go straight to one of the exits!"

Antonio Peduto approached the door.

Lorenzo's jaw was twisted, his eyes full of blood and smoke. Brambilla, small and bald, was crouching in a corner.

"Lorenzo, let me kiss your hands and feet. As you love

Christ, as you love your child, don't let me die of fear, don't let me disgrace our army. Do I have to die now, only a few days before our final defeat? Don't come near me! Let me go!"

Lorenzo flew across the table, overturning a heap of empty bottles, trampling over neatly arranged newspapers and maps, and landed on Brambilla's shoulders.

Brambilla screamed. Darkness frothed and the stars, deceptive and hot, wavered about his head once, twice, several times. He sought to break the skein of Lorenzo's fingers. He tried to save himself from the emptiness by screaming. The stars scattered and he vanished into an abyss.

Lorenzo felt the movement of Brambilla's throat. He had no desire to cut it. He lifted him and hung him on a hook like a rain-soaked coat. Brambilla's body jerked.

"Free at last," Lorenzo whispered, grabbing a bottle. "There's no one to tell tales on me any more. What a day! Oh, God, don't let me get drunk! If I'm to save my neck, I must run."

Major Peduto's heart was beating, and his eyes were veiled by a scum of sweet terror. He hid behind the door. Upright and surefooted, Captain Lorenzo Fioravanti rushed past him, and set off down the street that led to the river.

"What a man, what alcoholism, what courage!" Peduto thought. "He has made the war synonymous with the bottle."

Suddenly Lorenzo fell on his knees, as if shot, in front of the boy with the withered legs and buried his hands in the dust. He kissed the beggar's filthy hands.

"You again," the child groaned.

"My boy, my house has been destroyed, my children killed. I've strangled Brambilla, the one who gave you bread and sweets. Who will feed you now, poor child?

"Can you see me, or has pus blinded you altogether? Say something. Evildoer that I am! Tell me how to escape! Should I wade the river or run to the main gate?"

Lorenzo Fioravanti caught sight of the major and of the

Carabinieri approaching on his other side. He rose and wiped his hollow cheeks:

"Goodbye, my boy, goodbye shameful army, goodbye Brambilla! I am going to the mountains, to join the people whom I have been killing!"

Major Peduto followed him to the riverbank and watched him ford the rapid stream. As Lorenzo gained the reeds and thicket, the major raised his arm in salute. He paced up and down the river edge for some time and then walked back to the square. In front of the headquarters stood the *padre*, stroking the heads of Moslem children he had just baptized, distributing little yellow crosses. At the other end of the road stood the little mullah. The priest sat by the fountain, drunk and disheveled, yelling, waving his arms, pointing to the Malic posters. In a hoarse voice he cursed world communism and Gruban Malic.

Peduto went up to Salvatore and pressed his forehead against the warm butt of his rifle. The ugly square loomed before his eyes. "My filthy metaphors," he said softly, "you are all damned, damned and doomed."

CHAPTER 7

MALIC AND MARIJA lay in the corn. The sky above was vacant. Marija spread Malic's arms and lowered her head, trying to kiss him with her swollen lips.

"Control yourself. I'm a soldier."

"I love you and I'll die of happiness."

"You're not the only one, Marija," Malic said.

"I know," Marija said. "I know you have a woman in every village. That's what officers are like. Our poor husbands are dead or at the front, so you go straight between our legs."

"Being an officer is no fun, I tell you," Malic said. "Take me, for instance. I've been made a captain. Because of the bridge, I suppose."

"Why didn't you tell me before," Marija was kissing him again.

"I don't like to boast," Malic said, pushing her gently away, "particularly since this rank should have gone to somebody else. Besides, Communists are not allowed to boast."

"Why not?"

"For the sake of the masses," he said. "But sew on a third star for me anyway."

She sewed on the star and sang to him. Gazing at the barley, Malic caught sight of the woman with the cow. Her legs apart, hands by her sides, she was standing on a hill. The cow's horns showed black against the sky. They were both sniffing.

"Who is that woman, Marija?"

"From the next village," Marija said. "She wanders about with the cow. Never talks. Her name's Ana."

"Do you know her?"

"No, Captain," Marija said, leaning over him. "I want it here and now. You've been promising it since yesterday. You're a captain now and you must deliver."

"The woman is watching us," Malic said as Marija was unbuttoning his blouse.

"I don't care. I am happy for the first time in my life! Let them look! Where are you going? You can't get away from me so easily, my captain!"

"My wounds hurt," Malic groaned, pointing to a spot near his heart, "and I'm hungry. Marija, my wounds don't seem to matter to you!"

They walked down the road to the house. Marija looked at his badges of rank; he looked at Ana and the thick, firm stalks of barley between her legs. She was running after the cow.

In front of the house Marija's sons were waiting for them: the ten-year-old Banjo was waving his arms, telling his mother that somebody had stolen their pig; Suka, with a hooked nose and tight lips, was playing with an army knife; little Matija, with curly hair and laughing eyes, held a red rooster in his arms. Marija told them to go to the next village. The captain entered the house.

"Fine children you've got. They'll make good soldiers," said Malic.

"And officers too, I'll bet," Marija said. "I have great hopes for Matija: he's bright like his uncle. Do your wounds still hurt?"

"From time to time," Malic said, taking a sip of brandy. "I need a rest. I am exhausted. These Italians are swine." Marija pressed herself closer. The warm woman on top of him was combing his hair and kissing him. He knew he wouldn't be able to resist her for long.

"Whose side are you on?" she asked.

"I'm fighting for communism," Malic said, stroking her neck.

"What's communism?"

"The end of Italians!"

"Here or everywhere?"

"Most likely everywhere," Malic said wearily. "With a few exceptions."

"What's Italy like? Is it as beautiful as they say?"

"It's a Fascist country. Soldiers sing about it a lot, but who knows? It's long, Marija, and looks like a Montenegrin boot."

"When Communists come . . . "

"We shall all be equal."

"I don't believe it," the woman protested, kissing him on the chest.

"We will!" Malic whispered.

"You may be right," the woman said, unfastening his belt. "Everything is possible. Just don't turn away from me."

"Ok, but bring Jovan's medals first."

Marija obeyed. He looked them over carefully, chose a few for himself: they were the *Obilic* and *Karadjordjevic* stars, the Italian *Medaglia di Cavaliere,* the *Medaglia di Commendatore,* and the *Collare dell' Annunziata.* Finest of all was the Russian silver medal of St. George. Marija pinned them to his blouse, raised her skirt, and pushed herself hard against his knees. But suddenly they heard voices. The woman covered her nakedness and opened the window. Some twenty soldiers were advancing through the plum orchard, led by a middle-aged man with a long mustache and a red star on his round Montenegrin cap. They sat down under the plum trees, laid aside their rifles and sweat-soaked caps.

"Partisans!" Marija cried.

"Shut the window!" Malic was frightened.

"They may be your 501st," she said.

"Hide me quickly!" Malic said in terror.

Marija showed him how to get up into the attic. "I'm coming," she said to the man who was banging on the door with the butt of his rifle. "Just a minute!"

The lieutenant entered, followed by two young men.

"Anyone hiding here, Marija?"

"No, Lieutenant," the anxious woman replied. "You forget whose house this is."

"Any food for us?"

"All gone," Marija told him.

"You said that the last time," laughed the lieutenant, and motioned to the soldiers to climb up into the attic.

Before the men reached the attic, Malic with medals clinking pushed his way through the thatched roof. "They can't be from the 501st," he thought. Covered with straw, he scrambled slowly over the eaves and dropped down into the nettles. He was afraid Marija's sons might see him. They had just arrived with a rich loot: Banjo and Suka with a lamb and Matija with a huge red cockerel. "What a breed," Malic thought as he ran through the nettles and thorns. He gained the potato clamp and dived into it. He closed the cover and was overwhelmed by the smell of rotting potatoes. "They'll never find me here," he thought, "unless they want some potatoes."

"The attic is empty," said the soldier.

"What about the stable?"

"Nothing," another soldier said. "I've looked."

"And no potatoes either?"

"Go, look, Lieutenant," the woman said, glad to have them leave the house.

The soldiers went to the potato clamp but the lieutenant stayed. He told Marija that the Italians were repairing the bridge to facilitate their retreat, but that they had to be stopped. She glanced anxiously toward the potato clamp as a soldier bent down and lifted the cover. Malic released a loud miaow and then began to bark. The soldiers dropped their rifles and ran through the nettles. Malic quickly scrambled out, replaced the cover, and slipped off through the bracken above the house.

"There's something in the potato clamp!" a soldier reported.

"Surround the clamp!" the lieutenant ordered, and looked sternly at Marija. "Bring me the light machine gun!"

"There's no enemy here!" Marija said. "It could be one of my boys in the clamp . . . "

The circle around the pit grew tighter. The grenade throwers rushed the clamp, the machine gun spat fire, the lieutenant shouted: "Forward, comrades!"

A grenade hit the cover. The clamp released darkness and stench. Luca ordered a cease-fire. The soldiers gathered around him. They reported no casualties. But no creature underground either. The commander slapped his knee and shot a glance full of suspicion at Marija.

"Oh God!" one of Marija's boys wept in the grass, "Look at him running! Our little officer, our new papa!"

They all turned: across the clearing, Gruban Malic ran toward the woods.

"Who is that, Marija?" the lieutenant asked sternly. "Answer me quickly."

"A comrade . . . a captain from the 501st Montenegrin Brigade," the woman replied, and burst into tears. "Stop him! He shouldn't run away and leave me with my starving orphans. My Gruban, my love, the pride of our armies!"

Marija bestrode the machine gun and fell into the lieutenant's arms. The soldiers waited for orders. But the lieutenant was silent, feeling a warm, soft body against him.

"I go from bad to worse," Malic thought, thrusting aside branches and bracken, scaring hares that leaped out of the bushes. With a last vestige of strength, he ran toward a stream. He removed his Montenegrin cap, Marija's last gift. He had lost one of his medals: the *Medaglia di Cavaliere*. "It doesn't really matter," he thought. "One medal more or less . . . the war is coming to an end. There'll be plenty of medals and promotions."

"Halt!" a powerful male voice cried.

Malic turned and saw a huge man with long hair and beard peeking out of the ferns. On his fur hat he had a cockade and at his belt a long knife and several grenades.

"Halt, Communist!" the Chetnik cried, taking cover behind a beech trunk.

"I'm waiting!" Malic answered with bravado, drawing his revolver and taking cover.

The Chetnik fired first, but his bullet hummed high over Malic's head. "He can't be a good shot," Malic thought, answering him with a bullet. But his bullet missed too, knocking a piece out of a tree trunk. "I'm no good today, either." The Chetnik fired a second shot. It vanished with the wind and Malic took cover behind another tree and fired again.

"Communist, I'll skin you like a goat . . . this is our territory!"

Malic could not tell where the hoarse, menacing voice came from. He crouched behind the tree, counting his remaining cartridges and wishing one of them would pierce that huge, hairy head. The man's breathing sounded closer. Suddenly a powerful hand seized him by the collar. Malic squealed like a hare. He fired into the air and turned. The Chetnik counted the stars on Malic's sleeve, laughed at the medals that clinked as Malic drew himself up by the tree. Then he knocked him down, grabbed him by the throat, and removed his right boot.

"I got myself a left boot last week. Now I have both," the Chetnik said, and vanished into the bracken.

Standing on one leg, Malic fired after him and challenged him to a fight. "Come on if you dare, damned, filthy traitor! Swine! Bearded bastard! Lousy rat! . . . Our suffering people will show you!"

"Get out of our territory!" the deep voice roared, "they'll kill you . . . castrate you, if they find you here!"

"Why didn't he kill me, instead of just threatening?" Malic was overwhelmed with shame. The revolver in his hand looked pathetic. He saw a multitude of gunbarrels, and marsh birds and beards that moved and filled the air with tumult, he heard the voice of the man who had run away with his right boot.

Malic went down a path. "How can I go anywhere with just one boot?" he thought, casting a pitiful glance at his bare foot. "I must kill somebody now for a pair of boots. Forward, Communist avenger," and he plunged through the thorns.

Startled by a loud noise, Malic turned, his finger on the trigger. He saw a cow charging toward him, waving her tail, foaming at the nostrils. He leaped over a bush and fell into a sea of wild vines. The cow jerked the rope out of a woman's hand and charged at him. Malic crouched and the cow jumped over him. His arms and legs were now sinking into soft, liquid mud.

"Swine! . . . Damned swine!"

The woman crashed onto Malic's chest. Her one hand under his shoulder, she squeezed his throat with the other. She pressed her lips to his. She kissed his forehead, his neck, whispering into his ear: "Swine! . . . How warm you are, you filthy officer."

She was as damp as a frog. Too weak to defend himself,

his arms and legs limp, he watched her raving about him. Her upper lip was split, her one eye blue. "Still, it's better to surrender to a woman than to run through thorns with a bare foot," he thought.

The woman stripped him and seized him by the organ. He begged her to be careful. She mounted him: tears of joy wet her passion-torn face as she skillfully rode him and the cow licked her large white bottom.

Malic lay beneath an ancient plum tree, his head in Ana's lap. He watched the ants climb up and down the trunk with unvaried speed. The woman combed his dark hair, caressed his brow. Sleep pressed more and more heavily on his eyes. Guns roared in the distance. He pictured himself making a report to Communist generals about the bridge and about his battle with the Chetnik. The memory of the Chetnik sobered him up, and stroking the woman's hairy leg, he asked: "Ana, whose territory are we on?"

"Your own," the woman said, lifting her split upper lip. "I am your territory."

Her broad face was smooth and firm, her eyes full of smoke, of the reddening plums and the distant gunfire. He heard her big, wild heart beating.

"You know, Ana, we Communists own nothing."

"I am yours," the woman said.

"You mustn't think only of yourself," Malic said.

"And what are you thinking about?"

"I think of liberating the world from the Italians," Malic said, sitting up next to her.

"I love the dimple in your cheek more than anything. I want to eat it," and she embraced him with her powerful arms.

"Ana, control yourself," Malic said, giving way to her. "Have mercy on me!"

Afterwards they lay in the grass caressing one another. Malic watched an eagle circling above them, rising higher and higher. "It must be hard to be a proud and brave eagle," Malic thought and felt sad.

"Why are you sad?" the woman asked, stroking his brow. "For your village? Or for your parents?"

"No," Malic said. "The movement bore me and brought me up."

"What did you do before the war?"

"I was a student."

"What did you study?"

"I was at the military academy."

"Have you killed a lot of people?"

"I don't know," Malic said vaguely.

"Why did you live with Marija? I'm sure she fed you badly."

"On the contrary! Better than you do. We always had cockerels."

"Stolen food isn't the same as honest food," Ana said.

"To soldiers it's all the same."

"It isn't," the woman flared, jerking her harelip. "I have a lamb turning on the spit here. It isn't stolen, it's *mine*!"

"Good, Ana! You roast your lambs and I'll forget Marija."

"That's right," the woman said. "You must remember me for the rest of your life!"

Malic leaped to his feet and rolled a piece of old newspaper into a baton. He waved it in the sweating air and spoke passionately: "Nobody will stop the advance of my armies! We must cut off the Italian retreat, led by General Besta and Colonel Allegretti. They will try to break through our western front and reach the Adriatic. We must send the fat one and the redhead as reinforcement to the comrades of the 377th. They will halt the entire Venezia Division!"

"How far can you see, goat?"

"I'm no goat," Malic snapped, "I'm half Russian. I see as far as Russia."

"How big is Russia?"

"Big, almost as big as Montenegro," Malic said ecstatically. "All mountains, thousands of feet high on the highest peak, all in a bloody mist, lies Moscow. My Moscow! Ana, why is one of your eyes blue? The lamb's burning on the spit, Ana!"

Malic stood in the orchard, watching bees working among the laden plum branches. The day was hot, full of wheat ears and chaff. He walked to the house and saw Ana kissing the hand of a priest.

Round as a barrel, the priest gnawed passionately at the lamb's ribs, tossing the bones over his shoulder. He rinsed his throat with brandy, smacked his lips, and sighed. He praised his hostess and promised he would come again soon.

"I need you more today than ever, father," Ana said, snuggling up to Malic.

"Why today?" Malic asked suspiciously.

"Where are your children, Ana?" the priest asked, choking on a large piece of meat.

"In the mountains, with the cattle," the woman replied pushing a bowl of sour milk to the priest.

"They say the Italians are retreating," the priest said, "but I don't believe it. I don't believe anyone; and certainly not the Communists."

Malic pushed the dish of meat aside and put a hand on his holster. With small, greedy hands, the priest grabbed the lamb's head and quickly pulled it apart. "Italians just lie and steal. Communists don't believe in God: and all atheists will go to hell!" he added.

"I'm going for a walk," Malic said.

"Father!" Ana said, "he is going to escape!"

The priest overturned the wooden bowl in which he had been cooling his feet, drove aside dogs and cats, spat in a puddle, and wiped his hands. "So, Signor Captain . . ." he said in a thin voice.

"I'm no Signor," Malic answered in confession.

"That's obvious!" the priest said. "Nor will you ever be, or I wouldn't be here today!"

"Why are you here?" Malic asked.

"To bless the union that's the talk of this whole district!" the priest said, drawing a revolver from under his mantle, "a union which will serve as an example to all of Montenegro," he added, placing his weapon among the lamb bones.

"Go on, father," Ana whispered, hiding her upper lip. "Your words are soothing!"

"I'm a Communist and will fight against the church and old-fashioned customs," Malic said, stepping back.

"You will do as I say or I'll kill you," the priest said. "You bring shame on a house I have visited as a priest these twenty years. I'll kill you . . . stay where you are!"

"We'll see about that!" Malic barked, taking cover behind a tree. "I'll get you both with one bullet if you come any closer!"

"Fornicator!" the priest cried, waving the revolver.

"Fornicator yourself! I fight fascism and you stuff yourself with lamb and give children to poor widows!"

"Who told you that!" the priest howled, purple with rage.

"You gave her twelve, you sexual, religious maniac!"

"Marry her, or I'll kill both you and myself! Do as I say . . . because honor demands it, Communist! Ana, bring that machine gun, I'll cut him down!"

"Just you try! Several proletarian divisions are behind me."

"Damned Communist!" the priest screamed, and fired his revolver at the crown of the tree. "You've been on our territory all this time. We could have eaten you if we'd wanted to. You're on the land of a man who was killed fighting communism!"

"Traitors!" Malic shouted, firing over the table. "I'm ashamed of the food I've eaten in this house. I'll have you all hanged!"

"Don't go!" Ana whispered, lying on her back, "Oh, my precious one! . . ."

"Ana, my child," groaned the priest, "he's no jewel! I'm your jewel, your genuine pearl. Look at him running away . . . just as well, the Communist monster!"

Malic changed direction in mid-flight and found himself

above the house. Lying in the bracken, he watched the drunken priest on top of the woman's widespread arms and legs, rousing her with gentle words. Malic put his revolver back in its holster, steadied his medals, and cursed his right boot that was tight, an unwelcome memento of Ana's husband, the traitor.

He saw a crowd of people approaching her house. He knew them all: Masan Popovic, who had escaped from a whole squad of Italian riflemen. He was followed by Marija, dressed all in black, with her sons. From the bush Marika suddenly leaped, like a fish, dressed in a tight short skirt of red silk, her dark curls reaching to her waist.

"*O mamma mia!*" Marika said, "*che fanciullo, che galletto, che Mateo!*"

"I don't understand Italian," Matija said, hiding his nose in the cock's feathers.

"Come to me, Matija!" Marika said.

"Later," the boy said.

The priest hid his weapons in his breast and climbed up onto the trough. Ana sat on the ground where he had left her and looked at the sky.

"Who was here with you a while ago, priest?" Masan Popovic asked.

"No one . . . I fired at a hare," the priest replied.

"Where's the hare?"

"Gone. Ran off."

"Which way?" Masan Popovic asked. "We need him badly, priest!"

"Are you from the 501st Montenegrin Brigade?" the priest asked.

"From the 501st?" Masan Popovic exclaimed. "Which way did he go?"

"There," said the priest, pointing to the walnut tree.

"Are you sure you didn't wound him, father?" Ana asked softly.

"You say he went down to the stream, priest?" Masan Popovic said, pulling out the weapons from the priest's bosom. "This is our territory again. Since last night. Get off that trough!"

"I've always been for peace," the priest said. "Where are the Italians, Masan?"

"They're withdrawing to the sea, surrendering as they go. We don't know what to do with them all."

"God is great," the priest said.

The group walked off and the priest carried Ana into the house. Malic rose out of the grass and set off down the path. The woods were full of smoke. He counted the tree trunks scarred by bullets, he counted them for hours. He was tired and felt he would never get out of the forest, which grew denser and darker. A steep goat path led into a glade, full of grass and wild berries. He fell among the flowers.

On the other side of the hill was another village. In the distance the sky was on fire with the setting sun. He lay on the grass. As he fell asleep, he heard shrill female cries, at first soft and drawn out, then rising to the darkening sky, rough as the bark of an oak tree and warm as dusk. The rock under his head no longer felt hard.

In his dream Malic reported to the chief of staff of the 501st Montenegrin Brigade. He was standing at attention, his revolver on his right hip, the grenade on his left. He stood for so long that he fell to the ground. Even so, he went on saluting his unreal superiors and guarding his medals.

Sleep grew more and more tortuous: the earth had slipped away from under his feet. He saw Salvatore Paolone heading an ugly throng. Captain Brambilla and General Besta slit open his green sleeves. Masan Popovic removed his captain's ribbons and stars with a hammer and chisel. But Major Peduto, with an arm the like of which no human eye had ever seen, drove Masan away. Only one star remained on Malic's sleeve; he fell into the grass: "Oh, my good people, brothers and comrades, don't take every rank away from me, don't hit me on the head with cold steel! I did destroy the bridge!"

Malic woke up. His hand lay on the helmet he had picked up the previous day. He wiped the sweat from his forehead. The sun was high, fresh and dew-washed above the distant pines. Suddenly he caught sight of an old peasant.

"Captain, did we wake you?" the old man said timidly. "Forgive us."

Malic shielded his eyes from the sun with the helmet. "Don't worry. Just go on fighting, comrades," he said.

"But we are not fighting, Captain," the old man said. "We're old, and sick and unfit for battle. We are erecting a tombstone to our children and neighbors."

The peasant's left sleeve was empty; he didn't have a single tooth in his mouth. He was joined by several old men.

"We are going to eat. Join us, Captain."

They ate in silence, chewing their bread and meat, washing it down with brandy. A marble slab had a long list of the dead.

"Were you hit by the drought?" Malic asked to break the silence.

"Heh, that is the least of our problems," an old man said, gazing into the darkness of the grave. "Now we have to make a nice headstone for our children."

"I see a lot of names there," Malic said.

"Those are the ones we know to be dead."

"Carve in one more name," Malic said to the carver, who was covered in dust. "He's not from these parts, but if we don't include him, he will vanish without memory. He was my right hand."

"What was his name, Captain?" the stonecarver asked, taking up his chisel.

"Gruban Malic. The day after he was killed he was made a captain."

Malic saw his name being chiseled into the marble slab. Again, he was last. That made him sad.

"Glory to those who fell in the struggle against the Italians!" he said to cheer himself up.

"Glory to them," echoed the peasants.

They raised the heavy stone obelisk with its lopsided red star on top and fixed the marble slab in its center. When the last of them had climbed out of the hole, Malic asked: "Where are the bodies?"

"That can wait."

"Why is the grave so big?"

"Why not, Captain? Why not be prepared? There are beggars lying about in our streams and Italians rotting all over the place. We'll put them in all together. They are all Christians." The old man then waved his arms, beat his skinny chest, kissed the freshly dug earth, and made the sign of the cross over it. He turned to Malic abruptly: "Captain, where was Lieutenant Malic killed?"

"I can't tell you exactly," Malic said. "But he was killed by an Italian colonel, Spartaco Allegretti. When he falls into our hands he will tell us the day and the place. Unless he is dead, of course. If he is dead . . ."

"We'll bury him in this grave too," the old man said. "Why not have a colonel here too!"

The old man's face was hollow and firm, his eyes hard, his words cold. "You are a good man, Captain. You have plenty of medals, too many for such a narrow chest. Look at the silver medal of St. George! I had it too, Captain! I was decorated with it by Colonel Dolgoruky for having personally slain fifty Turks with my saber, including a Pasha whose filthy Moslem head I threw before the feet of our master, King Nikola of Montenegro, God rest his soul. Captain, tell me, how many Italians did you send under ground before you earned the decorations that once decorated my chest? Someone stole all my medals. I'd rather have my silver medal of St. George back than another ten years to live! Ah, that great Dolgoruky!"

"Look, old man, there'll be as many medals as you could wish for," Malic said. "Freedom is coming, old man. Be patient! The great Dolgoruky may come too!"

"Freedom, you say! What kind of freedom?" the old man challenged him.

"Real freedom," Malic said, stretching his arms. "There'll be no Italians, and red flags will fly everywhere!"

"Why so much color?"

"Freedom has to be maintained. Twenty thousand tons of red paint is assured to this country. Also, we must keep fit physically: like this; one, two, three, four! Breathe deeply and watch out the insects don't get into your mouth! Then, we'll practice jumping over the grave, hop! It's not so hard! We must be flexible and strong! We'll destroy churches and inseminate sheep and cows from an aeroplane!"

"Who will lift their tails, Captain?"

Malic had no time to reply. A crowd of people entered the graveyard. Masan Popovic, followed by Ana, Marika, Marija, the priest, and Marija's sons. Masan Popovic ordered them to raise their hands. He ordered Malic to surrender. Malic announced his surrender and demanded to be disarmed in front of the entire company.

"Do you remember me, Captain?" Masan asked.

"Yes," Malic said, steadying his medals.

"This woman says you worked for the Italian command."

"You don't believe that Fascist whore, do you?" Malic was upset. "They will tell you at the 501st Montenegrin Brigade how much I helped the movement. Ask them, not this whore!"

"I slept with them because I was ordered to," Marika hissed.

"Whore!" Ana and Marija shrieked.

"I may be a whore!" Marika said, "but why has he decorated himself with stolen rank and medals? What a fool!"

"Shut up, all of you!" Masan Popovic cut in. "Let's go!" He turned to Malic: "What made you eat Italian shit?"

"You're wrong," Malic said, gripping him by the arm. "Don't listen to the enemies of our movement. The whole town knows what I did!"

"Explain yourself to the movement," Popovic said, "not to me."

"I certainly will!" Malic said, "but you shouldn't lead me like a prisoner. And in the company of three women? Marika has disgraced our nation. She should be soaked in petrol and set fire to."

"*Che patriota!*" Marika exclaimed.

"Shut up," Masan Popovic told her. "I'll let Ana and Marija have their way with you."

"Surely not those peasants," Marika said, putting her arm round him.

"Don't let that muck embrace you," Malic cried. "That monster who has been in and out of Fascist beds for years!"

"Relax, Captain," Masan Popovic said.

They finally reached the hilltop. In the valley below, on the other side of the noisy river, they saw a mob of peasants chasing a man; they were brandishing scythes, pitchforks, and axes; women were shouting and throwing rocks. The huge man, in a torn Italian uniform, overgrown in hair and beard, hid in the corn, and reemerged on the other side. It was Captain Lorenzo Fioravanti.

"Brothers!" he shouted, "I've deserted to you . . . Spare my life!"

He was hit in the stomach. Flinging his arms, he slid down the steep riverbank. "Brothers, you mustn't kill me! I've got a son. He is mute and blind and he begs. I want to protect his eyes from flies and pus!"

A blade flashed in front of Lorenzo's eyes. The blow was dull and cunningly dealt. His body twisted to one side. Dogs were pulling at his legs and tearing at his wounds. Pierced by something that burned hot, he threw back his head and saw another pack of dogs, their hair bristling, their muzzles bloody, their teeth sharp as pitchforks. Then the barking of dogs and the howls of men grew weaker. The earth under his head no longer felt full of thorns, snakes, and fire.

The peasants drove away the mad dogs. They stabbed Lorenzo with their scythes, they struck him with axes, plunging blades into his flesh. They raised him up on their prongs, and marched slowly, taking care the body should not fall into the uncut rye. Women wept, calling the names of their dead sons.

They reached the steep edge of the riverbank. The men heaved both corpse and prongs, "Now, go, Italian!"

Lorenzo Fioravanti fell from rock to rock, dwindling as he went. The men and women tramped silently back into the clean corn, the children counted bones and ravens in the sunless gorge. Beneath them the river raged, its water breaking in a crest of damp light and pearls.

On the opposite bank a long column of Italian soldiers dragged themselves westward in silence. Masan decided not to fire at them.

As the peasants approached the town they were met by a mob of beggars, stretching out their skinny arms. Goitered lame children asked for bread.

"Kill me!" Malic said. "Put lead through me before we enter the town!"

"Not in a million years," Masan said. "If I deliver you to them safe and sound, I get a medal."

"Beat me to death like a dog!" Malic screamed. "Here, in front of these beggars. Have pity on me."

"I'm sick of killing," Masan Popovic replied. "I'd like to live a few years in peace."

"I can't live in shame," Malic moaned.

"Yes, you can," Masan Popovic said. "We're all shamed. So long as a man is alive, water tastes sweet!"

"To me everything is bitter. I want to die!" Malic roared.

"No, you don't," Masan Popovic was firm.

"Then bind me . . . lead me into town!"

Masan Popovic pulled a length of thin string from his pocket and bound Malic's hands.

"Tighter, Masan!" Malic said. "Till the blood runs!"

"There he goes again," Masan said. "I'm sick of blood."

"Put me on a donkey!" Malic shouted, letting his eyes rest on the donkey nearby. "There, on the packsaddle."

Masan laughed.

"Oh, let him, Masan," the women cried.

"The will of the people be done," Masan said jestingly.

Malic's face brightened. He mounted the donkey. Seated clumsily on the packsaddle, holding onto the wooden saddlebow, he looked larger. Masan struck the donkey's meager flank. The beggars multiplied.

They were entering the town, climbing up the dusty street that led to the Orthodox church. The church doors were securely bolted. Marika waved toward the empty barracks and said: "They've gone . . . the Fascist beasts have gone!"

"Someday we won't be here either," Masan Popovic said.

"I go that way," the owner of the donkey interrupted. "Give me back my donkey. He is all I have."

"We've got to keep going," Masan Popovic said. "Who cares about a donkey at a time like this?"

"I do. You have your victory, I want my donkey!" the peasant said. "I've got eight children. That donkey is like a mother to them!"

"Forward!" Masan Popovic ordered. "In the name of the movement."

"To the final victory of our movement and world communism!" Gruban Malic burst out. "We will not stop until we have destroyed the last Italian," he added, glancing at the peasant who had drawn in his head like a turtle. "Don't worry, old man, Masan Popovic and I will give you a receipt with a red stamp for it."

"You keep the receipt and I'll take the donkey," the peasant whined. "I've nothing left to eat, brothers, what good are receipts to me?"

"You can frame them and put them up instead of candles," Malic said.

"What candles?" the peasant objected. "I'm a pauper. The only candles I've seen are in church. Give me back my donkey, my children's provider."

"Forward!" Masan Popovic ordered, concealing a smile behind his thick mustaches. "To the bitter end!"

"Oh my poor baby!" the peasant moaned. "I managed to keep you for three long years, and now the devil takes you from me on the very day of liberation!"

They were passing down the main street. The fountain was in ruins. The trees lay heavy with the heat. Tiles had slipped from the roofs, shop windows were broken. Voices and cries swelled on every side, but did not carry far. The sweat poured from under Malic's helmet. He passed his saloon without so much as a glance: it had no door and no windows. From the poster on the wall, another Malic looked down—Malic the flyer who hurled bombs in every direction, Malic the tank commander. He noticed that several other houses were destroyed and was glad. "This whole stinking place should be knocked down," he whispered.

"Bravo!" a voice greeted him from the dust. "Bravo!" Others joined in.

Tears swelled in Malic's eyes as he listened to the invisible people crying out his name. One of Marija's sons was wailing; someone had stolen his cockerel. Marika was waving to the motionless crowd and shouting: *"Cari, amici fratelli, campagni!* We're together again, my Montenegrin people!"

No one returned her greetings. The dust grew thicker and Malic's donkey moved more slowly. Masan coughed and wiped his neck. The donkey owner following his poor asthmatic animal was drenched in sweat. Only Ana and Marija remained impassive, their crazed eyes fixed on the figure seated on the pack-saddle, on the small body that moved under the burning helmet.

"Bravo! . . . Our captain and liberator!"

"Look at all those medals!"

"A Russian . . . a real Russian!"

He raised his hands, regretting they were not bound in heavy chains, greeting the dark faces and clean-shaven heads of these human shadows. "You thought I had been killed," he wanted to say to them. "I haven't. I am alive, you scum. And on a donkey too, a hero with medals and a helmet, with my hands bound . . . if I survive this day, if ever I get out of prison, look out!"

"Malic is here!"

"Wait! Don't seize him now! The Italians may come again!"

"Our poor child!"

Malic guided the donkey across the square. He recalled that on this very spot, propelled by Brambilla's hands, he had lain weeping and swallowing the dust. It was on the day of the general's arrival. No more Giovanni Besta with his eleven suitcases! I, Captain Gruban Malic, I am the general today.

His heart leaped at the sight of Paolone's overturned tank. The barrel of its long gun was twisted into a knot and pointed at headquarters. Around the dented tank soldier's excrement lay scattered.

The eternal sentry with his staring Calabresan eyes was no more. But his rifle had grown more than thirty meters high. At the foot of the bayonet, which glowed like a flame, lay the carbonized headless body of the soldier. Malic threw up. "If ever I get out of prison, I'll come here to see him again."

Concealed in thick bracken, Major Peduto sat next to his rifle and knapsack. Through a telescope, he watched Masan Popovic escorting Malic. He counted Malic's glittering medals and the stars on the green rolled-up sleeve: "Not bad, as far as rank is concerned, though I think the rank of major would suit you better than it does me. Still, you've got two pregnant women with you and that's more than I've got! Malic, Captain Malic, you've justified my trust in you and all my prophecies. They are escorting you in Marika's company. Disgusting! Your tears wet the fragile string your hands are bound with. I foresaw an ending like this for you long ago. Yet today I feel sorrier for you than ever. This injustice should be set right. And I, your friend and double, will do it today before I leave this valley full of bracken and wild berries."

The square was full of human shadows. The dust rose from

the ground in a thick cloud. Major Peduto shifted his telescope lens from the square to the headquarters with its shattered windows. He thought of his last moments there.

"Today, gentlemen and friends, the eighth of September, Nineteen forty-three," General Giovanni Besta had said, "Today, our powerful leaders have signed a partial capitulation. I have known this for the last three hours, but I have had to give myself a chance to absorb the news of partial disaster. I repeat; *partial* disaster! As you know, nobody has ever completely defeated our land. We may have suffered momentary defeats, but we always recover quickly. This time too, I hope . . . "

The general stank of alcohol. "What are we going to do, Signor General?" Colonel Allegretti asked.

"I have already taken the first step," the general said, reaching for a fresh bottle. "But if you want me to tell you what to do about Malic, that great strategist . . . I don't know. Ask Major Peduto, his creator and friend."

"No army can resist Malic," Peduto said. "No power can kill him, except for me. But I'm not sure that would promote our cause. With Malic in their ranks, the red half of mankind will end up in the sea, in an ecstasy of intoxication."

"You're a poisonous reptile, Antonio," the general said. "While I am joking and Allegretti is wetting his trousers, you speak of ecstasy. You should be shot! But it's too late for that, so you can go on enthusing about your deformed monsters! We must not lose our nerve. The army still knows nothing. When the time comes, we'll prepare them and give orders for the final attack. We will overthrow communism and the resistance once and for all! Friends, let's drink to each other's health!"

"What if they've cut off our retreat?" Allegretti mumbled.

"What do we care!" General Besta said. "What can they do to us? In any case, there's your little plane, Colonel. No weapon can shoot it down! I can see the three of us. The nicest escape I've ever made! To the coast, and then straight into the arms of the English and Americans! Nothing but milk, chocolate, and clean trousers for us. They say the Americans are kind and the English are bad-tempered. I'll move their hearts with our Italian melancholy."

"What if we are greeted on the coast by Russians instead?" Allegretti was alarmed.

"We'll go sleighriding in Siberia," coughed the general. "Also I have a pair of the finest Swiss skis!"

"What if Germans are on the coast?" Allegretti fluttered.

"Miaou, miaou, miaou! What a question, Spartaco! I'll still manage; I've got a mistress in Munich, One, Maximillianstrasse 17. My dear Inge, my Bavarian lass! I speak German fluently. But why not talk about nice things? Since I learned about our *partial* fall, I've arranged a little sexual hors d'oeuvre for you. The women don't yet know we're . . . so let them be informed by our most wise Italian General Giovanni Besta, *Conte de Tirano* . . . Long live Tirano, long live its cows and flowers, long live lambs on the borders of unconquerable Italy and milk-laden Switzerland! There are three of them, one for each. Romana is here, my Italian girl for the last ten years. She came here to see me and to breathe the mountain air of Montenegro. Don't say a word to Romana about the capitulation. She has two million lire in the bank, which are now worthless. She may faint."

But the dark-skinned Romana neither fainted nor demanded a rope to hang herself with.

"Oh, my uniformed idiots," she said. "I've known about this for the last four hours. Don't ask me how, Nanni. Remember what I told you long ago in Africa: I've got a radio station and a goldmine between my legs."

Romana, who had the tinest waist and the roundest bottom anyone had ever seen, invited the three of them to join her in a retreat to the sea and across the Adriatic. She also invited the other two girls, but they said they would not leave their unforgettable Montenegro.

"How stupid!" Romana exclaimed passionately, riding the naked general. "You come with me, you two darlings, but first take a ride on your two wild goats. That's it, Nanni, my favorite general. Come on, remember what we did that time in Greece!"

"Miaou!" Giovanni Besta was on all fours. "Miaou! Miaou! Miaou!"

They rolled on the girls, poured brandy and cognac over them, and then licked one another. Giovanni was the most active: he crawled from one female body to the other, miaoued, bit the drunken girls, and blew between their legs.

"Don't forget our wonderful country," one of the native beauties said, watching as the officers dressed themselves.

Both girls were now crying. The general begged them not to cry; he told them they could stay in his room and take all his belongings, except for the butterfly-catching gear. The girls wept all the more passionately.

"I'd like a Montenegrin," Romana said suddenly. "I hear their balls reach to their knees. Get me a Montenegrin! I can pay you!"

"But Romana . . . our money . . . " Peduto began.

"I've thought of that, Peduto!" she stretched her thick, painted lips and displayed a heap of gold coins in her bag. "Hah! My name is Romana! I will employ you all in the brothel I am opening for the Americans and English!"

"My wonderful Romana!" Peduto whispered, "my most wonderful Romana!"

"You're a born pimp," she told him, "with that marvelous red beard! Spartaco! He could be our commissionaire in charge of chucking our drunks. And Giovanni, my Nanni, is going to give lessons in licking! Should we lose one another on the way, Romana operates near the Vatican! Via dei Serpenti, in the old part of our majestic Rome."

"Allow me to drink once more to your sacred golden name!" Peduto said, deeply moved. He knew now what chapter of his book would deal with her.

"Only to my name!" Romana said, opening wide her bright, intelligent eyes.

"To disaster!" Antonio raised his glass. "I drink to you and to disaster! Romana, allow me to kiss your penetrating sincere eyes. Romana, my unexpected and last love; let us embrace in the name of beauty, of war, and of pornography!"

"Miaou! Miaou! Miaou! How I love life!" the general said. "The sour flesh of women and the defeat of men! Antonio, if you write a book about Malic, you must write one about me too."

"To the general, my future hero!" Antonio raised his glass again. "And to the two Montenegrin girls who are now fighting over his suitcases!"

"Friends!" Giovanni Besta droned, "I've made a sudden change of plan." He stopped and looked at them all. "I won't travel in your aeroplane, Spartaco. Romana and I will go in my car, which is waiting downstairs. Colonel, you go by plane with Turiddu. For you, Peduto, there's room in Spartaco's plane."

"I'll go on foot with the soldiers," Peduto said. "That's the right kind of retreat. I want to see what it's like."

"On leaving, Peduto, I want to inform you that you have been promoted to the rank of colonel," the general said.

"You've missed a rank," Peduto remarked bitterly.

"Everything is possible, Colonel Peduto," General Besta said. "You have also been decorated with the *Ordine di Spanta Chiara!* Forgive me for not having given you these two bits of news earlier."

"Thank you, Signor General," Antonio laughed. "I'm happy!"

"Colonel Peduto, I order you . . . no, I ask you, to inform the troops of the partial capitulation and lead them to the sea."

"Yes, Signor General," he said. "But what should I do with my eighteen medals?"

"Show them to the Americans," the general said seriously. "And to the English. They value gifted soldiers. Tell them you fought Montenegrins and survived. They'll give you a seat in the House of Lords! *Bon voyage*!"

"Why not come with me, Antonio?" Allegretti asked. "You know I'm a coward. Come with me, let's share good and evil."

"You go with Turiddu. A Sicilian is a Sicilian's best friend, Allegretti."

"You are insulting even at parting," Allegretti snarled and walked away. "Swine! Don't forget the general's orders! Good-bye!" He turned once more and looked at Peduto with hatred. "Good-bye, sexual kleptomaniac!"

"Good-bye, Signor Colonel!"

Antonio crushed the bracken under him and watched the deserted square. He recalled how he had ordered the junior officers to move the troops westward. In a disorder that reminded him of the panic-striken flights of the Abyssinians, the soldiers ran off to the outskirts. They threw away their rifles or sold them for food. "The most peaceloving, disgusting army I ever saw," he had thought, watching them abandon their machine guns and their banners.

He had been the last officer to leave town. He was on the other bank of the river when the peasants smashed through the triple fence of barbed wire and broke into the narrow side streets like water flooding in. Armed with guns, with axes and hoes, they had charged the headquarters, hurling grenades and rocks. They overturned the mast and tore at the Italian flag with their teeth. It took them a while to notice the rifle, now thick as an oak tree and over fifty meters high. At first they thought it was an ancient monument and then they caught sight of Salvatore close to the top. They asked him to come down, they showed him bread and water. But he held firmly to the rifle. Two peasants climbed up the rifle. Salvatore's heart beat violently against the warm barrel. They stabbed him repeatedly and threatened to set him on fire. But Salvatore didn't budge or move his eyes from the bayonet that burned in the sky. One of the peasants waved his ax back and forth and hacked off Salvatore's head. The small body, stinking of shit, remained above, its arms clutching the rifle barrel, its long neck resembling a stripped stump of alder.

"Forgive me," Antonio Peduto had said to himself. "Forgive me for not having sent you relief. Had you run away I would have lost one of my finest metaphors. This way, my little Calabrese, you will always be remembered. Rest there, burn dark, and don't worry about your head! I killed you so I could put you in verse."

The mob then turned on the tank. They spat on its tracks, pounded its steel sides with axes, bent its sun-melted ribs. Foaming at the mouth, the women screamed. With skirts raised, feet astride, they urinated against the tank. Thousands of them, naked and strong, leaped on the tank, their rectangular peasant thighs covered in dark hair. Dark hands and iron crowbars easily overturned the tank. The mob ran away. Dust and shame settled on the steel.

Major Peduto rose from the bracken. The tortoise had crept out of his pack. He wanted to crush it, but the sight of an egg it had laid between two strands of wild strawberries stopped him. He bent down and stroked its shell.

"Hah, my little one," he said, "I've carried you for three years, my *Anna Maria Cattolica*. No, you're no *cattolica*; you're Greek, a little Greek Orthodox whore, laying an egg and leaving descendants! Today of all days! You little cheat, you Balkan prostitute!"

The tortoise moved carefully, its neck outstretched, in a northwesterly direction. It shook off the wild strawberries Antonio had placed on its shell. "You are *Anna Maria Cattolica* nevertheless," he said bitterly. "You were Orthodox once, but sleeping with me changed your faith. You are Romana, *Bolognesina*, Eleanora, the most marvelous thing I have ever possessed, another of my hateful metaphors. Go! Someday you will reach the Adriatic. I will too, but further south. Wait for the sailors on the shore, show them your hairy Greek parts, sleep with every one of them, but wait for me. I'll find you and take you to my little house just south of Rome."

Major Peduto climbed up the slope and reached the hilltop sooner than he had expected. The town below was in ruins, the barracks and fortifications on fire. Mobs were flooding the town from all sides. "That's Malic's division, the most glorious and powerful 501st. Major Peduto, behold the divisions of your enemy and blush in shame!"

On the road west trucks were moving, full of food. "The army of shame," Peduto thought. His soldiers were intercepting women, beating and robbing them. They threw away their rifles, fell onto their knees, and shed tears. "The army of shame," Peduto repeated.

"But I must get back to Malic, my bastard son. I don't like his end. Why bring him into town on the back of a donkey? It doesn't make sense! It's disgraceful! Doesn't this hardened champion of freedom, this unequaled genius, this bridge destroyer, this charmer of snakes and hungry widows, doesn't he deserve a more fitting end? Yes, he does! I shall see to it."

Captain Malic looked around his prison cell. In the far corner he saw Marika in conversation with the priest, the mullah, and Mustafa Agic. He wanted to beat them all, but his hands were still bound. He was disgusted by the whores and spies who crowded near him. "Why did they put me in the same cell? I am an officer, after all. Gruban Malic deserves to wear fetters, heavy chains, and not this miserable string. I've been in this darkness for three whole hours and no one has come down to talk to me."

In this unsavory crowd of gamblers, pimps, and whores he suddenly caught sight of the redhead and the fat one. "It can't be true," Malic gasped.

He pushed his way to the door and told the sentry he was going to the headquarters of the 501st. Impressed by his rank and medals, the sentry saluted him and let him go. On the way Malic asked a soldier how to get to headquarters. The soldier laughed. Malic hit him hard on the face. The soldier no longer laughed. Malic ran into a group of high officers. They saluted him. He didn't bother to return their salutes.

Antonio Peduto lay on his back in the grass. His eyes were wide open. Through the fir branches he saw a patch of the earth, and Malic striding boldly across it. In his thoughts, he guided him down a narrow street; "Malic now wants to do what I've long been aiming to do. Let one of us do it," Antonio whispered.

Malic reached the edge of town. He thrust himself into a henhouse full of eggs and feathers, drank an egg, catching the shell with the tip of his boot. "My insult is so deep that I'll find peace only when I am dead," he said quietly, making a loop out of an old strip of wire. "I am better off ending my own life than waiting for Partisan generals to do it for me. I've given everything I own to the movement. Today I give my life."

It was humid in the henhouse. "He may change his mind," Peduto thought. "Then I will have to think of something else for him."

Gruban Malic raised his hands, glanced at his insignia and his medals, and placed the loop around his neck. He saw a woman standing under the plum tree calling her hens. "Another widow," Malic thought, and kicked aside the packingcase on which he stood.

"One more civil metaphor is gone," Peduto thought, as the sky grew lighter and clearer. "Now I must write a farewell letter in the names of General Besta, Colonel Allegretti, and myself, explaining to the Montenegrins why we had to kill their hero." Antonio reached for his pencil.

"We had to kill him," the letter said. "We are leaving this country as a defeated army, due largely to his dark powers. He destroyed bridges. Charging, he never could stop. He knew far too much. He did what he liked with us. Fury, thy name is Gruban Malic. His Communist intrepidity bordered on insanity. He carried on a fight against the local population as well. Few people on earth have not felt Malic's boot. Colonel Allegretti, General Besta, and I have shouted his name in our sleep. Sailors feared him more than a typhoon. When we expected him from the sea, he came out of the air, like the wind. Italy will remember him. Millions of mothers will know who scattered their sons' bones across Montenegro, Africa, Scandinavia, and India. For the Communist idea he did not mind destroying the world and, in the end, himself. With his teeth he tore the throat of the soldier who placed the loop around his neck. With his last gasp he shouted Communist slogans. Now we wish to live in peace. But if Malic had lived, there would have been no peace anywhere in the world.

"A list of things we found on him: A Russian revolver; a globe, painted red; and twenty thousand tons of red paint we were unable to destroy. We leave this unpleasant legacy to the Montenegrin people. We dismantled his small but powerful radio by which, for years, he had aroused Americans, Japanese, French, Serbs. We shall never forget the tiny pocket telephone manufactured in London, a gift for his thirty-fourth birthday from a famous Finnish general. Wonderful too was his idea for the division of the world: Montenegro was to receive Italy, half of France, Spain, and all of England. Russia was to get Moscow, New York, and several other cities. The Africans, the Chinese, and the Germans were to get all the rivers, waterfalls, and jungles. We confiscated, thank heaven, the button which he was to press in order to blow up Italy and Sicily. We also succeeded in destroying his aircraft. Had we failed to do this he would have reached London, Madrid, Washington, and other Communist centers. But we were unable to uncover the numerous bodyguard that watched over him wherever he went."

Peduto was crying. He beat his fists on the moss and watched the wind play among the pine branches. Guns roared in the distance. Peduto rose: down a narrow, dusty road the last remnants of the Venezia Division were withdrawing. "How many of them will ever see home?" he wondered as he climbed up the hill. "How many will end like Lorenzo, Augusto, or Salvatore? Open your notebook, find a clean page: It is September the eighth, Nineteen hundred and forty-three, a clear day, but too hot for this time of the year." Again the sound of an explosion and human cries. "No," he said, feeling the mountain sun scorching his eyes. "I can't write . . . my fingers will no longer hold the pencil: everything I've done has been a mistake, my bitter books, my senseless warfare, my morbid life! Nor have I killed the greatest hero of all time, Gruban Malic. General Besta photographed him and that film has been smuggled into Italy. Malic will emerge from the celluloid and again threaten mankind. If I live, we will fight once more. My country is spacious and surrounded by the sea. When I think how you will pursue me, that is my only consolation."

He stood in the clearing, his forehead raised toward the sun, listening to the bullets humming about him. "They've spotted me, they're shooting," he smiled. "I will not defend myself." Lead continued to fly about him, hitting trees, the earth, the air he breathed. One bullet knocked a splinter out of his rifle butt. "I won't let them smash my rifle," Peduto said, searching for the marksmen through his telescope. "I'll do that myself."

He grabbed his rifle and brought it crashing down: the butt split in two. He took out the bolt and hurled it into the stream. "I must make this rifle useless," he told himself, and banged its barrel against a rock. One by one he threw the cartridges away.

He threw his rifle and his revolver on a heap of dry branches. He struck a match and the flame quickly leaped upward, but the steel would not melt. He tied it with a piece of wire and set off, grunting with exertion. He walked through the woods. Shots echoed from the nearby hills. He came across a large, muddy pool. He dropped the remains of the rifle into the water. "Sink into the mud and stay there until the purpose you served is forgotten." Bullets plopped into the water.

"Except for my manuscript 'The Age of Shame,' I am harmless," he thought as he reached a village path. He paused, as if gauging where the shot came from. "From all sides," he decided. His pack fell on the ground. His manuscript fell out. He took a drink from a large bottle of brandy. His heart ached. He had emptied half the bottle in one go. He tottered in the dust and collapsed in a bush by the road.

His arms and legs outstretched, he lay on his back. He sank deep into the thorns, but made no attempt to protect himself. He had a good view of the mountain, its blue sides, ribs, and shoulders, its sharp summits capped with snow. Nearby he heard shooting and human cries.

A deer regarded him with slanting, unfaithful eyes. A bullet had torn her left thigh and opened her flank. "My poor darling, my poor wounded thing," Antonio wailed. "Let me bind your wounds!" The deer moved away from the path and he heard a dull thud. The deer was panting and beating its leg against the ground.

Peduto took another drink from the bottle. He saw a dog and a bitch stuck together. When one of them moved, the other released a howl that split the heavens. "I know you," Peduto said, "I've seen you before. Two weeks ago. Running through the burning forest. No, two years ago, and you've been stuck together like this ever since. I wish I still had my rifle. I'd aim straight at her stinking bottom. I'd feed him, stroke him, and tell him not to get nervous when making love."

On the path the tortoise appeared. "*Anna Maria Cattolica,*" he said, looking at her, full of tenderness. "What are you doing here? Get off the path, you naughty little thing . . . you're ill, there's something oozing out of you: it's Greco-Albanian or Montenegrin-Italian gonorrhea." The tortoise suddenly looked three times its normal size. Peduto wanted to strike it with the bottle but took a drink instead. "Go, my faithless little syphilitic." The tortoise departed with quiet, measured steps.

He thought of the boy with the crutches. The crutches had grown into huge, slanting scaffoldings that protected the town from the sun and the foul wind. His rifle sprouted from the mud and joined Salvatore's. Together they were a hundred meters high. Whose corpse was under the bayonet? Salvatore's or his?

"How much more will you grow, oh my metaphor? Peduto, your poetry will kill you!"

He drained the bottle. The sky and the earth spun around him. He opened his eyes and again saw the boy with swollen knees and skull. His hand was full of blackberries.

In the distance peasants were pursuing soldiers who had dropped out of the column. The peasants were like the insects that crawled under his nose and behind his ears. They carried machine guns and tools taken from fields. "I'll surrender quietly," he whispered. "Come quickly. I won't weep nor will I admit our guilt, though I've always believed in it. I'll wait calmly for the bullet or the ax blow that will spill my infected brains. I will not ask for pity although I have several families, five or six illegitimate children, and many men whom I love. I'll grit my teeth and wait for you to tear me to pieces!"

"And you will tear me apart," he whispered with a shudder. "The monster between my legs . . . you'll tear it out and throw it to the dogs! You'll pull my legs apart and cut me in half with your knives! Come! Disfigure my face with your bare feet! Come quickly, and destroy my book, which pours filth on both our peoples! Stick a handful of your earth down my throat, throttle me. I should no longer be on this earth, especially not on yours; everything I've touched has turned to evil. Why did I write it all down? Now nothing will ever be forgotten."

He heard the roar of the earth mixed with human cries. His eyes were open, his lips cracked: "I beg to be forgiven for having gathered so much filth together in one place. Don't bury me where people are buried. Try to forget my name. In the name of the Venezia Division, in the name of my beloved pornographic people, in the name of all my forefathers, my illegitimate sons and daughters, I ask forgiveness."

He heard someone's heartbeat. "Whose heart is that? Who are you?" he wondered. "What's your name, you drunken, crazy fellow?

"I am Antonio Peduto. I am thirty-seven years old, or one

hundred and seven. I have taken part in all the wars Italy has ever fought. As of today, I, the tamer of stars and of tortoises, bear the second name of Gruban. Antonio Gruban sounds good, thirty-seven years of age, already a general, an admiral, the bearer of every medal under the sun, by day a member of the Italian senate and by night a sexual consultant of the Via dei Serpenti, not far from the Vatican."

Peduto felt his face. "Thick eyebrows, a good nose, once Roman but now broken to make it resemble Gruban's, sensual lips sharply defined, a greasy beard full of blackberries, impressive mustache, a strong chest.

"I'm rather pleased with the description," Peduto said.

The cries faded into the distance. The earth shook. "Antonio Gruban Peduto is finished! More than a thousand bullets have pierced his heart, ravens are tearing at his bowels and liver!"